Also by Theresa Breslin:

GHOST SOLDIER
A thrilling, poignant story of hope and loss
set during the First World War.
'Another must-read novel by one of Scotland's finest writers' *Scotsman*

SPY FOR THE QUEEN OF SCOTS
A story full of secrets, betrayal and murder, set in sixteenth-century
France and Scotland.
'A gripping historical thriller from the brilliant Breslin'
The Bookseller

PRISONER OF THE INQUISITION
A gripping tale of fire, fury, love and revenge, set during the
Spanish Inquisition.
'Unputdownable' *The Times*

THE NOSTRADAMUS PROPHECY
A dramatic adventure story set in sixteenth-century France.
'Terrific novel . . . Enormously enjoyable' *Guardian*

THE MEDICI SEAL
A gloriously rich and authentic story set in Italy in 1502.
'A superb historical thriller . . . An enchanting novel about genius,
and a gift to an enquiring mind' *The Times*

REMEMBRANCE
An epic tale of young lives altered by the First World War.
'Immensely readable, passionately written' *Guardian*

SASKIA'S JOURNEY
A haunting tale of self-discovery.
'Mesmerising . . . Truly memorable' *The Bookseller*

DIVIDED CITY
Two young rival football supporters are caught up in an
attack on an asylum seeker.
'A cracking good read . . . A book with far-reaching appeal
and universal themes that will encourage young readers to
challenge bigotry' *Guardian*

KEZZIE AT WAR
A spirited young girl fights to keep her family together.
'A remarkable story of hope and determination' *Val Bierman*

THERESA BRESLIN

CORGI BOOKS

CORGI BOOKS

UK | USA | Canada | Ireland | Australia
India | New Zealand | South Africa

Corgi Books is part of the Penguin Random House group of companies
whose addresses can be found at global.penguinrandomhouse.com.

www.penguin.co.uk
www.puffin.co.uk
www.ladybird.co.uk

First published 2017
001

Set in 11.5/15.5 pt Bembo Std by Jouve (UK), Milton Keynes
Printed in Great Britain by Clays Ltd, St Ives plc

A CIP catalogue record for this book is available from the British Library

ISBN: 978–0–552–56525–7

All correspondence to:
Corgi Books
Penguin Random House Children's
80 Strand, London WC2R 0RL

Penguin Random House is committed to a
sustainable future for our business, our readers
and our planet. This book is made from Forest
Stewardship Council® certified paper.

This book is for TRB

PROLOGUE

RUSSIA

ST PETERSBURG

Sunday 22 January 1905

STEFAN

We were singing as we marched along.

Hymns at first — for many people carried icons and holy pictures: images of Christ Jesus, His Blessed Mother, the Apostles and Martyrs. I had no use for minor saints. I'd made my own banner where I painted a portrait of the Emperor of Russia. We called him our 'Little Father' and, as I had no father of my own, Tsar Nicholas was the face I held aloft.

Workers were streaming from the factories and houses, and my mother and I merged with the main flow heading towards the royal palace in the centre of the city. Flags were waving, and the clamour grew louder as the Tsar's imperial anthem rose into the bitterly cold air.

My mother took my free hand. 'Stay by me,' she said.

I scarcely heard her. My heart was beating to the sound of the singing and tramp of shoes on snow. We surged onwards.

'To the Winter Palace!'

'What will happen when we get there?' my mother asked a tall man, who was leading a section of the crowd.

'The Tsar will give us tea and cake!' It was a joke. But I half believed him. Today, the twenty-second of January, was my birthday. I was twelve years old and dizzy with excitement.

My mother laughed. 'There are thousands upon thousands here.' She indicated the crush of bodies. 'Not everyone will have cake.'

'We only want enough bread to stop us starving. And fair working conditions. Men and women must not work an eighteen-hour shift for a pittance.'

There was a rumble of support from those around us.

The tall man was suddenly serious. 'A delegation from the head of the procession will present the Tsar with our petition asking for a people's council to be part of the Government.'

'The Winter Palace!'

A shout went up as we entered the square before the palace. Now I could see how enormous it was! Line upon line of shining windows, with pillars and arches and statues. Rooftops a hundred foot high, shimmering like frosted icing under a thick covering of snow.

'The Tsar! The Tsar!'

Was he really there? On the balcony?

Instantly I dropped my mother's hand and began to burrow through the masses to the front. If I could be part of the delegation I might eat cake on my birthday with Tsar Nicholas!

'Stefan. Where are you?' my mother called after me. 'Stefan!' It was the last word I heard her say.

Soldiers were waiting in the square.

Cossacks and Hussars – with rifles ready.

They did not order us to disperse.

Without warning bullets thudded into the marchers — men, women, children. The singing stopped and the screaming began. Those unharmed scattered and ran. Others hobbled or crawled on all fours to get away. Banners and bunting lay torn and discarded. In the midst of the melee I stood alone, rigid in terror. An easy target. Another round of fire rattled out, spitting death. Then I was slammed to the ground as my mother threw herself across me like a human shield.

And she fell down, her face close to mine, her blood staining the snow bright red.

RUSSIA

SIBERIA

Summer 1916

Chapter 1

NINA

'I murdered a man.'

'What!' I exclaimed.

My papa's eyes, wild and staring, fixed on my face. 'He threatened my family . . . said he would do them harm. So I went to his house and I stabbed him to death!'

'No!' I gazed at my father in horror.

'I did, Nina. I stuck a knife in his chest!'

'Don't say such things.' My voice was high with shock. 'You could never stab someone.'

'I am a murderer,' he sobbed.

'No, no, Papa.' I tried to calm him – and myself – my fingers trembling as I reached to stroke his forehead. 'You are ill with a fever which gives you bad dreams.'

'Listen to me, Nina,' my papa insisted. 'I am dying and I want you to know the truth.'

'This cannot be true.' I spoke to reassure us both,

for nothing much happened in our sleepy village in a remote part of Russia. 'No one has ever been murdered here.'

'It was sixteen years ago, not long before you were born. I still have the dagger!'

'Papa,' I soothed him. 'Be quiet now and rest.'

'I did it for you, Valentina. For you! If this man had lived he would have destroyed you!'

'You are confused,' I whispered, for in his delirium Papa had called me by my mother's name.

My father groped at his neck and pulled off the chain he wore, upon which hung a tiny golden key. 'Take this,' he said, 'but don't unlock the casket unless you have to. And' – he gripped my hand tightly – 'do not ever leave our family home, Nina. If you do, then your life will be in peril!'

Chapter 2

NINA

After the funeral the family lawyer came to sort my father's papers and read his will.

This man, Viktor Ilyich Volkov, was a forty-year-old widower. With his dark hair and trim beard he considered himself handsome; but his mouth was often drawn down in a mean expression, and Dmitri, our steward, had noticed his eyes were full of envy whenever he walked around our house and grounds. In the past, when the lawyer visited my father to help him conduct the business of running our estate, he had often brought his two small children. Although my sixteenth birthday had passed I was happy to spend time with them, and read aloud stories from Papa's collections of Russian folk tales. My mother died when I was born and I was a lonely child, so I enjoyed the boys' company. I did not enjoy the company of the lawyer. Recently, as my father's health worsened, Viktor Ilyich had become more familiar in his ways.

'Such pretty things you have here.' As he entered my father's study the lawyer picked up a silver-framed photograph from a side table.

'That is an image of my mother.' I spoke briskly, irked that he'd been so bold as to lift it from its appointed place.

'Yes,' he said. 'The beautiful and richly dressed Valentina, who died so tragically young. 'Not many people knew your mother.' He hesitated. 'I suppose your father told you of their early life together . . . ?'

I didn't want to share any personal memories with this man and so I said, 'Would you be so good as to return that to me?' I held out my hand.

'Of course!' As he put the photograph in my palm the lawyer wrapped the clammy fingers of his other hand around mine in a caressing motion.

'Sir!' I pulled my hand free of his.

'I wish to express my deepest condolences, Nina, on the death of your father.'

'I thank you.' I bowed my head, overcome with the grief of my great loss.

'Ah, I see you are full of sadness. You must allow me to comfort you, Nina. Please . . .' He moved nearer.

I struggled to regain my composure for I wanted to be left alone to mourn in peace. 'May we proceed with the matter of the will, Viktor Ilyich? And . . . I am proud to carry my father's name, so you must call me "Nina Ivanovna".'

'My dear Nina, it is not necessary for us to use our formal middle names. From now on we should speak to each other by our given names. Please call me Viktor.'

'It is not appropriate,' I replied.

'But it could be!' The lawyer's manner was friendly. 'I thought you liked my sons?'

I nodded cautiously, for I'd no inkling why the lawyer should suddenly make a remark about his children.

'I could do with some help there,' he sighed. 'I am a mere man. They need a woman's touch.'

'They may visit me,' I said. 'And I will visit them, if you permit?'

'A better arrangement would be that we all live together.'

It was such a ridiculous idea that I tried not to laugh. Did he think that because I had agreeably watched over his sons when he was with my father, I would want a position as their governess? I strove to be polite. 'I cannot leave my home.'

'I'm not suggesting that you should leave here.'

'I thought that you were proposing that I should become a governess to your children?'

'Not at all – I am proposing that you become my wife.'

'Your wife!'

'Why not?' He gave me an ingratiating smile. 'You like my boys and they love you. I can sell my own house to live here and run the estate. I'd give you an ample house-keeping allowance and I'd permit you to keep these storybooks' – he waved his hand towards the bookcases which held Papa's precious manuscripts – 'that meant so much to your father. And' — his eyes roved over me — 'we'd get to know each other better too.'

'This is preposterous!' I bit my lip to quell the sense of nausea at the thought of Viktor Ilyich Volkov any closer to me than he already was. 'Even though I am a young woman, I can, and I will, run this estate as my father would have wished.'

At my response and obvious revulsion the lawyer's smile became thinner. 'As soon as the will is ratified *I* will manage this household.'

How dare he! It was for *me* to decide who would be my estate manager. I resolved to sack him and appoint another lawyer immediately. 'This was my father's household,' I said. 'It is mine now.'

'The first part of your statement is true. The second is not.'

It took a moment for the sense of what he was saying to sink in. 'I fail to comprehend,' I said. 'My father told me the terms of his will. He bequeathed all his possessions to me — and me alone.'

'Indeed that is true, but' — the lawyer spoke distinctly — 'only after his debts are paid.'

'What debts are these?'

Viktor Ilyich shook his head. 'I see that I will have to explain things to you, Nina, as obviously your father did not have the time or the inclination to do so.'

'Explain what things?' I asked with increasing impatience. 'Let us finish our business and you may be gone.'

'Our business, as you call it, will take some time.'

'It doesn't have to. Let me see my father's will and whatever else is attached to it so that I may take over the running of the estate.'

'The estate is too complex for you to manage.'

'No it is not,' I said. 'My father shared his skills and encouraged me to think for myself. You believe that I'm not capable because I am a woman and I am young.'

'Apart from those reasons there is also one insurmountable obstacle which prevents you from running this estate,' Viktor Ilyich replied. 'When the Imperial Government took men for soldiers to fight against the German Kaiser, they requisitioned horses and grain stores as war supplies. Your father had to borrow money to maintain your buildings, livestock and workers. The estate was signed over as surety and the money has never been repaid.'

'Who loaned my father this money?'

'I did.' Viktor Ilyich coughed. 'We had an understanding . . .'

'What kind of understanding?'

'That after your father had departed this life – may God keep his soul safe until we meet again' – he made the sign of the cross – 'our agreement was that you could not live by yourself in this house, so it would be better if you came under my protection.'

'I have all the protection I need,' I said. 'My father's workers are loyal.'

'But diminished in number. Our war with the German invaders does not look to end soon. The army will come again for more horses and men. There is no money available to clear your father's debts. Therefore I own the estate, this house, and everything in it.'

Viktor Ilyich went behind my father's desk and sat down in Papa's high-backed leather chair. 'And everything in it,' he repeated.

His face showed triumph.

'I own *you*.'

'No one owns me!' I cried out.

'There, there.' He placated me as one would a child. 'I should have used a different phrase. I apologize. I was attempting to make the situation absolutely clear to you.'

'The situation is far from clear!' What Viktor Ilyich said could not be true, yet he was so assured, so confident, that a worm of fear entered my soul. 'I want to see the official documents.'

'Of course you may see them.' His tone was patronizing. 'But I doubt if you will follow their meaning.'

'My father was a scholar, and he educated me himself, so I will follow their meaning well enough,' I snapped.

'Try not to sound so harsh when you are speaking, Nina. It is unbecoming in a lady.'

For answer I went and tugged on the cord to ring the bell to summon our steward. 'Dmitri will see you out,' I said. 'And I will inform you of what I intend to do.'

'Hush, Nina. There is no need for us to argue. Your problem is real and I want to offer you a solution. If we were married then you wouldn't have to leave your family home.'

'Lady?' Dmitri appeared at the door. I suspect he'd

been hovering in the hall since Viktor Ilyich had arrived, as I knew he liked the lawyer even less than I did. 'You rang for me?'

'Yes!' I could scarcely speak. 'Mr Viktor Ilyich is leaving. Would you please escort him to his carriage?'

'My pleasure.' Dmitri's eyes met mine, and in them I saw a gleam of approval.

Viktor Ilyich glanced at Dmitri, whose bulk filled the door frame. 'This is foolishness on your part, Nina,' he said. 'There is no way that you can live without accepting my offer.'

'I do not need your offer of marriage in order to survive.'

'Actually, you do!' the lawyer spat at me. 'You own *nothing*. You have no source of income for food or clothes. Your father spoiled you and shielded you from the hard facts of life. It has made you proud and haughty, Nina.'

Dmitri coughed and opened the door wide. The lawyer ignored him. 'A woman has not the strength of will to manage anything other than the housekeeping duties and childcare. Neither has she the wit to choose who would be a good match for her in marriage. It is a man's place to decide such a thing. In the absence of your father and, being appointed by him as your family lawyer, then I am making that decision.'

'I dismiss you as my lawyer.'

'By dismissing me you are acting like a selfish child!'

Dmitri took a few steps into the room. The lawyer started in fear. Then he recovered himself and said, 'I am prepared to put up with your lack of respect, but only for a certain length of time. Within a week the local magistrate will ratify the will and then I will be back to claim what is mine.'

'I bid you good day, sir,' I said.

'There is nowhere you can go, Nina. No one here may give you aid. I now own this estate: the land and everything on it.' Viktor Ilyich gave Dmitri a vicious look. 'If any servant or estate worker shelters you, then I will evict them out onto the public road. I will seize their goods and burn the roofs of their miserable hovels over their heads. They and their children will become worse than serfs.'

I heard Dmitri's intake of breath.

'You have seven days to reflect upon your situation,' the lawyer went on. 'Bear in mind that your father has no relations you may ask for help. On your mother's side there are none who will take you in — or even acknowledge your existence.'

The fact that my mother had family connections at all was news to me. I'd always believed that neither of my parents had any living relatives.

'Ah!' Viktor Ilyich said softly. 'I see you do not know your own personal history.'

My heart began to beat more rapidly. There was something sinister in the way he spoke, and it made me afraid.

'Your mother's background is obscure, but I do know that her family cast her out in disgrace when she ran away with your father. Indeed,' he continued spitefully, 'as there is no certificate among your father's papers, there is some doubt as to whether or not your parents were ever married.'

My parents not married! I looked at Dmitri in alarm. He was avoiding my gaze. Was it true? If so, then I was illegitimate!

'Consider this, Nina. Why was it that, despite your age, your father never sought to see you married or encourage suitors? You cannot lawfully bear the name "Ivanovna" for there is no proof that you are indeed Ivan's daughter. If you are the child of an unlicensed union, no respectable person would want you as part of their family, and so, in view of your circumstances, you must see that my offer is generous.'

I'd always thought Papa loved me too much for us to part. But if the lawyer spoke the truth, then it would have been impossible to make a betrothal contract for me without revealing that he and my mother were unmarried. As an illegitimate child I had no social status, and probably none legally as my father's heir.

'I will take my leave of you.' The lawyer's eyes lingered on my face and neck, and I saw an expression there that I'd never noticed before.

A greedy hunger.

I crumpled backwards, clutching at the gold chain my father had given me on his deathbed.

Viktor Ilyich nodded in satisfaction at what he took to be my compliance. 'While I'm gone you may make yourself busy by stitching up a wedding dress. For upon my return we *will* be wed.'

Chapter 3

NINA

All that day, and late into the evening, I sat reading at my father's desk. Outside the bees busied themselves among the flowers, and the sound and scent of it came to me through the window.

The lawyer was right. Over the last year the army's requisition of our horses, grain and other goods had left us with nothing to feed our people or livestock. My father had borrowed heavily, using our home and the estate as surety for the loans that Viktor Ilyich arranged for him. There were half a dozen contracts to prove that this had happened. And despite thorough searching I found no marriage certificate among my father's papers.

My father had told me very little about himself or my mother. I knew that they were both from St Petersburg and that his parents had left him enough money to attend the university there. But Papa brushed away any questions

I asked him about his time in the city, saying the facts were too dull to recount. He referred to himself and my mother as 'orphans of a storm' and I'd pictured them romantically huddled together in a blizzard. Perhaps he'd been speaking metaphorically – Viktor Ilyich said that her family had forbidden the marriage. They must have eloped to this remote place as a sanctuary to share their lives. I was glad they'd had time with each other before I arrived, but their flouting of the rules of society meant that I was now disinherited and vulnerable.

The thought of becoming the wife of Viktor Ilyich, subject to his every whim, was repugnant to me. But what other option did I have?

When Dmitri brought my supper he spoke to me gently. 'The passing of a person you love leaves a hole in your life. But we must allow that space to be filled with the memory of their wisdom, and act in a manner that shows we are living in the light of their spirit.'

I laid my head down upon my father's desk and wept openly in front of him. I was not embarrassed to do this for our relationship was more than servant and mistress. When I was growing up Dmitri had been like a nanny to me in the absence of my mother. He'd held the reins of my pony as I learned to ride and bound up my knees when I scraped them falling from the apple tree.

'Shush now, Nina Ivanovna,' he murmured. 'I have been thinking on the problem. You may have no relatives to give you shelter but your father had a dear friend, Konstantin, from his student days. Your father sent for him when your mother was nearing childbirth for he'd qualified as a medical doctor. He arrived too late to help her, but nursed you back to life when we'd given up hope and feared that we might lose both of you.'

'I remember Dr Konstantin!' I cried. 'He lives in St Petersburg but would visit four or five times a year when I was small.'

'You are his godchild and it may be that he would offer you assistance.'

'But he hasn't been in touch with us for a long time,' I said. 'It would seem he has no enthusiasm for being a godfather.'

'There are reasons why he stopped all contact.' Dmitri lowered his voice. 'The State Secret Police had begun to follow him and investigate his friends because he is an adviser to the Duma Council of the People and speaks up for the poor and ill.'

'Why should we worry about investigation?' I asked Dmitri. 'We are country mice. My father's sole interest was collecting the traditional tales of the peasants.' I looked around at the books and manuscripts we'd amassed over the years. 'Stories, not politics, were Papa's abiding passion.'

'Sometimes it doesn't matter what you do, or do not do.' Dmitri's voice held fear within it. 'One can be punished for even talking with a suspected person.'

'There were old letters from the doctor among Papa's correspondence,' I said, 'which have his address on it. I'll write to him at once.'

★

The following day Dmitri rode into the nearest town, Yekaterinburg, to post my letter. When he returned he had a worried expression upon his face. 'I don't believe that you will receive a reply very soon. Transport is disrupted. The town is full of refugees and soldiers – the one lot fleeing from the war, the other travelling reluctantly towards it.'

'What should I do?' I paced the room in agitation. 'Do you think I'll be able to stall Viktor Ilyich past the end of the week?'

'I don't know,' Dmitri replied. 'He is a cunning man and may suspect you've sent for help so he'll be inclined not to wait.'

'Then I must go to St Petersburg and speak personally to the doctor.'

'He was your father's friend so I doubt he would turn you away,' said Dmitri, 'but let us make a plan in case that happens.'

We decided I should leave the next day, taking only what I myself could carry.

Dmitri prepared food while I packed a hairbrush and basic clothes. In the early hours of the following morning I went to my father's study. It was my favourite place in the house, and where I felt closest to both my parents. From when I was young Papa had always involved me in his life's work. In the warm weather he and I would travel the countryside, stopping to speak to villagers and towns-folk. Wide-eyed, I would listen to their stories as he scribbled them down in his notebooks.

'Russia is the most ancient of lands,' my father told me, 'consisting of many peoples, each with their own language and culture. Our ancestors made up Folk and Faery stories as accounts of their fears and hopes, and their striving to explain their own nature and that of the wider world. Stories are what we are – and also what we might become.'

I loved these tales so much that sometimes Papa hardly needed to refer to his notes, for I could recite them by heart when we got home.

'You are the child of a beginning' – he patted my head – 'born at the start of this new century. It is appropriate that you become a Keeper of the Old Tales.'

In the winter months we'd stoke the stove with apple wood, and the smell of it would fill the study as we sat through the dark days, sharing and shaping the stories.

I ran my hand along his books. The larger anthologies he'd had printed up into bound volumes. Smaller collections and single stories we'd sewn into thin pamphlets handwritten by one of us. There would be space in my travel bag for a few of these. If I took them, then a part of my father would come with me on my travels. I selected my favourites: *The Frog Princess*, *Kolobok*, *The Wooden Eagle* – and some unfinished adventures of *Masha and the Bear*.

As I gathered them up they revealed an object, hidden from sight, lying at the back of the shelf. I drew it towards me.

It was a box. An oblong carved casket.

I examined it curiously for I'd never seen it before. The lid was locked. I set it aside while I packed my selection of pamphlets. It was only when I'd finished that it came into my mind that this might be the casket Papa had said I should not unlock unless I had to. Perhaps he'd hidden money there! I took the chain from my neck and put the key to the lock. With a click the casket opened.

Inside lay a dagger.

The handle was set with a huge round ruby. Fire blazed in its dark depths. Tiny seed pearls encircled the stone, lending it a false air of innocence. As I reached to pick it up I noticed the blade: curved and sharp. I hesitated. The polished steel was marked with spots . . .

Blood? Surely not! My father's wild words – *I stabbed a man* – they couldn't be right. In amongst that rambling nonsense were other flights of fancy. He'd also described himself and my mother skating on the frozen River Neva and him and his best friend dancing at a grand ball in the famous Winter Palace of the Tsar. I'd dismissed all these wanderings as fantasies – my father had been an unimportant university student and wouldn't have been allowed inside any imperial palace.

I lifted up the dagger and the strangest sensation thrilled through me. A shiver of ice and fire. At once frightening and compelling.

I gazed on it, hypnotized.

The ruby's light exploded like a firework in my mind. And instantly there was sound there too. Voices – men's voices: one angry, shouting; the other reasoning . . . And then a woman, pleading . . . The howling of a wolf which changed eerily into a thin, distant, high-pitched scream.

The dagger dropped from my hand. My whole body was trembling. Fingers shaking, I replaced it on the bed of white silk, locked the casket and put the key and chain round my neck.

'Lady, the sun is rising.' The door opened and Dmitri's voice brought me back to reality. 'We must leave to catch the first train.'

'I will be with you in a moment. Wait for me by the horses please, Dmitri.'

I stuffed the casket deep in the bottom of my travel bag then wrapped my Siberian shawl around me and tied it at my waist.

There was one more thing I wanted to do before I left my father's study. In a corner of the room hung a holy painting; my father was not religious but he kept this near him for it had belonged to my mother. This *Strastnaya* icon had been her favourite portrayal of Mary and Jesus. It showed the mother holding her son as a toddler. Their dress was formal and sober, except that one of the child's sandals was falling off his foot. Growing up, I had identified with this image, for often, in warm weather, I'd slip off my shoes to run barefoot in the long grass full of meadow flowers.

I knelt to ask my mother to watch over me and I lit the candle that was set in front of the painting.

By the time the candle burned down I would be far from here – perhaps never to return.

Chapter 4

NINA

Papa and I had often visited Yekaterinburg and the stationmaster knew me well.

'I will get you a good berth,' he said, 'away from this riff-raff.' He indicated the crowds of refugees sleeping on the station platforms.

'What is the Government doing to help these unfortunates?' I asked him.

He rolled his eyes. 'The Government can scarcely do anything to help themselves. See there . . .' He pointed to my ticket. 'When the war began they decided that "St Petersburg" sounded too German so they changed the name of the city to "Petrograd". But, two years later, have they issued us with new stationery or rubber stamps? Oh no! That would be too efficient for them.' He laughed. 'So please don't get distressed, my lady; although your ticket says "St Petersburg", you will arrive in the city of "Petrograd"!'

'I suppose things are as bad as ever in the capital,' said Dmitri.

'The Tsar is at the Front, making a mess of running the war, while his wife, the Tsarina, is at home in Petrograd, making a mess of running the country.' The stationmaster gloomily puffed on his pipe. 'Government ministers are sacked and replaced on a monthly basis for she listens to the ravings of the Siberian monk Rasputin, who claims to be inspired by God.'

'What are the Duma saying about this?' Dmitri asked.

'The so-called "people's" Council of the Duma has been suspended, then reinstated, on numerous occasions – not that the Tsar or the Tsarina or the ruling elite in the State Council ever listen to them anyway.' The station-master looked directly at me now, as he got into his stride. 'We were allowed a Duma Council, my lady, in order to forestall riots and rebellion after the murder of peaceful protestors in 1905. But it has no real power. And with the ongoing war the workers' conditions are even worse than before. So they strike; the army break up their marches and shoot a few protestors. The Okhrana – the Tsar's Secret Police – under the orders of the Government, imprison and torture the ringleaders. So it goes . . . on and on.' He spat a long squirt of tobacco juice onto the tracks and said more quietly, 'If you want to cripple a country then you look to the transportation.

28

If the trains stopped running, all Russia would grind to a halt. Whoever has the nous to seize control of the railway system will be the one who holds the winning cards.'

I could sense tension building in Dmitri while we listened to the stationmaster. He was beginning to rethink our plan of my travelling to Petrograd.

'I'd like to get on the train now,' I said firmly. I'd set out on this course in order to escape from Viktor Ilyich, but was now keen to venture out on my own and see the city of my parents.

'The journey will last several days,' Dmitri told me as he ushered me aboard. 'I'd like to come with you, but I believe I should stay here and protect what is yours. Find a family group and attach yourself to them so that you're not alone when stretching your legs or visiting the tea urn. Engage with the children and share your food, and they will be glad to take you under their wing.'

'I am very comfortable with children,' I said. 'But my father made me independent. I don't need to be under anyone's wing.'

'You are a lovely young woman,' said Dmitri. 'And there will be soldiers about. Dashing officers in gold-braided uniforms, with an eye for a pretty lass.'

'Dressed in these clothes' – I indicated the long plain grey dress and coat which Dmitri had insisted I wear – 'I am definitely not a pretty lass!'

He sighed. 'They will spot your flaxen hair a mile off.' He adjusted my green and purple shawl so that it covered the curls which fell over my forehead. 'It is good that you do not see how attractive you are.'

The sun had come up by the time the train chugged out of Yekaterinburg. The engine heaved and clanked. The houses and churches slipped past, and soon we were crossing the great flat plains of Siberia. I did as Dmitri advised and struck up conversation with a family. I told stories to the children and we passed an uneventful, if long and wearisome, journey to arrive in Petrograd in the late morning four days later.

I had never been in such a press of people before. I gripped my bag to my chest, remembering Dmitri's dire warnings of pickpockets, swindlers, slave traders and a dozen other dangers a young country girl might encounter when visiting a big city. But I was ignored. Far from greeting each other as they passed, the citizens appeared to avoid eye contact. No one seemed to have any time to spare — being solely intent on their own business.

Dmitri had copied a route for me from a city map in one of Papa's books and I'd studied it during the train journey. I made my way onto the main street: the Nevsky Prospekt. Filled with shops and traders and stalls selling goods of every kind, its width and activity took my breath away.

There was so much to see that I was tempted to browse. But Dmitri said that as I was a girl alone in a strange place then I shouldn't dawdle but go straight to Dr Konstantin's house without delay. He was confident Papa's friend would take me in and find me work. My father had taught me arithmetic, mathematics and scientific subjects. I had a wide general knowledge and my writing was neat and legible, and we expected a doctor to have some influence as regards getting employment. I would have endless days ahead to explore the sights, so I told myself that I mustn't stop on one of the many bridges, or look at the expanse of the river teeming with barges and boats, or listen to the captains calling orders, or pause in wonderment when the bell tolled from the immense domes of the cathedral.

And I did try to obey Dmitri . . . until I reached a vast square.

Before me was the Winter Palace. The intensity of the light reflecting from the building hurt my eyes, and I had to shade them to look at it. I'd seen images of this residence of the Russian Tsars in books and journals, but no painting or photograph captured by a camera lens did justice to its magnificence and magnitude. Stretching the width of Palace Square with a splendour of three hundred rooms, the huge emblem of Imperial Russia blazed from the facade – a twin-headed eagle with wings outstretched and the Crown of the Romanovs resting on its head. There was the balcony where, at the beginning of the war with Germany, Tsar Nicholas and his wife, Tsarina Alexandra, had come out to greet a crowd of cheering thousands.

My shawl slipped back from my head as I walked forward and tilted my head to look up.

'Good day to you!'

I hadn't noticed the two young army officers approaching. Their eyes flashed mischief as they saluted smartly and bowed. My eyebrows flew up in confusion and my face went pink with embarrassment.

'Oh, Anton!' One of them nudged the other. 'It's so long since I've seen a girl blush when a lad simply says "good morning" to her.'

'You are from the countryside, aren't you?' the one called Anton asked me. 'Is it your first time in the city?'

'Yes.' I nodded. 'No!' I added quickly as I recalled Dmitri's advice: *If a stranger asks, always pretend that you know the city.*

'In that case,' the first soldier said, 'maybe you would be good enough to be our guide, for this is our first day in Petrograd.'

'I cannot talk to you,' I said, following Dmitri's instructions as to how I should treat a stranger in the street, 'for I am on my way to meet my husband.'

'You are married?' The first soldier clasped his hand across his chest in a dramatic gesture. 'My heart is broken and it is not yet noon.'

'Do not fret for him, my lady.' Anton gave his friend a rough shove. 'Pavel's heart gets broken a dozen times a day. I am the one who needs your attention.'

'May I at least have a smile?' Pavel went on his knees before me. 'We are being posted out tomorrow. To the war. But I could die happy on the battlefield if I had the memory of a smile from a beauty such as you.'

I giggled. I couldn't help myself.

'Have pity on us,' Anton chimed in. 'We've just returned from the Front after fighting in mud and slime for weeks on end. Surely we deserve some reward?'

Their uniform was far too clean for them to have been on active service. I opened my mouth to point this out, but again Dmitri's voice was in my ear: *If you are accosted by any young men, ignore them. Given the slightest encouragement they will follow you for the rest of the day.* I ducked my head and pulled up my shawl to re-cover my hair. Then I walked away determinedly.

'We are devastated!' they called after me merrily. 'You have crushed us completely!'

I wondered what would have happened if I had accepted their offer to be their companion for the day. Inwardly I was pleased that they'd picked me out from among others in the square. Viktor Ilyich had indicated that he was offering me marriage as a favour – I'd no idea if I was pretty or not. Papa and Dmitri said I was, but then they'd hardly tell me if I was ugly, would they?

Totally exhilarated by the encounter, I arrived at the address I sought with a light step and full of hope.

Dr Konstantin did not live there!

The owner of the house told me that the doctor had moved to another area of the city. She gave me the name of a particular street but did not have a number for the house. It took me over an hour to get to the place, crossing several bridges as I did so. It was a different city that I saw as I went deeper into the industrial quarter. Gone were the wide avenues of beautiful residences fronted with pretty pink plaster. Steelworks and sawmills, with many factories and family dwellings packed densely together, took up all available space, shutting out the daylight. The buildings hemmed me in and I was relieved when I finally reached my destination. I walked to the end of this long street, examining nameplates and making enquiries. No one knew of a Dr Konstantin or any doctor ever living there. By now it was late afternoon. I sat down by a fountain to think what to do next.

In the purse pinned to my underclothes I had a return railway ticket to Yekaterinburg. Dmitri had insisted I buy one so that, in the event of not finding Dr Konstantin, I would be able to go home again. Although the ticket was valid for a week, Dmitri's plan was that I should come home if I did not find the doctor within three days.

I unfastened my food bag and began to eat a slice of the soft white bread that Dmitri himself had baked for me. The smell of it reminded me of our warm kitchen and tears rose into my eyes. The place where I found myself was so alien to my usual surroundings. Houses closely built with no trees or grass to be seen . . . I glanced around. A little girl stood a few paces off, watching me.

'Hello.' I smiled. 'My name is Nina. How are you this afternoon?'

I had a great liking for children and usually they took easily to me. But this child didn't smile in reply. She continued to stare without speaking.

Then I understood that she was not staring at me, but at the bread I held in my hand.

'Oh!' I said. And I was aware of her peaked face and scraggy body, with skinny legs poking out below the ragged skirt.

I broke off a piece of the bread and held it out to her. She snatched it from me and darted off, swifter than a bird pecking a crumb from my hand in winter time.

I could not, in good faith, eat any more in front of this starving child. I emptied the contents of my food bag onto the bench and walked away. When I glanced back it had disappeared. I'd decided that if I couldn't find the doctor then I would find work, and make a new life for myself here. But as I went through the city streets I realized that there might be no employment to be had. Below the superficial appearance of a busy, affluent city the people's clothes were worn and they looked lean.

My steps were leading in the direction of the railway station and I stopped at a newspaper stand to read the headlines. The war was going badly, and the workers were striking. Evening came on, and groups of men and women gathered on street corners, discussing and arguing. Overheard conversations shocked me:

'*Death to the German-born Tsarina!*'

Growls of agreement came from the throats of the listeners.

'*She is a cousin of the Kaiser and a German spy!*'

'*The Mad Monk Rasputin should be burned alive!*'

At the railway station, I went to the toilet where I counted my money. I reckoned that if I lived frugally it would last me one week. My face was reflected in the cracked mirror above the broken wash basin from whose taps no water issued.

'Seven days, Nina,' I said aloud, 'that's all the time you have.' In my heart, however, I was prepared to be destitute rather than go home to marry Viktor Ilyich.

Surveying the main concourse, I picked the oldest and kindest-looking porter I could see. In answer to my query he gave me directions to a cheap boarding house, which was still a suitable place for a respectable young woman to lodge.

On my way there I passed what looked like the main hospital of the city and, on an impulse, I went inside and found the offices. Boldly I asked the clerk if there was any record of a Dr Konstantin. I showed her the last letter Papa and I had received from him. She became sympathetic when I explained that my father had died and I didn't want to marry the older man who'd taken our house and estate.

'Being in the city for a while could change your mind,' she called to me as she riffled through a drawer of record cards. 'Food prices are rising by the day and the workers' hours have been increased, but not their pay. My body is aching for a decent meal and a warm fire.'

I shook my head.

'Got it!' Laying a card on the counter, the clerk then brought a piece of paper and a pen for me to copy out the details. She wished me luck and winked as we parted, saying: 'If you decide not to marry the lawyer, then stop by and give me his address so I can try my hand!'

My spirits lifted as I set out from the hospital. I would neither starve in this city nor be forced to go back home. In my hand was the present address of my father's closest friend, who would look after me. I was supremely confident that I would be safe for evermore.

I'd forgotten my papa's dying warning:

Do not ever leave our family home, Nina. If you do, then your life will be in peril!

Chapter 5

NINA

Dusk was settling over the city when I eventually reached the house of Dr Konstantin.

I was immensely tired, for I'd had little sleep over the last five days. My face and hands were grubby and my coat and dress travel-stained. The house loomed over me, narrow but high, consisting of two storeys, with attic rooms in the roof. Wearily I trudged up the front steps and sounded the bell.

'What do you want?' A young man asked the question as he opened the door. For a servant his manner was abrupt, but perhaps city customs differed from those of the country.

'My name is Nina Ivanovna Izmailov,' I said. 'I have come to see Dr Konstantin.'

'Dr K is a busy man, but he sees patients in his weekly clinic tomorrow morning from six until eight.

The entrance is at the side of the house.' He pointed to show me the way and made to close the door.

'I don't want to be his patient,' I said. 'I have—'

'No money,' he cut across me, finishing my sentence with what he thought I was going to say. He glanced at my clothes. 'Dr K doesn't charge factory workers.'

'I'm not a factory worker!' I said indignantly. 'I am a lady!'

'Are you indeed?' he replied with an edge to his voice that I'd never before heard in any servant. 'For your information, female factory workers are ladies too – by right of their own birth and body.'

'I-I only meant—' I stammered.

'Whereas,' he continued, ignoring my protest, 'I doubt if a so-called "lady" could be a factory worker. They'd have neither the wit nor the will to be capable of the tasks involved.'

This was the second time within a week that I had been dismissed by a man as having neither 'wit' nor 'will'. I felt my temper rise in response.

'I have both wit and will to know that you are exceptionally rude. And also to know that you are not Dr Konstantin. I wish to see him at once.'

'Well, you can't; he's not at home.'

'I will come in and wait.'

'You will not,' he retorted. 'I am not here to be commanded by the likes of you. The days of masters issuing orders to servants and serfs are drawing to a close.'

I swallowed my annoyance. 'I am not giving you

orders. My father was a friend of Dr Konstantin and I have come to visit him.'

'How do I know that you are who you say you are?' He scrutinized me. 'Have you proof of this?'

I hadn't thought too much about what kind of reception I might expect at the home of Dr Konstantin, but I was unbearably disappointed with this reaction. The young man, who I now thought might be the doctor's son rather than his servant, kept me standing on the outside step while I searched in my pocket and gave him the letter I carried with me.

'Anyone can forge documents, and anyhow' – he thrust it back at me – 'your letter is many years old.'

'I was told that Dr Konstantin stopped writing to my father because he knew his letters were being censored.'

A look of alarm crossed the young man's face. 'That is a rash thing to say!'

'It was your lack of manners that forced me to say it.'

He studied me more closely. 'You have come here to spy on us.'

'Don't be ridiculous!'

'If you are not a spy, then I'm guessing you're looking for a free handout of some sort. Go to the back gate via the lane at the side of the house and ring the bell. The housekeeper will give you bread and soup.'

I caught my breath. 'We haven't met for years but I can tell you enough about Dr Konstantin to convince you that he does know me,' I said.

'Ha!' he said. 'If you knew him as well as you pretend then you'd know that he's never referred to as "Dr Konstantin". Everyone calls him "Dr K".'

'My father used his full name when he visited us. Surely you can appreciate that would be the case with old friends?'

He shrugged. 'It wouldn't take a lot of inquiry on your part to uncover suitable information. Until you can definitely prove who you are I cannot welcome you into this house.'

'Then I will not stay where I am not welcome,' I said stiffly. I fought away my tears. I would not give this arrogant person the satisfaction of seeing me break down. 'I will trouble you no further.'

I turned and bumped into a tall man who was coming up the steps with head bent, reading a leaflet he carried in his hand. 'Ho!' he said. 'My pardon.'

Clutching my bag, I brushed past him and walked on.

'What did that girl want?' I heard him ask the young man.

'She claimed her father knew you. I sent her to the back door to get some food.'

'Did she give a name?'

'Nina . . . something or other. Probably another agent sent by the police to plant themselves amongst us. Although' – he laughed – 'she's prettier than any of the others.'

Face burning with humiliation, I increased my pace so as to avoid hearing his unkind remarks.

I barely heard the tall man repeat my name. 'Nina . . . ?'

Chapter 6

NINA

'*Nina!*'

Footsteps were running on the pavement behind me and someone caught at my sleeve.

'Nina Ivanovna? Is it really you?' The tall man who had bumped into me on the steps swung me round and looked into my face. Then he drew me to him and kissed me on each cheek. 'Your mother's eyes! Of deepest blue. I would know them anywhere on earth!' Before I could speak he seized hold of my bag and tucked my arm through his. 'Come in! Come inside the house!'

The rude young man held the door open and then, without apology, he nodded and left us in the hallway.

'Forgive that ignorant boy,' Dr Konstantin said as he hung up my coat and led me through to a large kitchen. 'Stefan is intelligent, therefore there's not a drop of common sense inside his skull.' He took tea glasses from their hooks to place upon the table. 'Let us have tea and you can tell me what brings you to my door.'

'It was complicated for me to discover where you live,' I said. 'I only had an old address . . .'

'I'm sorry. I should have found a way of letting your father know where I was. But you look weary; please sit down.'

'I am told that you are busy so I won't stay long.' I was not ready to forgive the hurt I felt at being so shabbily treated.

'Not so busy that I cannot spend time with my own goddaughter whom I have not seen for many years.' The doctor patted my hand. 'I have missed you and your papa very much.'

'It was you who lost touch with my family,' I accused him.

'Yes.' The doctor nodded. 'Quite deliberately. I became an adviser to the Duma Council and was told that the Okhrana, the Secret Police, would begin to keep me and the people I met under surveillance. I destroyed the letters your father sent me and advised him to destroy those he'd received from me. My breaking our contact was to prevent any harm coming to either of you. And yet' – he smiled – 'you managed to seek me out.' He poured hot tea into the two glasses and sat down. 'Is there a particular reason why you have come to St Petersbu—' He corrected himself. 'Or rather, as we must call our capital city now, "Petrograd"? How is your father?'

I bent my head and stared at my tea, unable to say the words, unable to tell him that my papa had died.

43

'My poor child! I'm so stupid!' His own tea glass clattered onto the table. 'I should have guessed that your father's passing would be why you are visiting me. If he were alive he'd never have permitted you to come to this city.'

'But he's not alive!' I raised my tearful face to his. 'Couldn't you have come to Yekaterinburg at least once in a while?'

'We live in critical times, Nina. I did what I thought was best to keep you both safe and secure in your hiding place.'

'Didn't you know how much your visits meant to me? To us? Lately my father needed help, someone he could trust — but the friend of his youth abandoned him.'

'I am sadder than you will ever know that I had to lose the companionship and correspondence of you both. Your papa was my truest friend.' Tears formed in the doctor's own eyes and he got up quickly and stood at the window with his back to me.

And now I felt guilty that I had misjudged my godfather when he was so obviously upset at hearing of Papa's death. I righted his glass and wiped up the spilled tea and then asked politely if I should pour him some more. He inclined his head and said he'd like to hear of my father's last days and my present circumstances.

And so I gave Dr Konstantin an account of the stroke that had paralysed my papa and eventually killed him. I informed him of the debt owed by the estate, and told him about the actions of the lawyer Viktor Ilyich. I did not mention the carved oblong casket, nor the dagger it contained.

'The truth of the matter is that I have no money. To pay off my father's debt I will have to hand over everything I own: the estate, the house and the goods within it. I came here in the hope that you would be able to find me work to do, and that I might live modestly.'

The doctor sat down beside me. Then he said, 'You must stay for a few days at least to recover from your journey, Nina. But, honestly, I do not know if this is the best place for you to seek sanctuary on a long-term basis.'

This was not the jolly friend of Papa's that I recalled from my childhood. This man was far removed from the one who had hoisted me on his shoulders and carried me about our orchard so that I could pluck fruit from the trees.

'I see you are disappointed and upset.' He spoke kindly. 'But you are old enough to be aware that the war is going badly for Russia, which affects those at the Front and those at home. Our Government is sliding into chaos and the people are ready to rise against them. This is a city of strikes and shortages and I am concerned for your well-being.'

'There is another reason I came,' I said. 'I want to get to know the city where my mother and father lived and met each other – the St Petersburg of my parents.'

'That St Petersburg is no more,' he said. 'Neither in name nor in nature. Its name was considered too German by the powers that be, and so it was changed. Its nature is considered too corrupt by the powers that hope to be, and so they are attempting to change that too.'

I slumped in my chair. I believed that my father had educated me well but I lacked any real knowledge of politics. Of course Papa had told me of our war with the German Kaiser. We had noted the absence of young men on our travels through Siberia, and I was aware that Russia had allies in France and Britain who were also fighting to contain the German invaders – but I was ignorant of how the war was being conducted or how it affected the mass of the Russian people.

'You may use our upstairs guest room,' the doctor went on. 'Rest and refresh yourself and I'll discuss the situation with Galena when she returns.'

'Is Galena your wife?' I asked.

'I never married and I have no children,' he answered. 'Galena runs my house and everyone must obey her rules. Apart from Stefan,' he added, 'who is completely spoiled – for when he was a small boy she punished his disobedience by only pretending to strike him . . . with a feather duster.'

'So Stefan is not your son?'

'No – not of the blood anyway. I met him years ago under . . . difficult . . . circumstances. He lives on the attic floor and I am sponsoring his studies in medicine. You will meet him again tonight at dinner.'

Chapter 7

NINA

I had wrapped my Siberian shawl around my body and was resting on top of the bedcovers when Galena came to the guest room to speak to me.

She was a sturdy woman with a direct manner. 'I would have expected a pretty girl of your age to be betrothed.'

'No one I met appealed to me.'

She raised her eyebrows. 'These matters are usually decided by the girl's father.'

'My father said I should marry whom I please.'

'That is . . . unusual.'

'In any case,' I added, 'no young man ever showed much interest in me.'

Galena laughed out loud. 'You have an honest way with words. But I imagine that in the countryside the young men have gone to war?'

'There is also the fact that I have no dowry. Who would want a pauper wife?'

'Dr K mentioned an older man, a lawyer, who has proposed to you?'

I shuddered.

'Ah . . .' she said. 'Is that the way of it?'

I was conscious that she was assessing me as we chatted and I sensed that she respected openness and plain speaking. 'I cannot bear him near me,' I replied. 'He is greedy and domineering and would destroy my spirit.'

Galena nodded slowly. 'We cannot allow that to happen to the child of an old friend. I will remind Dr K that, as your godfather, he has a duty of care. Nina, you may live in this room in this house for as long as you want. One morning a week, in the shed at the foot of the garden, Dr K and Stefan, our medical student, treat patients who can't afford to pay to see a doctor. Tomorrow is clinic day so you'll see for yourself how busy we are.' She paused. 'Be aware too that the city is becoming more unruly. You must be mindful not to get caught up in any disturbance on the streets.'

'I will be careful,' I promised her.

Galena gave a rueful sigh. 'You will be as careful as any of us were at your age – which is not at all.'

Relief washed through me and I might have hugged her, but she was already on her way out of the door. I was left to hug myself. And so I rearranged my shawl to tie the ends like a belt around my waist – and immediately felt more secure than I had for many days. The room was smaller than my own at home and the window view was to the rear of the house, but I would have happily slept in a cupboard to avoid marrying that lawyer. I put my travel bag on the bed and unpacked my belongings. At the bottom, nestled among Papa's story pamphlets, was the carved wooden casket.

I don't know what made me take the chain from around my neck and insert the key into the lock again. I only know that, when I laid my eyes upon it, the dagger drew me like a magnet. The ruby absorbed light into its heart and seemed to grow larger. Fighting my fear, I reached out to it. No visions came to disrupt my mind. All was as it should be. And yet . . . not quite – the jewel was warm under my touch. Obeying an inner urge, I lifted the dagger and tucked it in amongst the folds of the shawl gathered at my waist. I swung round to see myself in the dressing-table mirror.

'Oh!'

The Nina who looked back at me was taller, straighter, different . . . A ray of light from the ruby reflected in her eyes and a strength grew within me. I thought that, were Viktor Ilyich to stand in front of me now, tarnishing my honour and defiling my father's name, I would grasp this dagger and plunge it deep into his wicked heart.

The dagger was in my hand!

With a cry I flung it from me onto the bedcovers and stood, panting.

The dinner gong sounded through the house. I fumbled the dagger into the casket, locked it and put it away in my travel bag. With it gone, the mood left me as quickly as it came. But it was some minutes before I was composed enough to go downstairs.

To my surprise, at dinner Galena seated herself at the opposite end of the table to the doctor. Dmitri, our steward in Siberia, was a single man who, from boyhood, had dedicated his life to me and Papa, but he would never have eaten with us.

I sat opposite the medical student, Stefan. He was several years older than me and would have been attractive in a darkly handsome way were it not that his features seemed drawn in a perpetual scowl.

'I don't want to be a burden to the household,' I said as we sat down to eat. 'Please let me be useful in any way I can.'

'Have you ever worked before?' Stefan asked abruptly.

'I have not.' I bit back a sharper reply, for the tone of his voice verged on a sneer. 'But I can, and will, learn to do so.'

Stefan turned his eyes towards heaven.

Dr Konstantin flicked a glance at him but spoke to me. 'I've missed so much of your personal history, Nina. Tell us what's been happening in your life since we last met?'

'You know that my mother died as I was born.' I made the sign of the cross. 'By the grace of God she and my father are now reunited for eternity.'

Stefan cleared his throat but Dr Konstantin silenced him with a look.

'My father indulged me. I was constantly in his

company. From an early age I sat with him at table and he taught me to ride my horse and lots of other things.'

'And as you grew older? How did you spend your time?'

'Mainly helping Papa. I minded the lawyer's children while he conducted the estate business with my father. But Papa left as much of that work as he could to this lawyer, for he was more interested in researching native cultures.'

'It was his focus,' the doctor agreed. 'He studied language and literature at university and at one time was destined to gain a professorship in that subject.'

'I travelled with Papa through the countryside as he collected songs and tales from the villagers. When we got home I'd transcribe his notes and we'd write up the stories.'

'You can read and write?'

'Of course I can read and write!'

'Tush! I did not mean to offend you. It is a scandal that so many women cannot. If you mix in the elite society of Petrograd, you will find elegant women who are able to sing or dance to perfection yet cannot read or write.'

'They at least have the opportunity to learn,' muttered Stefan. 'The peasants are not given even a basic education.'

'Some peasants are.' I was thinking of how my father had taught lessons to the children of our workers. 'But, apart from learning skills to fulfil their function in life, it is not necessary for them to have an education – neither men nor women.'

'Such snobbery!' Stefan spluttered on a mouthful of cabbage.

'What?' I looked from one to the other. 'Is there something wrong with what I said?'

Dr Konstantin pressed his lips together as if he was trying not to laugh. 'Why do you think that peasants shouldn't be educated?'

'Yes, Lady Nina.' Stefan's eyes glittered with fury. 'Please share your insights into the life of a peasant or a worker. Do tell us why you think they should not learn to read or write.'

'I didn't say that they *should* not,' I replied. 'I said that it was not *necessary* for them to be educated in order to do their daily tasks. I have no moral objection to everyone being educated.'

'Oh well, that's all right then,' Stefan said sarcastically. 'Perhaps you might like to share your thoughts on that matter with our government ministers?'

I stared at this angry young man. Why was he so hostile?

Dr Konstantin pointed his fork at me. 'Your turn, I think.'

'Given the opportunity,' I said, 'I would share my opinion with the Tsar himself.'

'Unfortunately that won't be possible,' said Dr Konstantin. 'His Imperial Majesty has chosen to stay away from the city to be nearer the Front and show leadership to the troops.'

'He might return later in the summer,' said Galena, 'for there will be festivities to mark the day his son becomes a man. In August the Tsarevich Alexei will be twelve years old.'

'It will be a crime if the Romanovs spend money on fripperies with the country in the state it is.' Stefan seemed to throw this out as a challenge to test my opinion.

'Can a father not have a party for his son's birthday?' I countered his remark with a question. This forward young man had beaten me into submission at the front door, but I would let him see that I was as capable as he was to take part in a debate.

'Well said, Nina!' Galena exclaimed. 'Stefan can acknowledge no good in the Romanov family. But my grandfather was a serf; he owed his freedom to Tsar Nicholas's grandfather, who liberated the peasants and gave them citizenship. Without such leadership my family would still be slaves of the landowners. Russia needs the Romanovs to curb the power of those who would exploit us.'

'But those initial changes weren't followed through,' said Stefan. 'Russians are citizens with no voice. Tsar Nicholas – or, rather, his wife now – chooses our government ministers.'

'There is a reason for that,' said Galena.

'As a young man Tsar Nicholas saw his grandfather die a horrible death when, in the name of civil rights, an assassin blew his legs off with a bomb,' Dr K explained.

'It's understandable then,' I said, 'why he is afraid of more reform.'

'It makes him an incompetent leader,' said Stefan.

'But not an incompetent father,' said Galena. 'It is fitting that the Tsar should join his family to celebrate his son's twelfth birthday . . .'

Chapter 8

STEFAN

While Dr K and Galena and the girl, Nina, continued to talk, I dropped out of the conversation. My mind tracked back to my own twelfth birthday.

I recalled the joy in my heart as my mother and I linked arms with the workers of St Petersburg to bring our petition to the Tsar. I recalled the singing, and the chanting, and the waving flags, and the snow.

The snow . . .

My mother's face is inches from my own. She lies with her eyes open. It begins to snow. Flakes settle on her nose and eyelashes. I expect her to wipe them away with her hand. She doesn't move, so I take off my mitts and do it for her.

'Mama,' I whisper.

I wait. Any moment now she'll blink and start to scold me for running off.

'Boy! Are you hurt?'

The tall man who'd been beside us in the crowd earlier was standing over me.

I stared up at him.

'No?' he said. 'Good. Stand up and follow me.'

I shook my head.

'Come away, child.' He spoke urgently. 'Quickly now!'

'I need to help my mama,' I told him.

The tall man knelt down beside my mother and put his finger to her neck. 'She has no pulse.' Gently he closed down her eyelids. 'I am a doctor and I am sorry to have to tell you this. Your mother is dead.'

For a single second the world stopped. Somewhere inside me I knew that I was denying the evidence of my own eyes. Like a child playing make-believe, I'd been pretending that my mother was still alive.

'The Cossacks are marshalling their horses for a charge.' The doctor-man was talking again. 'They will scythe down what is left of us. A bullet might miss its target. A Cossack wielding a sabre will not.'

'I won't let the horsemen ride over my mama.' I set my chin in determination. 'She requires a proper burial. With prayers, and, and . . .'

'Your mama gave her life that you might own yours. Is this what a son does to his mother? Throws her most precious gift back in her face?'

'I . . . I—'

'What is your name?' he interrupted me.

'Stefan,' I replied. 'My name is Stefan Petrovich Kolodin.'

'Take my hand, Stefan Petrovich Kolodin. It is what your mother would have wanted you to do.'

As I stood up I heard the clatter of horses' hooves. The Cossacks were lining up at the corner of the square. 'May God save us!' My voice shook in fright.

'I doubt if the Almighty will intervene directly, but let's hope He gave you a good pair of legs for running. You are going to need them when they begin their gallop.' And saying that, the doctor yanked on my arm so hard as to almost wrench it from its socket and we raced down the Prospekt. 'Follow the tram lines!' he yelled at me.

'The staircase!' I cried out. 'To the narrow embankment!'

'Good thinking!'

All around us people were fleeing. As we reached the steps to the river we saw, running towards us, a group who'd been marching to the Winter Palace from a different part of the city.

'Soldiers!' they shouted. 'Behind us!'

We went towards the cathedral.

'They have cannon on the steps!' Another warning cry.

The tall man swore. 'They are trying to corral us like cattle!' He dived down a nearby lane. At the end was a stone wall.

We were trapped.

He pulled me into the folds of his coat as uniformed horsemen trotted past the end of the street. 'Stay quiet.' Only when the man put his hand over my mouth did I realize that I was sobbing aloud. The Cossacks had almost gone past when one of them swivelled his head and spotted us. With a loud 'Halloo!' he alerted his companions and tugged at his horse's rein. Two or three more turned to join him.

The doctor bent and, lifting me in his arms, he heaved me upwards at the wall. Desperately I flailed out, found a crevice and clambered to the top. A pile of manure was stacked against the other side. A soft landing for me. By releasing my grip I'd tumble to safety.

'Go on!' the doctor urged.

'No!' I swung my legs to sit astride the wall and reached down to hold out my hand.

'Stupid boy!' He glanced behind him. The Cossacks were cramped in the passage. It wasn't wide enough to allow a full charge but they came steadily onwards.

They had drawn their sabres.

The doctor shed his coat upon the ground, took a few paces back, and raced forward to leap upwards. I grabbed his collar as he scrabbled madly with his hands and feet to the top of the wall and hauled himself over. Together we toppled into the dung heap.

'How appropriate,' the doctor commented as he removed a lump of foul-smelling manure from his hair. 'It is how they treat us – as excrement to be swept from the streets.'

Chapter 9

STEFAN

Leaving the midden heap, we ran through wynds and alleys until we came to a wider street of individual houses. By a side lane we entered the back garden of one of these.

'Don't chide me, Galena!' The doctor addressed the severe-looking housekeeper who opened the door. 'At least I had the decency to avoid the front entrance.'

'Because you knew I would not let you in that way to make a mess of the hallway.' She sniffed. 'Both of you wait here in the scullery' — she inspected me with disapproval — 'while I sort out some clean clothes.'

I wondered at her attitude. Some of Mama's friends were servants in large houses and they'd never dare speak to their employers in such a manner.

'I'll change later.' The doctor was already scrubbing his hands at the sink. 'Fetch my medical bag — as fast as you can. The

army broke up the procession with rifle fire. I cannot help the dead and the dying, but many more are wounded.'

She put her hand to her mouth. 'The Tsar would never give that order. To murder his own people.'

'Nevertheless, it is happening as we speak. The Cossacks are riding roughshod over them, trampling women and children under their horses' hooves. I must go out again.'

'If you are killed the people will have lost a leader.'

'There is something else I have to do.' He glanced at me. 'I want to find this boy's mother and bring her body home.' The woman hurried off while the doctor took another coat from the hooks at the scullery door. 'Look after this young man, Galena,' he said when the woman returned. 'Give him hot tea and add two tablespoons of brandy with plenty of brown sugar.'

'I've been your housekeeper long enough to know how to deal with shock,' the woman said in indignation. 'Here is your bag. And wear these too.' She ran an armband up his sleeve. It had a red cross on it, as did the cap she placed on his head. 'They may give you some protection against murdering Bolsheviks.'

'Galena, it wasn't political agitators who did this,' said the doctor. 'It was uniformed soldiers.'

'Get along with you, then.' She gave him a tiny push. 'There will be stew and dumplings on the stove when you return.'

It was years since I'd allowed even my mother to see me naked, but I was so distressed that I didn't protest when Galena stripped and sponged me and helped me into an over-long flannel nightshirt.

She heaved me over her shoulder like a sack of coal and carried me upstairs and put me to bed. Despite the brandy and the sugar and the hot tea, a numbness descended upon me and I lay with eyes wide open, neither speaking nor sleeping. The doctor came in later to listen to my chest with his stethoscope and give me medicine – for the chill had seeped from my heart and head into my lungs. But my jaw locked and I stared out fixedly on a different world. In the darkness beyond the lamplight monsters lurked – misshapen beasts with fangs that dripped blood. They prowled and growled, and I knew that if I closed my eyes they would pounce and tear me to pieces.

By nightfall I was struggling to breathe.

'We're losing him,' I heard the doctor mutter as, once again, he failed to force liquid into my mouth.

'Let me try.' Galena's voice softened. She sat on the bed and, taking my hands, rubbed them between her own.

The texture of her skin was rough. Whereas the doctor's hands were smooth and his nails clean and neat, Galena's were coarsened with manual work. They felt like the hands of my mama. I began to tremble.

Galena peered into my face. 'You are frightened,' she declared in sudden realization. 'Dr K! There are too many shadows in this room. More lamps!' she ordered him. 'Let us make this place as bright as day.'

And while the doctor did as she bade him, Galena crooned over me, stroking my forehead and singing snatches of lullabies. When the room was to her satisfaction she propped me up and, holding out the medicine spoon, recited the same nursery rhyme my mama had chanted when coaxing me to eat as a child.

'Part your lips — prepare to chew
Some specials treats are here for you!
All the way from far Cathay
A little man has come today
To bring you soup and bread and bun
For you to eat — beloved son.'

Automatically I opened my mouth. With a deft movement Galena emptied in the liquid and it slipped down my throat. I sank back on the pillows and closed my eyes.

For twelve days and nights I drifted in and out of delirious sleep. But I never awoke except that one or other of them was there, sitting in the chair beside my bed. I was reassured by the sound of their voices and their footsteps coming and going.

When I was able to speak I told Dr Konstantin where I lived so that he might go there and gather my mother's things. But the Secret Police had rampaged through the workers' accommodation, including the single-room block of apartments where Mama and I lived. They broke up the furniture and threw our possessions into the street, where scavengers made off with everything. Father Galen, the priest who had organized the march, had disappeared. It was claimed that he was really a government spy who'd organized the protest so that the Okhrana could identify troublemakers and revolutionaries.

We never did find my mother. The army shovelled the bodies up and took them away in trucks. This was to conceal from the world how many had been killed. They buried these people outside the city in a pit filled with lime so that their very bones would dissolve.

And so I became part of the household of Dr Konstantin. Galena made me new clothes from a jacket and a pair of trousers which had belonged to the doctor.

'You might have used an old outfit,' he grumbled at her, 'and not cut up my best suit.'

'You never wore it,' she replied, 'and, anyway, it looks better on the boy than it ever did on you.'

I ate the tastiest food and received the best of what could be spared from the household budget. My mother had taught me my letters and counting numbers, but Dr Konstantin sent me to higher-level school, and I often accompanied him when he was treating patients. He expanded my mind and I excelled enough to gain a place, with his sponsorship, in the medical faculty of the city's university.

He spoke to me about how his work as a doctor had made him aware of the suffering of ordinary Russians. Dr K felt that Russia might be more democratically ruled by the Duma Council, but at the moment the Tsar gave them little power and appointed his own Ministers of State. The leaders of the Duma, in particular the socialist lawyer Alexander Kerensky, often sought Dr K's advice on welfare provision and the organization of health services.

As I grew older I began to lose hope that the Duma would ever achieve even basic civil rights for us. The councillors seemed badly organized, divided and ineffective. Besides which, Bolshevik ideas of complete democracy – overthrowing the ruling elite and all adults voting for a people's government – were infiltrating the university and converting students to the Bolsheviks' cause.

In recent years the household had to cope with increasing food shortages and other effects of the bungling conduct of the war against Germany. We never actually fell out, but the discussions were lively, for the three of us were on differing sides.

Galena held stubbornly to the belief that the Tsar was doing his best. She had faith in the Romanov leadership and believed that Russia could not be governed without a monarchy. Nothing would sway her from this opinion.

'If it ever happens that the Imperial Family are deposed, then people will turn on each other like rabid dogs,' she stated firmly.

'The French did it,' I protested.

'Exactly!' Galena said triumphantly. 'And replaced their royalty with a Reign of Terror.'

I was about to point out that the French now had democratic rights, when Dr K touched my arm. 'Galena prefers to live in the past. She refuses to move into the twentieth century with the rest of us.'

'Anyhow, the Tsar could not have ordered the army to fire upon the citizens.' Galena was unyielding. 'When the 1905 slaughter happened he was in his country house.'

'There is some doubt as to whether he knew what was happening, but perhaps our Tsar should not have remained inside a country house while he had a country to run,' the doctor observed mildly.

Now, eleven years after that march, the Tsar was still hiding away. The Imperial Family was in permanent residence at the Alexander Palace, fifteen miles south of the city, on their estate of Tsarskoe Selo. When war broke out Tsar Nicholas had the best excuse for avoiding the seat of government in Petrograd – he took over as Supreme Commander of our armed forces, and spent his time near the Front, leaving his wife to make foolish decisions in his absence. Meanwhile a wing of the Winter Palace was turned into a military hospital.

During those years, deep inside me I nursed a bitter hatred. He may not have given the actual order, but the Tsar had refused to condemn the actions of his army commanders who had murdered my mother. He and his Tsarina, Alexandra, gave a sum of money to help those who'd been hurt. But this did not wash away their guilt or erase the blood that stained the hands of the man I'd revered as our 'Little Father'.

Their imperial line was tainted. For over three hundred years they'd squandered the blood of countless slaves, serfs, peasants and soldiers in wars fought for greed and false glory. They were poisonous to Russia. When I was a child my thoughts on this were simple and straightforward – and as I reached adulthood I did not change my opinion. I believed that the Russian people would only be free when the Romanov family was gone. And so the logical solution was to get rid of the Romanovs – every last one of them.

Chapter 10

STEFAN

The day after her arrival I thought our guest, Nina, would lie abed, expecting someone to bring her a glass of hot tea and a basin of warm water to wash her face.

But she appeared early in the kitchen and said, 'When our estate workers were sick Papa and I would tend to them until a doctor arrived. So I thought I might be able to help with your clinic appointments this morning.'

I sniggered. I couldn't stop myself. What could she do? She looked as though she might pass out at the sight of blood. 'If you want to be useful you could make our breakfast,' I said.

She blushed, for I spoke to her as if she were a servant, and I enjoyed her discomfort.

At this point Dr K came in, saying, 'It would be helpful if you did that, Nina, please – if you don't mind.'

'I don't mind,' she replied. 'It will give Galena a longer rest before she starts her duties.'

At that I did laugh out loud, for Galena had gone out an hour before we rose to see if she could get some bread.

'The oatmeal has been soaking in that jug,' said Dr Konstantin.

Nina picked up the jug and peered into it.

'Galena usually puts it in a pot,' he prompted her.

The pots hung above the stove. She took down the nearest. It was the wrong size and weight and it was clear that she didn't know what to do.

I tilted my head to watch her in amusement.

Dr K handed me the keys of the shed we used as a consulting room. 'Stefan, please go and open up.' As I left I heard him instruct Nina in how to add the water and salt, then he gave her a wooden ladle.

Imagine having to be told how to stir a porridge pot! And she didn't do it well, for when we came to breakfast at the kitchen table it was half cooked and lumpy.

Galena, who had returned home with the bread, hissed at me, 'If you say one word to Nina about this breakfast, either now or any time hereafter, I will box your ears.'

Box my ears! Box *my* ears? Galena had never laid a hand on me in her life, through all the years since I'd arrived unexpectedly, a shivering orphan on the doorstep. Despite my tricks and naughtiness, the broken dishes and stolen sweetmeats, the cracked windows, the torn trousers and lost shoes, not once had she disciplined me with any force.

Worse was to follow. When we'd finished breakfast Galena spoke out in the sweetest tones. 'Nina,' she said, 'Stefan has no lecture until noon today, so I'm sure he'd be happy to show you the famous places of Petrograd this morning.'

I opened my mouth to make an excuse or invent an appointment, but then Dr K joined in, saying, 'I would expect nothing less. Stefan has been well brought up and knows how to behave to a guest of this house.'

So I was stuck with her for a whole two hours and had to make the best of it. 'I suppose you want to visit the cathedral and the Winter Palace and the famous bridges?' I asked as we left the house.

'Yes,' she replied, 'but firstly I would like you to show me the way to the bread shop where Galena queues in the morning.'

We walked in silence until we reached the bakery. I could barely control my disgust at her wish to view the sad sights of the city. 'You won't have an opportunity to ogle at the starving masses,' I said. 'By this time it will be shut.'

She surveyed the empty street. 'Why do the shops close so early?'

'Because within a few hours they run out of food and they have nothing more to sell.'

She gave me a peculiar look and fell silent.

From there we went to the cathedral. I stood at the back, keeping a wary eye out for aggressive beggars while she lit her candles and prayed.

'Why do you follow that custom?' I asked. Galena had warned me to be on my best behaviour but I felt it was a reasonable question to ask.

'It calms my soul,' she replied.

'What makes you think you have a soul?' I demanded.

'It's complex to explain and may not be worth the effort to do so to someone who has no real interest in the answer, or is perhaps only enquiring in order to mock my beliefs.' With that tart reply she marched ahead and I had to chase after her to catch up.

In a thoroughly bad mood, I took her to the Winter Palace.

'Have you ever been inside?'

'Oh, yes,' I said grimly, 'many times.'

'Is it very beautiful?'

I looked at her, so soft and fragile with her large blue eyes and blonde hair, and I wanted to fracture that glass bubble in which she lived.

'Would you like to see the wondrous Grand Halls, where the royalty of Europe processed, and the sumptuous Nicholas Hall, where two thousand people could sit for dinner?'

'Yes please,' she breathed, turning to walk towards the main entrance.

'This way,' I told her, and went instead along the riverside until we came to a small door set in a wall. She glanced at me in surprise when the sentry saluted as I approached.

We went by the servants' stair to the first floor.

The three main reception halls had been adapted to function as a military hospital. The wounded soldiers lay in beds crammed so closely that there was hardly space for the medical staff to walk between. The greater part of these beds contained patients who were the most grievous cases. Wretchedly ill and horrifically mutilated, the noise of their yowling moans rose to the splendid chandeliers and vaulted ceilings.

I offered her a handkerchief, for the smell of the rotting leg stumps and suppurating wounds was overpowering on this hot day. She gave a tiny shake of her head in rejection. I thought she would avert her eyes and hurry through, but she went on slowly, gazing attentively at the men and the nurses and the doctors and the walls and the roof and the windows and all about her.

We walked the length of the enormous Nicholas Hall, and by the time we reached the end of the room, the rosy bloom had vanished from her cheeks.

Chapter 11

STEFAN

That night I missed dinner.

I knew that Galena would leave something on the stove for me. In part I was late home because I wanted to check up on a few of my patients in the Winter Palace. But I also thought Nina would have given an account of where I'd taken her, including the military hospital. And while I didn't care a fig for Nina's opinion, I did mind that Galena would think me discourteous.

When I returned the women had gone to bed, but Dr K was in his study writing up medical notes. I saw the light on and went in and sat with my dinner plate and we discussed cases. Then he said casually, 'How went your outing with Nina this morning?'

'Why?' I asked suspiciously. 'What did she tell you?'

'Nothing much. That you showed her some interesting places and it was very pleasant.'

'That's all?' I asked.

'That's all,' he replied, then looked hard at me. 'Why did you want to know what she told us?'

'No reason.' I shrugged.

'You've always been a poor liar, Stefan. She didn't betray you, but I'm curious to know – where did you take her that you shouldn't have?'

'She asked to see the Winter Palace.' I spoke in a neutral voice. 'And so I showed her the Winter Palace.'

'Did that include a tour of its interior?'

I nodded.

Dr K studied my face. I shifted uncomfortably.

'You knew she would expect to see the glory of the grand apartments and you took her through the hospital wards.'

He made this statement in a flat tone, and I recalled from my youth that, on occasions when I'd misbehaved badly, he'd call me to his study and state my offence. Then he would wait to hear what I had to say in mitigation. Usually I was silent – as I was now. His method had the effect of shaming me, and was a better aid to improving my future behaviour than being belted or denied a treat.

'Perhaps you believed it to be right that Nina should know the truth of the situation in the city and the times in which we live?'

I accepted his lifeline and nodded my head. But we both knew that I'd been unkind. I mumbled, 'Good night, sir,' and went to bed.

★

I should have guessed what she was up to when she'd asked me the location of the bread shop. I came down the next morning to be confronted by Galena. 'Nina has gone out onto the streets by herself! See!' She waved a piece of paper in my face. 'She has written here that she rose early and went to queue for bread. Is this your fault, Stefan Petrovich? Is it? Did you make some remark that caused her to do this?'

'No!' I replied honestly. 'I did not. And if she'd asked me I would have told her that the rule of the house is that you claim that task as your own.'

'Nina is a green country girl,' Galena fretted. 'She doesn't know Vera or Duscha, or the rest of us who queue as a group. The rougher women might jostle her out. If she does manage to beg a loaf from that ill-humoured shopkeeper she'll be set upon by rogues on the way home. Nina won't know that she must hide the bread about her person and carry a stick to show that she's prepared to fend off hooligans.' She collapsed into a chair. 'We have a guest for one day. One day! And we lose her!'

'Yet here she is!' Dr K, who'd been keeping lookout at the kitchen window, strode through the scullery and flung the back door wide open.

Nina stumbled into the house with a heap of bread wrapped up in her green and purple shawl. 'I had not thought to bring a bag,' she said. 'I had to use this instead.' She emptied several loaves onto the table and shook out the crumbs.

'Nina, in future you must always forget to bring a bag

when you shop.' Dr K picked up a warm loaf and held it to his cheek. The air filled with the smell of freshly baked bread. 'You uncovered your head, and so dazzled the baker with your golden curls that he seems to have given you extra rations.'

'No, no,' she protested. 'I explained that I was new in the city and I didn't yet have an allowance. I told him that I didn't want to impose upon the family I was staying with and asked what I should do; and he said he understood perfectly.' She smiled brightly. 'He asked if I was coming back tomorrow. He is a lovely man.'

'That same person is the grumpiest baker in the entire city,' said Galena. 'Your grace must have melted his heart, but you mustn't trouble yourself like that again.'

'I'm happy to fetch the morning bread,' Nina said. 'The women are friendly and keep each other up to date with city news. And it means that Galena can make breakfast so that Dr Konstantin and Stefan don't have to endure my lumpy porridge – which they bravely ate yesterday . . . even though it was truly terrible.'

We sat down at the kitchen table to eat, with them laughing and chatting and me glowering into my bowl of oatmeal.

Chapter 12

STEFAN

I gobbled my breakfast and made to leave the house.

'One moment, Stefan!' Dr K waved a letter under my nose. 'Please give this to your Head of Studies. I've written to ask him if Nina may attend lectures with you today.' There was a smile on his face but a glint of steel in his eyes. 'I've altered her family names so that there will be less fuss with bureaucracy in registering for rations. From now on Nina will assume a position as my niece and be known as Nina Andreyovna Loskov, the daughter of my dead brother Andrey. Please bear that in mind when introducing her to anyone.'

'Oh! Oh, I thank you.' Nina jumped up from her chair and kissed Dr K on his cheek. 'That would be wonderful. Thank you so much – Godfather, my new uncle!' She rushed off to collect her coat.

'I'm not sure that's a good idea,' I appealed to Dr K.

'We are preparing for final exams and may have dissections today, or possibly a surgical session. And by late afternoon my year group often find themselves working in the wards of the Winter Palace.'

I thought he hadn't heard me for, as Nina left the room, he was looking after her like a fond father at a favourite child. But then he turned a piercing stare upon me and said: 'Nina mentioned an interest in medical matters, and that should include her becoming acquainted with the gruesome side of the subject.' He paused before continuing, 'You believe it to be right that a person should know the truth of a situation and the times in which we live, don't you, Stefan?'

I saw that if I didn't stop this at once, then I would have Nina with me all day. *All day.* I sought help from Galena. 'If you think the city is unsafe and Nina might come to harm there,' I said, 'may I inform you that the university is even worse. There are constant demonstrations and rows, with running battles between the different political factions.'

'Then you must stay close to Nina,' Galena responded in her 'this-argument-is-now-ended' voice, 'and protect her.'

'But—'

'Here you are.' She handed me and the girl – who had reappeared – a bag of food. 'I have made each of you a lunch. I wish you a pleasant day.'

'As do I,' said Dr K. 'And,' he added, 'we look forward to having dinner with both of you tonight so that we may hear every detail of it.'

My gaze went from Galena to Dr K and back again. They smiled serenely at me and I saw that they had plotted this entrapment in tandem, and I was defeated.

When we were out of sight of the house I lengthened my step so that Nina had to half jog to keep up. I decided that I too could make plans to have what I wanted. At the earliest opportunity I'd have a quiet word with my friends and tell them to ignore her, and also that they must, when we were together today, speak solely on subjects of which she would be ignorant, and at a level she couldn't understand. I reckoned that she'd become bored, and tire of pursuing what was surely a feigned interest in medicine. In future she'd want to remain at home with Galena and not bother me again.

I soon learned how traitorous friends can be. We had scarcely reached the university when Tomas, Eugene and Fyodor hailed me. These three were my closest companions. Having enrolled for medical studies on the same day, we'd gone in fellowship through our university years; falling out of taverns and into trouble and rescuing each other from awkward situations. Tomas was an amiable person who generally saw the humorous side of life, while Eugene increasingly kept to himself, poring over his textbooks in the hope that he might singlehandedly cure the ills of the world. Fyodor was the one I clashed with most, for we ceaselessly argued politics. I thought of him as a lumbering hothead who wanted social change by any means, fair or foul. Upon seeing us, they bounded across the avenue to greet me and I was forced to introduce Nina. Within minutes she was laughing at a joke of Tomas's and I felt myself edged aside as they engaged in animated conversation.

This proved to be the pattern for the day. Everywhere we went she charmed those we met.

As we were gathering up our notebooks at the end of the Anatomy lecture, the elderly Professor Kirichenko addressed her personally. 'Would our visiting student like to ask a question?'

Nina stood up from her bench. 'I'd like to thank you for allowing me to attend.'

'As long as you are a guest of Dr K' – the professor beamed at her – 'you may be here whenever you choose.'

Please don't say that, I thought to myself. *Please do not say that.*

'You know, you remind me of someone' – he peered into her face as she descended the steps towards the exit at the front of the lecture theatre – 'but I cannot remember who, exactly. What is your name?'

Too slowly I recalled Dr K's instruction to me that I should always use his family name when introducing Nina. I opened my mouth to do this but she was already speaking.

'Nina Ivanovna Izmailov,' she replied.

'Izmailov . . . Izmailov. Yes, that name. Of course! Was your father Ivan Sergeyevich Izmailov?'

'He was indeed!' she exclaimed. 'Papa attended this university to obtain a degree in language and literature.'

'I have the ability to detect similar bone structures in humans.' The professor was pleased with himself. 'The shape of a cranium, the set of the jaw.' He nodded vigorously. 'The skull has the framework of inherited genes.'

'How is it that you knew my father if he was in a different faculty?'

'Ivan Sergeyevich Izmailov was a noted brilliant student – graduated with distinction and began research for his Doctorate. Even though he wasn't studying medicine, I was aware of him. However, I'd say that in soft tissue you favour your mother in looks, especially regarding your eyes.'

'You knew my mother?' Nina moved closer to Professor Kirichenko.

'She was very beautiful. And gentle. Ivan had a promising career ahead of him. Such a shame that they—' He stopped.

'Please tell me more.' She laid her hand on his arm. 'I know practically nothing of my father's youth and even less of my mother's. My mama died when I was born, you see.' Her face coloured slightly, as if she were embarrassed about something.

'So, then, you have no knowledge of her early life . . .' Professor Kirichenko's voice tailed off.

'Only what my father told me. He said Mama was like him, an orphan with no family, and that she came from a distant place and was a stranger in the city.' Nina looked at the professor expectantly.

'I shouldn't say. Or rather, I *couldn't* say.' Suddenly Professor Kirichenko appeared stressed. He rubbed his forehead. 'My dear, I am chattering like a gossip. I am getting old. I talk too much, things mix themselves up in my head. As you said, your father wasn't one of my students, so I didn't really know him. And if I did, my brain is shrinking with age. Most days I hardly remember where I laid down my hat.' He gathered his papers and scuttled off.

Here was a puzzle! Professor Kirichenko's mind was sharper than any of his students'. He appeared to have knowledge of Nina's mother but was not prepared to share it; it seemed that there was something untoward in her ladyship's family background. Obviously Nina had drawn the same conclusion for, although she said nothing, she was biting her lip.

I tried to find an unobtrusive spot to eat lunch but, despite my asking for their co-operation in ostracizing Nina, my supposed friends clustered around her, offering to share their food. I ground my teeth in frustration while she commandeered their attention. It became apparent that she'd been highly educated by her father, for she was ignorant of little within our conversation. She had a wide-ranging knowledge of world geography and history. It was merely in modern politics that she was lacking.

'Didn't your father tell you what was happening in Russia?' asked Tomas, who, much to my annoyance, had appointed himself her personal mentor.

'As you say that, I see that it *is* odd.' She smiled at him and he smiled back and moved closer to her. 'Neither did Papa ever bring newspapers to the house. Yet I know that he was aware of the latest news, for he visited the stationmaster at Yekaterinburg each week to play chess, and railway staff are always up to date.' She puckered her brow as she thought about this. 'I wonder why he never broached the subject or spoke of his time as a student. Considering St Petersburg was his home city, and this' – she raised her long eyelashes and surveyed the buildings – 'was the university he attended.'

'Petrograd,' Tomas corrected her. 'Try to remember to call the city "Petrograd" in case someone accuses you of treason or being a German in disguise.'

'My country accent would let them know that I'm a Siberian Russian.' Nina laughed. Tomas and Eugene, and even the normally grumpy Fyodor, laughed with her.

But it was no laughing matter. Throughout the city the Okhrana – the Secret Police – had infiltrated the places of work and of learning. We joked that this year there were more Okhrana spies than students enrolled for courses in the university.

And so it was not just because her presence irritated me that, after classes, I told Nina to wait in the refectory while I attended a political gathering. It was to take place in an old wine cellar below the kitchens. Such assemblies were banned by the State, so were held in out-of-the-way places. This meant I was genuinely following Galena's instructions regarding Nina's safety – and in any case I'd

80

only been tasked with acquainting her with my medical studies. 'You could go to the library with Eugene,' I suggested. 'It's where he spends most of his free time, and he'd be pleased to introduce you to the staff.'

'I wouldn't dream of keeping him from his studies.' Nina regarded me steadily.

'Tomas will be in the refectory,' I said. 'You'd enjoy listening to one of his tall tales.'

'He *is* amusing,' she agreed, 'but I'd like to come along with you.'

'You can't.'

'Why not?'

'Because it's – it's it's . . . not suitable.'

'Why not? I think it's eminently suitable,' she replied. 'Today it has been revealed that I'm appallingly ignorant of what is going on in my own country.'

'I don't think Dr K and Galena will approve of my taking you to a political husting. Inflammatory statements are made. Accusations and threats of murder are commonplace. They'd be cross with me when you relate this at dinner this evening.'

'I will give them a report on the medical lectures I attended, nothing more.' She faced me squarely. 'I haven't yet said anything that might cause them to be displeased with you. Have I?'

Her meaning was clear and her dart struck home. 'Well . . . I don't want you getting into any bother.' I flung the words over my shoulder as I walked away.

'I won't,' she said meekly, following behind.

She appeared compliant, so when we reached the meeting place I said, 'You must wait outside. You'll hear clearly enough. Most of the speakers shout loudly.'

'Mmmm,' she said, and walked straight past me into the cellar.

Fyodor was handing out his Bolshevik propaganda. Nina took a leaflet and proceeded to engage him in discussion.

'We need a social revolution!' It took only a passing interest from someone to send Fyodor into one of his rants. 'You should read the writings of Lenin,' he told Nina. 'He lives in exile but his thoughts are published and sent to us secretly. Lenin believes that the people must mobilize. Our aim is to have our own troops, for socialism will not be achieved without military action.'

'Do you think that too, Stefan?' Nina asked me.

'It may be necessary,' I said reluctantly.

Fyodor was agitating on behalf of a group called the Bolsheviks and had taken to wearing the same red shirt as the factory workers to show his solidarity. I thought it pretentious, yet despite Dr K's moderate outlook my own mind had moved away from the idea of gradual liberalization via the Duma. I now believed that the total overthrowing of the Tsar's State Council was the best solution to Russia's problems. Ordinary people needed to take control and set up a completely new form of government – to establish a democracy. But Fyodor was more extreme. He'd make joining his Bolshevik political party compulsory and shoot anyone who refused.

'I'll take these home with me to read later.' Nina sat down beside me with a bundle of the leaflets she'd collected on her lap.

'Not that one, you won't,' I said, extricating a scurrilous drawing of the Tsarina consorting with Rasputin. 'Unless you want to give Galena a heart attack.'

'Don't *you* find it shocking,' she said, 'that people write such things about them?'

'Are we not allowed to criticize the nobility or the Government?' I retorted. 'Don't you believe we should have a free press?'

She thought about that. 'I believe in the ideal of a free press, but we must have restraints.'

'Here is someone who would have no restraints whatsoever.' I indicated Fyodor, who had got up to speak.

'Lenin, our leader, is calling upon us to form civil brigades.' Fyodor struck a pose in the middle of the room. 'By arming ourselves we'll be ready to fight in the glorious revolution.'

'How can Lenin lead the Bolsheviks when he is in hiding?' a member of the audience heckled loudly. 'Lenin is a coward who expects others to do his dirty work for him.'

'This won't be a debate.' I glanced around the room, which had filled up with unfamiliar faces. 'I suspect there are supporters of other political factions here to cause trouble. We should go.' I touched Nina's arm.

'No.' She moved away from me. 'I want to hear the debate.'

'When the time is right Lenin will return,' said Fyodor.

'You are a liar!' the heckler shouted and pulled a stick from under his coat.

'And you are a spy!' Fyodor leaped to grapple him by the throat.

The next second a fight broke out. A bottle flew past my head to crash against the wall. I swore aloud. 'Get down!' I pushed Nina to the floor. Among the turmoil of overturning chairs and scuffling feet we crawled into a corner.

'Will Fyodor be all right?' Nina peeked out from our safe spot.

A broken stool landed near, spraying us with splinters.

'He'll be fine,' I snapped, peeved that while I protected her in the midst of this mayhem Nina's concern was for someone else. Fyodor was roaring out some Bolshevik slogan while he and his political allies knocked their opponents' heads together. 'Let's see if we can get out of here.'

Hugging the wall, we slid round towards the door. A gap opened amongst the heaving bodies.

'Now!' I sprang up and turned to help Nina to her feet. But she'd been alert enough to see the opportunity, and was beside me. Shielding her as best I could I hustled her to the door – and this time she did not resist.

'You don't want to pay any attention to Fyodor,' I told Nina on our way home.

'Why not?'

Her habit of doing this – responding to statements I made with constant questions – was taxing my brain.

'You saw what happened,' I said. 'Fyodor preaches sedition, follows it up by trying to throttle someone, and a riot starts.'

'Fyodor was about to be attacked. What was he meant to do?'

'Not talk such arrant nonsense.' I slowed my pace. Nina was removing a fragment of wood from her shawl. 'Hold still,' I said. 'There is more scattered about your head.'

It was the first time we'd ever been so physically close. Her hair was burnished gold like the leaves which fall by the River Neva in autumn. My fingers were unexpectedly clumsy as I picked out slivers from among her curls.

'Let me return the favour.' Nina stretched to brush debris off my shoulders, and I was looking down into her face, long lashes framing brilliant blue eyes . . . 'That's better.' She stepped back. 'So, tell me. Why do you think Fyodor's beliefs are nonsense?'

'Because . . . because Lenin wants the whole world to revolt. It's an impossible proposition.'

'But what makes it impossible?'

'Oh,' I cried in exasperation. 'I can't begin to explain how futile that would be.'

'Why do you dismiss other people's opinions so readily?' She rounded on me. 'Surely we should listen to everyone's point of view?'

And we continued along the street, arguing.

Chapter 13

STEFAN

As the days lengthened Nina often sat apart from me in classes and found her own company between lectures and at break times.

Sometimes I saw her strolling with Tomas under the blossoming trees in the quadrangle — he, no doubt, entertaining her with his fund of funny jokes. And once, wearing a pretty floral patterned dress, she was sitting on the grass reading newspapers and political journals with Fyodor.

'Watch out, Nina!' I called. 'My friend will convert you to his cause and soon the colour of your clothes will be Bolshevik red!'

The sound of her laugh sparkled in the balmy air. I turned my head as I passed them and saw her gaze following me, her eyes a deeper blue than the summer sky.

Then I noticed that Nina was skipping more and more lectures. One morning when we left the house, instead of starting in on her usual list of enquiries concerning politics, she asked, 'Would you mind if I stopped attending classes with you?'

'What?' I was taken aback. To mask my confusion, I replied quickly, 'I don't mind at all!'

'I'd prefer it if you didn't mention our new arrangement to Galena and Dr K. Will you let me know the hours you intend to keep so that we can enter and leave the house about the same time each day?'

'Uh. If that's what you wish.' I was glad Nina had said that, for Dr K and Galena might blame me for her defection from the university. They'd suppose that I'd been rude or offhand with her. 'Where do you intend to go during the day, or the evening, for that matter?'

'I've haven't quite decided yet.' She smiled, and we parted company at the corner of the street, with me feeling a strange sense of disappointment.

It was the time of the 'White Nights', when because the city lies so far north towards the Arctic, for a week or so in high summer the sun barely sets. I was returning home late one evening, having stayed on at the university to work – and suddenly there was Nina ahead of me on the street. She was with two or three other women, chatting as they walked.

'Oh!' I heard her exclaim as a shaft of iridescent light turned the furrows of white cloud above us to glowing pink.

The group stopped to look at the view. I didn't especially want to meet them so I was forced to do likewise. The sky was cream and lilac, with the outline of the main bridges, which connect the two halves of the city like heavy lace fringing the horizons.

'The city is so beautiful,' her voice carried to me. 'Despite everything, it is lovely to see.'

Fair enough that she'd lost interest in studying medicine but, rather than gadding about amusing herself with her friends, the very least she could have done was to stay home and help Galena with the housework. Her attitude confirmed my first impressions – Nina was spoiled and didn't care to exert herself too much, either academically or physically. For the immediate future, with degree exams looming, my focus was on intensive study sessions and I should have been glad not to act the part of nanny. But, in truth, I missed the friction between us, and her constant barrage of questions, which I'd initially found annoying. I began to wonder what she was doing each day and who she might be with.

Three days later I found out how Nina was spending her time.

An influx of wounded soldiers meant that anyone with medical experience, including senior students, was deployed to the wards in the Winter Palace. I was doing post-operative dressings on an amputated arm when I noticed, six beds away, an auxiliary nurse pouring water into tumblers. Something about her movements as she lifted the jug caused me to pause. The white cap which was meant to cover her hair had slipped back, and blonde curls were springing loose.

How dare she take up a post here without informing anyone! I marched up the ward. 'What are *you* doing here?' I demanded.

Startled, she slopped the water over the trolley, but recovered enough to state calmly, 'Replenishing the water tumblers for our patients.'

'*Our* patients? These men are not *your* patients. You're not qualified to attend to patients. You shouldn't be here.'

'Why not?' There were red spots on her cheeks, but she stood her ground. 'You are.'

'I am a doctor!'

'And I am training to be a nursing auxiliary.'

'Who said that you could do this?'

'I made that decision for myself.' She drew herself up so that her face was almost on a level with my own. 'The social and political ideology which you so slavishly follow asserts that women should have equality with men. If your great revolution takes place we may even be the first women on earth to vote in a government election.'

I raised my voice. 'I don't "slavishly follow" anything!'

'What is the problem?' Neither of us had seen the approach of the Matron. 'Is there something amiss with this patient, Doctor?'

'No, no,' I said hurriedly.

'You are not talking on medical matters?' The Matron arched her eyebrows. Then she spied my badge, which showed her that I had not yet attained my degree. '*Student*

Doctor?' She voiced her disdain. 'You must not harass the female staff, else I will report you to your Head of Studies at the university.'

'I—'

'With respect, Matron,' Nina said swiftly, 'we are cousins, and although' – she assumed a look of wide-eyed innocence – 'we long for each other's company, we seldom have time to spend together.'

Nina's big lie made me irritable and failed to impress the Matron.

'Even so, it is not appropriate for nurses and doctors to fraternize. I will ignore your conduct on this occasion but there has to be no recurrence. Now, carry on with your work, both of you.'

I waited for Nina's shift to finish and then waylaid her as she left the Winter Palace.

'Why have you not said anything about this new career?'

'I didn't want to offend Dr K as he'd arranged for me to sample the classes at the university. Also, I thought that he and Galena wouldn't want me to work in these conditions. But I'm doing more good on the ward than sitting in advanced lectures and encumbering you with my presence.'

I opened my mouth to protest but found I couldn't disagree with anything she'd said.

'You have been attentive to me . . .' She hesitated before continuing, '. . . as much you could be. And for that I thank you, Stefan.'

My breath caught. It was the first time she'd addressed me using my name. Her saying it like that, with the lilt of the countryside in her accent, caused me to swallow the smart reply which was forming on my lips.

'I know you need to focus on your final exams, so this way of working will suit us both.'

We walked in silence for a bit and then I asked her, 'When are you going to tell Dr K and Galena what you are really doing every day?'

'Another week perhaps, when your lectures end and exams begin. Will you keep my secret until then?'

I nodded. She was right. It did suit me to say nothing and have no interruptions for a week.

But certain events unfolded which meant that, before two days had passed, Dr K and Galena were, quite abruptly, made aware of Nina's presence in the Winter Palace.

Chapter 14

STEFAN

One hot afternoon, when Tomas and I came on duty, the ward was a flurry of activity. Orderlies were rushing to and fro, sweeping floors, tidying beds and disposing of soiled dressings. Officials were gathered at the entrance to the Nicholas Hall.

'Important visitors,' the Matron snapped at us as she hurried by. 'Straighten your collars and mind your manners.'

We could hardly do our duties, as the wounded men had been so firmly tucked in their beds. I was told off when I loosened a soldier's clothing to listen to his breathing.

'Leave off medical examinations for now,' a doctor instructed me. 'See! They have arrived.'

I glanced to the main door. Two young girls were presenting gifts to the Matron while senior staff spoke to two older ones. Then our Chief Medical Officer assembled an escort to take them into the ward. A tall, ornately dressed lady stepped forward to the head of the procession.

Her image was known throughout Russia and she was unmistakable by her height and bearing. Advancing towards me was the Tsarina Alexandra Fedorovna Romanov!

With no wish to stand to attention, and bow my head or bend my knee as they passed, I slipped into the wide alcove of a grand window, still curtained with the heavy drapes which had adorned the room when it was used for royal receptions.

From my hiding place I could see the Imperial Family. Leading her daughters, the Tsarina paused now and then to give a prayer card to a wounded soldier. These feeble souls would grasp at her hand and ask her to bless them. This she did with a show of graciousness which I found infuriating.

A minute later I was joined by Tomas, who'd been working further along the line of beds. 'We are being subjected to an Imperial Inspection. I hope you wore a clean shirt today, Stefan Petrovich,' he joked.

'If only this was an explosive device' – I indicated the catheter bag I held in my hand – 'then a well-placed lob could wipe out the Romanov succession.' I was enraged by the Tsarina, in her exquisite hat with plumes of feathers wafting in the air, and the four girls in their dresses bedecked with frills and tucks and flounces, each wearing shoes of fine leather, with strings of pearls encircling their necks. Their faces were plump with good feeding, their hair and skin shining with health.

They were almost parallel with us when an order rang out.

'Put me down!' The voice was reedy, but the tone imperious. '*Now!* Nagorny, do as I say. At once!'

'It's him!' said Tomas. 'The child we rarely see or hear of – the heir to the imperial throne.'

At the rear of the entourage was the Tsar's son, the Tsarevich Alexei, borne aloft in the arms of a man in sailor's uniform. With his thin nose and oval face topped with reddish-brown hair, the Tsarevich resembled his mother, the Tsarina. When the sailor hesitated to obey him the boy cuffed his ear. With a sigh the man set him down upon his feet. The reason for him being carried became plain – one leg dragged slightly as he moved. Immediately he hobbled off to catch up with his family.

'Alexei!' his mother chided him. 'Your leg has yet to recover from the last blow. I asked you not to walk today.'

'But I want to walk. And I *will* walk. And run too, if I wish.' And saying this, he darted off between the beds.

'Be careful!' she called after him.

Her son laughed and moved faster. Then he swivelled round to make a defiant face at his family. The next instant he tripped and fell, his knee colliding with a washstand to land him on the floor with a howl of rage and frustration.

'Aieeee!' the Tsarina screeched.

The sound was taken up as a refrain by her daughters. 'Alexei! Alexei!' they wailed in unison like a bizarre Greek chorus, wringing their hands and clutching at each other.

Doctor and nurses flocked to his side. Among them was Nina. A bruise was rising rapidly at the spot where the child's knee had been knocked – unlike any bruise I'd ever seen before.

'A bed! A bed!' The Tsarina's voice, strident over the rest. 'Lay him upon a bed!'

For an awful moment I thought they were contemplating tipping a patient onto the floor to make room for the child.

'There is a long cushioned bench in this window alcove.' The Matron pulled aside our curtain, and Tomas and I were pressed into the far corner as they bore the boy in and laid him down.

'Pillows!' the Matron called. But Nina had anticipated her wishes and was there with pillows in her hand.

'My darling!' The Tsarina showered kisses on her son's head. 'I've told you many times that you must allow Sailor Nagorny to carry you whenever you are in unfamiliar surroundings.'

'I hate it!' the child said in a pettish voice. 'It makes me feel like a baby.'

'He *is* a baby,' Tomas whispered. 'His parents call him "Baby" rather than by his given name. They treat him like one and so he behaves like one. If this petulant child is the future of Russia then we are doomed.'

'It is they who should be doomed,' I replied tersely. 'Let us do away with the Romanovs.'

'Stefan, hush!' Tomas warned me.

But I couldn't, for in my head my twelve-year-old self once again saw his mama lying dead in the snow. I spoke louder. 'Let us do awa—'

'Tsarevich Alexi.' A pleasant voice cut across me. 'If you are being carried by the sailor, Nagorny, does that not mean that your head is higher up than everyone else's?'

'Nina!' Tomas breathed in my ear.

She'd been helping the Matron place the pillows behind the child's head and turned to address him with her question.

'I suppose it does,' the Tsarevich replied.

'Above your four *older* sisters?'

The boy nodded.

'Your mother too? The Tsarina?'

'Yes.'

'Even above His Imperial Majesty?' Nina's voice was tinged with awe. 'The Tsar of all the Russias?'

A look of triumphant pleasure appeared on the boy's face. His lips curved in a smile.

Nina opened her eyes very wide. 'Why, that is just like the famous Russian folk tale!'

'What folk tale is that?'

'*Masha and the Bear of the Forest*. Do you know it?'

'I do not.'

'It is a most exciting and intriguing story. My papa told it to me, and his papa told it to him, and on and on, so far back that it is a tale as old as Russia.'

'Was the bear very big?' the boy asked.

'The bear was gigantic!' Nina spread her hands upwards to the ceiling. 'As tall as that chandelier. And' – she poked the sailor gently in his stomach – 'five times as fat as your friend.'

'Did the bear eat Masha?'

'Ah . . . in order to find that out, you would have to hear the whole story.' Nina gave an impish smile. She lowered her voice to a whisper. 'On the edge of the forest, on the edge of the world, there was a teeny-tiny cottage. And inside this cottage there lived a little old couple. A man and his wife. They had but one child, and her name was . . . ?' Nina paused and held her chin as if thinking deeply.

'Masha!' cried the boy.

'How *did* you know that?'

'I am the Tsarevich. I know many things.' He waved his hand at her. 'Come, be seated and tell me this story.'

Nina glanced at the Tsarina.

'Yes, yes! Do as my son wishes!'

The Matron herself brought a chair for Nina to sit upon.

'Once upon a time,' Nina began, 'the rivers of Russia were as wide as the ocean, the mountains as high as the moon, and the forests full of trees and bushes with the finest berries you ever did see. There were blue berries and black berries, pink berries and ruby-red berries. The berries were plump and juicy, delicious to eat, sweet to spread on bread and scrumptious when baked in a pie.'

'I like berries,' the boy said.

'So do I!' Nina leaned in as if they were in conspiracy together. Taking advantage of their nearness, she subtly adjusted his pillows so that he reclined more upon the bench.

'See what Nina is doing,' Tomas pointed out in a low voice. 'How clever she is!'

'From the window of her teeny-tiny cottage at the edge of the forest Masha could see these berries shining brightly among the trees. Her mouth watered at the sight of them glistening on their bushes, ready ripened for her to pick. Bu . . . ut . . .' Nina pronounced these words in a tone of ominous warning: 'Masha had been told by her parents never, ever, ever to go into the forest on her own. And the reason was that in the deepest, darkest part of the forest there lived a great big—'

'Bear!' the boy supplied the answer.

'You are an exceptionally smart young man.' Nina stroked his forehead; tension eased from the child's body and he sank back into his pillows.

'Did Masha disobey her parents and go into the forest?'

'I am sorry to tell you that upon this occasion Masha was a disobedient child. In her defence, I should say that usually Masha *did* do as she was bidden. She set the table at mealtimes, helped cook dinner, washed dishes, chopped wood, hung out wet washing and folded it when dry. And she brushed her hair one hundred times before going to bed. As a rule Masha was well behaved.

'However' – Nina shook her head sadly – 'this time Masha was *not* a good girl. She longed to sample the tasty berries and feel the flavour on her lips and in her mouth. She thought that perhaps she could do this by taking only the eeniest-tweeniest step into the forest . . .

'Surely there could be no harm in that?'

Nina slowed and quietened the pace of her storytelling. 'Masha knew that her mother and father were having their after-dinner nap so she decided to go off on her adventure. She tiptoed out of her room and down the stairs. She tiptoed past her parents snoring loudly in their chairs by the fire. She tiptoed out of the front door and crept towards the forest—'

'Your Imperial Highness!'

A senior doctor – an eminent professor at the university – had come onto the ward. He called for a screen to be placed around the alcove. 'I am here to examine your son.'

Nina stopped talking. The child Alexei's attention wavered. He saw the professor in his white coat and his face registered stark fear.

'Mama!' He began to thrash about. 'Don't let the doctors hurt me!'

'Hush, hush, my baby, my pet, my lamb.' The Tsarina flew to his side, where she cooed and fluttered like a pigeon. 'I won't let anyone harm you.' She turned to the professor and asked him to leave.

'I am aware of your child's condition,' the professor said in a low voice. 'It would be best if I could look at the damaged area.'

'Mama, no!' The child's agitation increased. He wriggled and tossed on the bed. 'No needles. No tablets. No spoonfuls of nasty medicine.'

The Tsarina waved the professor away. 'A close friend of the Imperial Family, a person that the Tsar and I trust absolutely,' she stated, 'has advised me not to let doctors bother my son.'

'She's referring to that charlatan Rasputin.' Tomas spoke in my ear. 'The Siberian monk claims that his power is greater than any medicine on earth.'

'At least allow me to administer a painkiller,' the professor tried again.

Nina stood up, and aside, to give him room.

'Bring back the nurse with the blonde curls!' the child demanded in petulance. 'I want to hear the rest of the story.'

The professor and his colleagues left, with strict instructions from the Tsarina that they must not return.

Nina was reseated and the story resumed: 'Masha had brought a basket with her and she went among the bushes collecting and sampling the berries. It wasn't until sunset that she thought of going home. But when she turned round she realized that she'd wandered off the path and was now lost in the deepest, darkest part of the forest!'

The Tsarevich gasped. 'Where the bear lives?'

Slowly and deliberately Nina nodded, and a curl of hair fell over her forehead. I checked an impulse to reach out and tuck it under her nurse's cap.

'There was a light glimmering ahead. Masha walked towards it and saw it was lamp set in the window of a *very* high house with a red roof. Masha thought aloud: "I hope some kindly person lives there who will help me find my way home." And she went forward and knocked on the door.

'Three times she knocked, but no one answered. Masha peeked in the windows. The house was empty. So she opened the door and stepped over the threshold.'

The boy's sisters had moved to form a semicircle around their mother. The five women fixed their eyes intently on Nina's face.

And I realized that I was doing the same . . .

'Masha took seven small steps inside when . . . suddenly there was a tremendous roar! The most enormous bear appeared behind her. It leaped into the house and slammed the door shut! "I am ravenous," the Bear growled. It reared up on its hind legs and clawed the air. "I'm going to eat you for my dinner!"

'Now any other person in the same predicament might scream or shout or dissolve in tears. But Masha was brave and resourceful. She knew that she must think of a plan to rescue herself — very quickly indeed! "I am small and thin," she told the Bear. "Two bites and I'd be gone. A meal of me will hardly fill a hole in your tooth, far less your tummy. I have a better idea." She held up her basket, which was overflowing with berries. "I could use these to make you a tasty pie for your dinner."

'The idea of a warm pie appealed to the Bear and he agreed to Masha's suggestion. The pie was made. And while the Bear was eating it Masha looked for an opportunity to escape . . .'

Nina's voice tailed off; for her web of words had brought peace to the child's mind and the boy was slipping into sleep.

Chapter 15

STEFAN

'It was the most curious thing,' I told Dr K as we chatted in his study later. 'I wouldn't have believed it if I'd not seen it myself. Nina spun the story out as long as possible until the child, Alexei, became drowsy enough to sleep. And over the course of the afternoon the swelling actually subsided. It was a marvel to watch.'

'And another marvel that it has engendered in you some respect for Nina,' said Dr K, 'albeit grudging.'

'I do not disrespect Nina!'

'Stefan, you constantly disrespect her. It's a tribute to her good nature that she does not lose her temper with you. You act as though she is personally responsible for all Russia's woes.'

'I don't think so,' I protested. 'But clearly Nina thinks she is of a different class, for when she first arrived in this house she expected Galena to serve her and didn't intend to clear her own dinner dishes. She has no real notion of how people struggle each day to obtain enough food to eat. Even her action in seeking you out is evidence that she anticipated you providing for her. Her attitude to life was that a certain position in society means certain needs should always be met by others.'

'It's to her benefit then,' Dr K replied, 'that she is living with us and we can educate her properly. And it is perceptive of you, Stefan, to see how those who are spoiled expect things always to go as they wish them to.'

Afterwards it occurred to me that this latter remark might have been directed at myself, rather than at the girl.

As we rose to go for dinner Dr K asked casually, 'Am I right in thinking that today is not the first time that Nina has worked in the wards of the Winter Palace?'

The question was too direct for me to avoid.

'Em . . . I . . . I couldn't say,' I said, flustered; I realized that by speaking of the incident I'd inadvertently given away Nina's secret.

'I'm glad to see that you are at least attempting to be honourable, Stefan.' Dr K placed his hand on my shoulder. 'Of course Galena and I knew what was going on,' he said as we entered the kitchen, where Galena and Nina were transferring food from pots to serving dishes. 'My friends and fellow doctors have already complimented me on my niece's good work in tending wounded soldiers.'

Nina raised her head and looked at me.

Dr K exchanged a look with Galena, lifted the stacked plates and carried them through to the dining room.

'Naughty children!' Galena wagged her finger at both of us as we sat down at the table. 'Did you think that in this city, which is really a large village, we wouldn't find out what you were doing?'

Once she'd reprimanded both of us, Galena was eager to hear about the Imperial Family.

'Are they truly beautiful?' she asked.

I pretended I didn't hear the question and it was left to Nina to answer her.

'The Tsarina seems too haughty and cold to be truly beautiful.' Nina's reply was thoughtful. 'But her daughters are lovely. They were very considerate of the suffering of our patients. Olga and Tatiana, the elder girls, spoke seriously to the doctors, while the two younger ones, Maria and Anastasia, gave parcels of cake to the Matron to be shared among the wounded. And they chatted to the men and asked them about their families. I saw tears in their eyes as they heard how bravely the men endured their suffering.'

'And their clothes?' Galena wanted to know every detail – their jewellery, hairstyles, how they walked and what they said. 'Is it true that the Tsar's daughters are always dressed exactly the same?'

'Overdressed, I'd say,' I answered shortly. I'd no wish to waste time discussing the fashion of these parasitical people.

Nina, however, was happy to provide Galena with the

information, and although I wasn't interested in this, it made me realize how acutely observant she was. She could tell the type of cloth, describe the stitching and embroidery, the fullness of the skirts and the length of the hem, and whether gloves were worn.

Eventually I was forced to interrupt. 'That they should display such opulence when their subjects are starving is an offence against humanity.'

'What would you have them do?' Nina challenged me. Irritation was in her voice – no doubt due to the fact that she suspected I'd told Dr K what she was doing instead of attending lectures with me. 'Dress like paupers and depress the soldiers even further? The atmosphere in the ward lifted immeasurably when the imperial procession passed through. Whenever they stopped, the wounded men in nearby beds begged for the blessing of the Tsarina.'

'Alexandra Fedorovna Romanov is a housewife – not a divine deity that can bestow a blessing on anyone.'

'But my father blessed me as he lay dying,' said Nina. 'I did not believe he was divine, but I was glad to have his benediction upon my head.'

Dr K winked at Galena, and I spluttered a reply – I wouldn't be bested in an argument with this ignorant girl. 'The point is that the value of one of their rings would feed a family for a week.'

'If they dressed as ordinary folk, then they'd lose their aura of majesty.'

'Which is exactly what should happen!'

'People need leaders,' Nina said waspishly. 'Also,

Matron said to me that the Tsarina and her two older girls are training as nurses. Most days they don their uniforms and spend hours working in a military hospital which has been set up in the village at Tsarskoe Selo.'

'We should not be fooled by this token attempt to identify with the masses. The Tsar is leading his army to disaster.'

'The German Kaiser wanted to expand his empire and intended to take Russian property,' Dr K pointed out. 'We had to defend ourselves.'

'The ordinary German does not want this war any more than we do. Neither do the citizens of Britain, Belgium and France. Wars are caused by the greed of royal ruling classes who send their subjects to be killed that they may acquire more land and possessions. Perhaps Lenin is right, and the workers of the world should join forces across national boundaries and refuse to fight.'

Nina seized on my statement. 'Are you now agreeing with Fyodor's opinion when previously you said that he talked nonsense?'

'Was the boy there?' Galena interrupted to forestall yet another argument between us. 'The Tsarevich Alexei, was he with them?'

'He was,' Nina answered her.

I waited to see how she'd relate her part in the drama of the afternoon.

'He was dressed in a sailor suit. Most becoming,' she added, and then bent her head to her plate.

'Is he as weak as is rumoured?' Galena looked from

Nina to me. 'It is said one leg is so twisted that he has to be carried everywhere by an officer of the navy.'

Still I didn't speak.

'I believe his health is precarious,' said Nina. She made a gesture to indicate that she would say no more.

'The child's health *is* precarious,' I said, 'and his manner is precocious. He has a definite weakness, but upon entering the hospital he refused to be carried and subsequently tripped and struck his knee. A common injury for most children, but in his case . . .' I hesitated, unsure whether Dr K would want to pick up on the discussion we'd been having in his study before dinner.

'The Imperial Family does not wish it known openly,' Dr K explained, 'but in medical circles it is suspected that the child has inherited the condition known as haemophilia. It means his blood lacks the ability to clot properly; therefore a bleeding of any type can be fatal.'

'So if he sustains a cut on his skin, he could bleed to death?' I asked.

'Possibly. Although it's an internal, not an external, bleeding that presents the greatest danger. Even an innocent knock against a piece of furniture could cause a deep blood vessel to rupture.'

'When he struck his knee the skin bruised, but not as you would expect.' I recounted what had happened. 'Cold compresses and elevation of the limb failed to halt the swelling. I suppose if the internal bleeding continues, as it probably has in the past, then a haematoma forms.'

'Sounds painful,' murmured Galena. 'The poor mite.'

Dr K nodded. 'The child must suffer agonies as the swelling grows and pushes on his joints and internal organs.'

With a look of intense pity Nina asked, 'Is there no medicine that can help his condition?'

'There's innovative work being done on blood transfusion, but we're not far enough down that road yet. The ordering of blood groups is complex.'

'The child's mother wouldn't allow the doctors near him,' I said. 'She claimed that sometimes they make it worse. She mentioned this advice had been given to them by "a special friend of the Imperial Family". It was obvious she was talking of Rasputin.'

'A Holy Man' – Galena crossed herself – 'can do God's work where humans on earth cannot. Reliable witnesses have said that the child improves when Rasputin lays his hand on him. And such are the monk's healing skills that he doesn't even have to be present in the room. Once he sent a telegram to say that he was praying, and within hours the boy was well again.'

'Medical science is more effective than any incantation.' I was struggling not to offend Galena.

'Maybe not . . .' Dr K spoke thoughtfully. 'If the preferred analgesic is aspirin as a painkiller, then in this case it could be detrimental. There is evidence that aspirin helps patients with heart disease as it thins the blood and promotes freer flow through the body.'

'Administering aspirin discourages clotting?' I queried him. 'If the child had haemophilia, then it would stimulate the condition – the very opposite of what is needed!'

'Aspirin would help to relieve the pain, which would cause the boy to be less agitated. So, in that way, the situation would ease, but it may prolong the actual bleeding. However, if left to natural methods' – Dr K counted the progression on his fingers – 'then the blood pressure drops, the patient becomes lethargic, and bleeding eases. As long as there's no major organ damage, then this could manifest as a type of cure.'

'The monk is both placebo and panacea!' I exclaimed. 'The boy's family witness this and believe in his power. And because they do, it becomes a self-fulfilling prophecy. He has imprinted a certain behaviour upon them. By advising the Tsarina to ignore the doctors Rasputin appears to heal him magically.'

'If she believes that the power of Rasputin's personality can cure her child,' said Nina, 'small wonder that the Tsarina is in thrall to him.'

'I believe you were telling him a story, Nina?' Dr K made his statement a question.

Nina flashed me a look of hurt betrayal. 'It was one of the tales about Masha and the Bear which my father and I collected.'

'I heard you spun it out and, by doing so, the patient's pulse slowed and the swelling subsided.'

'You mustn't compliment me,' she said, 'for it was happenstance and not forethought. I sought to distract him the way you do when a child is ill.'

'By extending the story you reduced his agitation.'

'I extended it,' she laughed, 'because I could not rightly

remember the details. I must look it up in Papa's story booklets.'

'I'd be interested to read through your father's work,' said Dr K.

'After we've eaten I'll go to my room and bring them downstairs.'

When we'd finished the kitchen work, Nina contrived to catch me alone in the hall. 'You told Dr K that I was a nursing auxiliary in the Winter Palace.' She glared at me, blue eyes blazing. 'I have never talked about your actions outwith your presence, so in future I'd be grateful if you afforded me the same courtesy.'

Her being vexed made me uncomfortable but I was not going to back down. 'You were not the topic of my conversation. It came up because I was discussing the boy as I would a patient's case with Dr K – as an exchange between medical *professionals*.'

'You agreed to keep it secret that I was working there. For all your high principles you have a tenuous connec-tion with the truth, Stefan.' Nina flounced past me to go to her room.

Huh! I thought. I was not impressed by huffy females. Yet . . . it was true that she hadn't mentioned me taking her to the Winter Palace on our first sightseeing day, or the breaking bottles at the political meeting, or the vulgar drawing which had been put into her hand.

Perhaps I *should* have spoken to her before telling Dr K of her involvement with the Romanov child in the ward. I recalled agreeing when she'd asked me to keep silent about what she was doing each day and I could see how she might believe that I'd broken my word. The correct thing to do was go upstairs and explain to her that it had not been deliberate – and that Dr K and Galena already knew what she was doing. I put my hand on the banister.

At that moment the doorbell rang and I went to answer it.

A coachman stood there. Behind him a carriage was drawn up in the street.

'I am the Imperial Coachman, Sergei Pavlovich, and I have come to transport the woman known as Nurse Nina to the royal estate at Tsarskoe Selo.' He handed me an embossed card. 'The Tsarina Alexandra Fedorovna Romanov has summoned her to spend some time there with the Imperial Family.'

Chapter 16

NINA

I spoke the truth when I told Galena, Dr K and Stefan that I couldn't remember the details of the folk tale about Masha and the Bear of the Forest. During the events of the afternoon I'd struggled to find the words as I tried to ease the child's distress.

My travel bag was stored under the bed. I knelt down and pulled it towards me. My hand, groping for Papa's booklets and manuscripts, connected with the oblong casket. Without thinking I drew it out and unlocked it.

The dagger lay quietly in its hidden home.

The sound of my breathing filled the room. The ruby beckoned me with its fiery light. I raised my hand. My fingers curled like a claw and hovered above the handle. I felt compelled, and yet terrified, to touch it. Part of my mind told me that an object had no power over a person.

Still I reached to pick it up . . .

A thrill went through me. I rocked back on my heels. The dagger was snug in my grip, as if it had been made to fit my hand.

It belonged with me.

And I belonged to it.

The sound of someone coming upstairs returned me to reality. I unclasped my hand to replace the dagger in the casket. The imprint of the ruby was embedded in my palm.

A knock upon my bedroom door prompted me to lock the casket and shove the travel bag under the bed. I thought it might be Stefan come to make peace with me and was pleased because, although we bickered, our conversations were very enlightening. I decided to make him wait while I smoothed my dress and sorted my hair. Then, with my head high, I opened the door.

It was Galena who stood there. In a voice loaded with apprehension, she said, 'Dr K would like to speak to you in his study.'

In the hallway at the front of the house was a man dressed in the livery of an Imperial Coachman. 'Is this the girl?' he asked as I came downstairs. When Galena didn't answer him he directed a question to me. 'Are you Nina Andreyovna Loskov?'

I hesitated before saying, 'Yes'. It was strange to be addressed by Dr K's family name rather than that of my own father.

'Her Imperial Highness, the Tsarina Alexandra Fedorovna Romanov, requests that you come with me,' said the coachman.

Despite her beliefs, Galena said dismissively, 'Coachman Sergei Pavlovich, you will wait here until further notice while we decide our course of action.'

'You cannot disobey the wishes of the Tsarina,' the man said nervously. 'Please understand my position.'

Galena ushered me into the study and closed the door behind us. Stefan glanced at me as I entered the room. Maybe he wanted to say something conciliatory? But I wasn't going to make it easy for him so I turned my face away.

'The Tsarina has issued you with an invitation.' Dr K handed me a card.

A crested emblem was embossed in gold upon the thick cream card – a double-headed crowned eagle – the Romanov symbol of Imperial Russia. A special monogram printed below it indicated that the missive was from the Tsarina, and that I was summoned to her presence at the Alexander Palace at Tsarskoe Selo. Handwritten along the bottom, in a bold, yet awkwardly formed script, was a personal note to me.

The special friend who watches over our family is on a spiritual retreat at the monastery at Verkhoturye and unable to be with us just now. My son, Tsarevich Alexei, is still recovering from his accident and would like to hear the end of the folk tale. While we await the return of our friend, your presence would be of advantage to Alexei, and appreciated by us all.

'How long do you think this visit will be?' Galena asked Dr K.

'Who knows? The "Special Friend" referred to in the invitation is the monk, Grigory Rasputin. He could be gone for many days.'

Galena looked at Dr K. 'Supposing the Tsarina decides she wants Nina to go and live there permanently? Supposing . . .'

'You said Nina made a connection with the child?' Dr K looked to Stefan for an answer.

Stefan nodded.

'I do feel sorry for the boy, and his mother,' said Dr K, 'but they cannot take Nina from us to play nursemaid on a whim. There's no indication as to how long this visit might last.'

'It will be for as long as she is useful and then they will cast her out,' said Stefan. 'It is the way of the Romanovs. They are a plague upon the earth.'

'The Tsarina is like every other mother who grasps at any straw to ease her child's pain,' said Galena.

'I appreciate that,' said Dr K, 'but there is another fear that gnaws at her mind. She is too old to have another child, so this single boy is vital to their continued existence as autocratic rulers. By a law made by their own ancestor, the Romanov succession cannot be passed down via the female line.'

'Nina calmed her son and the boy liked her' – Galena rummaged her hair with her fingers – 'but must we allow her to go there alone? It could be dangerous' – she paused – 'for more than one reason.'

'Possibly more dangerous to refuse.' Dr K began to pace the floor.

'This is exactly what I mean,' Stefan railed. 'We have no rights over our own persons. A Romanov issues a summons and we are obliged to obey! They think they can acquire whatever they desire and regard us as their possessions. We should flout their commands. Nina must remain here.'

'*Excuse me!*' I shouted, furious that Dr K and Galena, and indeed Stefan, knew what was written on the invitation. 'You are discussing me as if I don't exist. I am here in this room – not some object to be despatched or disposed of. And *I* will decide what *I* will do!'

My outburst shocked Galena and Dr K – and Stefan too, I was pleased to note.

'We only wish what is best for you,' said Dr K.

'You have read correspondence which was addressed to me!' The embossed card trembled in my hand as I held it up. 'Before even I saw it! Have I no right to privacy?'

'But . . .' Galena tried to explain. 'When he handed the card to me the coachman told me what it said.'

'I am very grateful that you have taken me in and provided for me in my need. But you must not make me feel so beholden to you that I have no control over my own actions.'

'Of course, of course,' Dr K said in a placating tone. 'It was remiss of us. I'm sorry to have intruded.'

'So am I,' said Galena.

Stefan's lips were thin. He had no intention of apologizing. I told myself that I didn't care. In future I'd steel my soul against him and his opinion would be of no consequence to me. Yet . . . there was a spark of something in his eyes. Admiration? Perhaps not. More like surprise at the change in meek Nina. I was glad that he'd witnessed my temper, for whereas up until now I'd been accommodating with his moods, henceforth I'd assert myself more strongly with this young man.

'I am not a "straw" to be grasped at,' I went on in angry determination. 'Nor do I intend to "play" at being a nursemaid. I will remain in the Alexander Palace for as long as it takes to finish the story.'

'Would it be an idea to give the coachman the booklet which contains the story?' Galena suggested. 'Then you would not have to actually go there. His mother or one of his four sisters could read the tale to the boy.'

I shook my head in frustration. 'You are charitable people. I see that by your actions towards the needy who come regularly to the back gate, and also how you received me into this house. But' – I gave Stefan a look so that he'd realize my next barb was aimed at him – 'but, as has been recently pointed out to me, you are medical *professionals*. Of course I'm a mere auxiliary but, like you, am bound to help the sick no matter what their station in life. I have seen it happen in the hospital where, on occasion, a German soldier is treated by a Russian doctor.'

'That is so,' Dr K said reasonably. 'However, these circumstances—'

'The boy needs help,' I broke in, too far into my rant to be mannerly. 'I may be a simple nursemaid, but they think I can fulfil that role. Would you prevent me from going to help a sick child?' I stared at them in turn.

Stefan would not meet my gaze. He stood by the stove, isolated in his pride, his fingers balled into tight fists.

'Nina.' Dr K glanced at the door and lowered his voice to barely a whisper. 'For . . . several reasons I would rather you were not parted from us for too long. The political situation is extremely volatile. The whole of Russia, and in particular our city, is a like a huge barrel of gunpowder surrounded by desperate souls brandishing lighted tapers. You know' – he appealed to Stefan for confirmation – 'there are those who would welcome bloodshed as the way to achieve democracy.'

Stefan nodded curtly. 'One of my university friends has that outlook.'

He means Fyodor, I thought. And I agreed with Stefan on this. Fyodor's Bolshevik Party seemed to relish the idea of an armed rising.

'Any innocents who are damaged or die will be deemed expendable,' said Dr K harshly.

'And yet' – Stefan stared at the floor as he spoke – 'I am beginning to empathize with the militant faction. Daily

I tend the broken bodies and minds of the men the Imperial Family send to fight a war to preserve their power. I am moved to believe the only way Russia will be free is to destroy the dynasty of the Romanovs. They are a malignance: selfish and uncaring. Everyone with the name of Romanov must be swept away.'

'Ah, no!' Galena wrung her hands together. 'Beloved boy, do not speak such words of hate.'

Stefan gave his head a shake, as if trying to rid himself of the storm of emotion that had taken hold of him. My heart contracted at the anguish apparent on his face.

'This rage will pass.' Dr K touched Galena's shoulder in reassurance. 'Stefan is an angry youth,' he said. 'With a right to be angry. As have all young people' – he glanced at me – 'who see their future prospects being squandered by an older generation.'

'I will go to Tsarskoe Selo tonight,' I said in a conciliatory tone. 'If I don't, then it might bring trouble to your door. I'll return when the boy recovers or when their friend, the monk, returns.'

Galena and Dr K exchanged a helpless look.

'Nina,' Dr K said seriously, 'it is very likely that you will meet this pseudo-monk in person. When you do, try not to be alone with him. With regard to women, Rasputin has a certain . . . unsavoury . . . reputation.' A furrow of worry appeared on his brow. Normally confident when speaking, Dr K was ill at ease as he fumbled for the words to tell me to protect my virtue. 'Bawdy cartoons circulate indicating that he and the Tsarina are more intimate . . . than . . . than is proper.'

'I am aware of how I should behave with regard to my person. Dmitri, my father's steward, gave me a similar lecture before I left home.'

'I have other concerns . . .' Dr K looked once more at Galena. He drew in a deep breath. 'There is the Imperial Family themselves. Please try not to become attached to them. Their glamour could become beguiling. They might draw you into their circle, and – and . . .'

Suddenly Galena clicked her fingers. 'If she goes dressed as a nurse . . . ?' Then, realizing her error, she turned quickly to me. 'Nina. I am sorry, I should have asked you this directly. If you wear your overall, apron and cap, they will see that you are a professional person. May I help you change and pack a bag?'

'Thank you,' I said, tears prickling behind my eyelids as I went with her.

Galena didn't speak again until she was fixing the white cap firmly to my head. 'That's better.' She surveyed me critically. 'Much better. This gives you the appearance of a nurse and less like . . . yourself.' She took both my hands in hers and was forthright in her advice to me. 'Nina, you were born and reared in the country, but are old enough to know certain practical facts of how life begins. You are young but have lived long enough to be aware that there are some men who desire to possess women, their soul and their body. They have no interest in your mind or your happiness. For them it is about dominance and control.'

'You forget that I suffered the attentions of my father's lawyer, who had no interest in my personal welfare,' I reminded her.

'It is said that Rasputin can hypnotize people with his voice or even by gazing into their eyes.'

'Well then, I will not look into his eyes.'

Galena nodded and then impulsively hugged me. 'I would not have you harmed.'

The coachman sighed in relief when I came downstairs. Galena handed him my bag to put in the carriage. Dr K came from the study to say goodbye, with Stefan hovering in the background.

The doctor kissed me on both cheeks and embraced me. 'Don't stay too long,' he said. 'Things are changing rapidly, and for love of my friend, your father, and also for love of you yourself, Nina, I beg you to return soon. In all sorts of ways you will be safer with us.'

Stefan made no formal farewell to me, merely murmured, 'Stay safe, my . . . friend.'

I allowed him a small smile, and he added lightly, 'At least you won't have to queue at the bakery in the early morning in order to bring bread to their table.' Then he turned on his heel and ran upstairs to his rooms.

Dr K and Galena stood at the front door to wave me off. As the carriage pulled away I glanced upwards at the attic windows of the house – just in time to see the curtain fall back into place.

Chapter 17

NINA

There were soldiers marching ahead of us on the road to Tsarskoe Selo.

The coachman stopped the carriage and came to speak to me. 'Pay attention to me, young lady,' he said, 'for I, Sergei Pavlovich, am old enough to be your grandfather.' He closed the window blinds of the carriage. 'Don't peek out,' he advised. 'And hold on tight, for when we set off again I'll be going at full gallop.'

'Why?' I wondered at his caution. 'Aren't these our own troops?'

'This lot are men from the unit based at the fortress of Saints Peter and Paul. Low-life irregulars,' he said scornfully, 'recruited because of shortages at the Front. Cut your throat as soon as look at you.'

Of course I slid the blind aside as we drove past at speed. The soldiers didn't seem threatening – they were thin and bedraggled, with patched-up uniforms, and mostly carrying long sticks rather than actual rifles.

It was different when we arrived at the gates of the royal estate of Tsarskoe Selo. The men on duty there were the famous Imperial Guard: the elite of the army, with an unwavering loyalty to the Government and a personal pledge to defend the Tsar and his family. Their Commander took the Tsarina's invitation and studied it. Then he opened the carriage door and demanded that I step out while he searched inside. He picked up my travel bag. For one agonizing second I thought he was going to ask me to open it. He would find the dagger – I would be regarded as a would-be assassin! There was no reasonable explanation for carrying a weapon with me into the presence of the Tsarina and her children. I should have listened to Galena and Dr K, and sent the story booklets rather than coming here myself.

In a stark moment of recollection my father's voice sounded in my head like a knell of doom: *Do not ever leave our family home, Nina. If you do, then your life will be in peril!* An unshakeable conviction swept over me. Papa must have had a vision, a dreadful precognition of my fate. This terrifying realization caused me to turn pale. In a semi-faint I leaned against the carriage.

'Don't be afraid, young lady.' The Commander of the Imperial Guard misunderstood the reason for my frightened look. 'The Tsarina is not as severe as people say she is. I expect she wants you to help with our Tsarevich.'

Acknowledging my nursing outfit, he returned the invitation card, replaced my travel bag, and allowed us into the estate.

I had not thought what to expect of the interior of the Alexander Palace but was surprised to find that the private apartments occupied by the Imperial Family were furnished somewhat like the house of Dr K. The furniture was grander and more expensive, but the general mode was of a family home. The rooms had comfortable armchairs, plain drapes at the windows, and dotted about were many family photographs.

I was ushered into a sitting room, the walls of which were covered with holy images of every shape and size: depictions of the Lord God, Jesus Christ, His Blessed Mother, and a cluster of saints. Votive lamps burned on shelves with prayer cards set beside them. Supported by cushions, the Tsarina lay upon a long couch, with her son cuddled close and his four sisters standing around her.

'Nina!' On seeing me, the boy, Alexei, feebly tried to squirm upright.

'Lie still, Baby.' His mother restrained him. 'Nurse Nina will come and sit by us and finish the story for you.'

I waited for her command to approach. The Tsarina did not speak. Six pairs of eyes stared at me expectantly and I realized that they wanted me to take the initiative.

I brought a chair closer to the couch and sat down. There was a tangible tension in the room and, as I looked in my travel bag to find the story booklet, I became aware that its source was the Tsarina. Although half prone, she held herself in an awkward position of stiffness; I'd seen similar cases in the hospital, where men, fresh from the Front and suffering mental trauma, had coiled their muscles into a rigor that they were unable to release. The military doctors described it as a type of 'shell shock'.

'We find that the Tsarevich Alexei is unable to fall asleep tonight.' Her voice vibrated with anxiety. 'The bruise from his recent fall is aching and his mind is bothered with unwanted thoughts.'

I was to learn that the Tsarina had a habit of talking about her son in his presence as if he wasn't there. It was as if she thought he couldn't hear her or was not sensible to these remarks. And so I, who'd just lost my temper at similar treatment an hour or so previously, was in full empathy with this child.

I switched my gaze to the boy to address him. 'Would you like me to tell you the remainder of the story?'

He nodded listlessly.

I winked in an obvious manner, leaned over and whispered loudly, 'This story is for you, Alexei. Should we let others be present while I tell you what happens when Masha meets the Bear?'

He regarded me with puzzlement.

'What do you think?' I said. 'It's your decision. The storyteller must abide by your rules. If you choose, you may dismiss these people and have a private audience.'

He gasped at the enormity of my impertinence. My own heartbeat had increased. It was an all-or-nothing throw of the dice. Alexei's eyes went to his mother's face.

Alexei's sisters glanced at their mama in consternation. Their hands fluttered to join up and interlock fingers as they sought to support each other. The eldest one reached out and patted her mother's shoulder. And in an instant I understood something about this family relationship. The girls were concerned for their mother as much as for their brother. The Tsarina was strained to the point of breaking. And the young boy was bearing two burdens – that of his own illness plus the effect that it had upon his mama.

The Tsarina gave a nervous twitch. Then she laughed. It was a merry sound, and immediately the atmosphere in the room lightened. 'Of course, my baby son! You shall have whatever you desire, Alexei.'

'Please may we stay?' the girls begged their brother.

'You may.' Alexei's eyes were more alert than they'd been a few minutes previously.

'Perhaps you should introduce me to your sisters?' I suggested.

'They may introduce themselves.' Alexei wriggled away from his mother to be free of her constricting hug.

And so I met the four daughters of Tsar Nicholas and his wife, Tsarina Alexandra: the eldest, Olga, straining to fulfil the role of mother to her own mother; Tatiana, dainty and decorous; Maria of the mischievous smile; and the youngest, Anastasia.

They listened attentively as I continued with the story of *Masha and the Bear of the Forest*.

'Well, as you know, Masha made a pie for the Bear and hoped she might escape while he was eating it. But the Bear locked the door of his very high house and told Masha that she must stay and look after him. He decided that each morning he would go and gather berries in the wood, and at night Masha would make delicious pies for dinner.

'Masha saw that, in order to escape, she would have to think of a more cunning plan. One night, in addition to making a large pie for the Bear, she made lots of little ones too. "We have been taught that we should share our extra food with those less fortunate than ourselves," she told the Bear. "I would like to take these small pies to a poor man and woman who live by the edge of the forest."

'Although he was fierce, the Bear had a kind heart. He said, "Then let us share what we have."

'But' – I paused and raised my eyebrows – 'despite having a kind heart the Bear was not stupid. He realized that when Masha left his high house she might not return. And so he also said, "Put the pies in my tall pannier basket and I will take them to the couple who live at the edge of the forest."'

The youngest girl, Anastasia, put her hand to her mouth. 'Masha will never escape from the Bear!'

'Masha had guessed the Bear might do this' – I spoke reassuringly – 'and so, after she made the Bear promise that he would not eat any of the pies, she jumped into the pannier basket and hid herself among them.

'The Bear strapped the tall pannier basket onto his back and set off for the edge of the forest. After a *little* while the Bear stopped, for he dearly wanted to eat one of the pies. He began to undo the straps to take the basket from his back. And as he did so he said:

"I'm so far from Masha, she will not spy
If I sit down and eat a pie!"

'Masha heard this, and, popping her head up above that of the Bear's, she called out:

"I can see you, for I have climbed so high!
Bear of the Forest, you must *not* sit down and eat a pie."

'"Oh! Oh!" the Bear cried out. 'If Masha can see me she must have climbed onto the red roof of my tall house."

'He quickly refastened the straps of the pannier basket and went on his way. After a *long* while the Bear stopped again, for he dearly wanted to eat one of the pies. He began to undo the straps to take the pannier basket from his back. And as he did so he said:

"I'm so far from Masha, she will not spy
If I sit down and eat a pie!"

'Masha heard this, and, popping her head up above that of the Bear, she called out:

"I can see you, for I have climbed so high!

Bear of the Forest, you must *not* sit down and eat a pie."

' "Oh! Oh!" the Bear cried out. 'If Masha can see me she must have climbed to the chimney tops of the red roof of my tall house."

'He quickly refastened the straps of the pannier basket and went on his way. This time he did not stop until he reached the cottage at the edge of the forest. The Bear unstrapped the basket and dashed off. Whereupon Masha jumped out of the pannier basket, ran into her home, hugged her mother and father and promised never again to wander away.'

'And the Bear?' Olga, the eldest girl, asked. 'What happened to the Bear?'

'There is a legend,' I said, 'that the Bear loved Masha's pies so much that he'd pile heaps of berries by the cottage door. Masha would make a pie with these and leave it outside for him to eat. And in exchange the Bear would protect Masha and her family and neighbours from the packs of wolves that roamed the land.'

We began to discuss the tale and whether Masha was meant to meet the Bear, and for what purpose.

'Wolves prey on the weak and would devour them,' Alexei said seriously. 'Masha trained the Bear and mastered it to protect her family and her people.'

Alexei fell asleep. A few minutes later the Tsarina's head lolled back. Lovingly the sisters rearranged the cushions and tucked the coverlets around their mama and brother.

'I'll summon Alexei's nanny to watch over them now,' Olga told me.

We waited while the curtains were closed, and then the sisters led me to the bedroom where I was to sleep. Despite their different personalities the girls formed a unique bond of sisterhood, living physically close and sharing strong emotional ties. They'd link fingers and converse with each other in undertones – slipping in and out of a secret language where they employed special words and phrases to exchange private messages.

'I hope Father Grigory Rasputin stays away for a month,' Anastasia whispered to me as we said goodnight.

Chapter 18

NINA

Several weeks passed before Rasputin reappeared at the Alexander Palace. In that time I discovered that the main preoccupation of the household was Alexei and his health. Of prime concern was what Alexei ate and drank, what he did, what he wore, and how he looked. Breakfast and supper were served to him privately, after which the family doctor took his temperature and surveyed his body for blemishes which might indicate a blood vessel had burst and was causing internal bleeding.

The mention of the word 'doctor' triggered an allergic reaction in Alexei, and he complained loudly when he had to undergo an examination. The family doctor was a dedicated physician. Frequently disrespected and on occasions insulted by the boy, Dr Botkin maintained a courteous manner. He supported the Tsarina as far as he was able, but she was a woman of absolute opinions, and when she set herself on a course of action she refused to be diverted from it. In the absence of Rasputin the doctor quietly persisted in trying to turn the Tsarina's thoughts outwards to improve her frame of mind.

He did not openly decry the monk, but when she mentioned that Rasputin's method of dealing with one of Alexei's previous falls had been to ignore symptoms and effect a cure by prayer and the laying on of hands, Dr Botkin commented, 'We must not mistake a well-meaning amateur for a professionally qualified medical specialist.' He said this in such a way that the Tsarina did not bridle. But although she inclined her head to the doctor, it was plain that she had no intention of breaking her link with Father Grigory Rasputin.

Initially suspicious of me as another 'well-meaning amateur', Dr Botkin grew to trust me. We soon became friends and allies in keeping the emotional environment in the Alexander Palace as stable as possible.

While the weather stayed warm the girls went with their tutor into the extensive gardens to draw and paint. My papa had taught me to embrace difference and learn about the customs beyond our borders, but the daughters of the Tsar had no real knowledge of the wider world. Their pursuits were designed for them to be decorative, not useful, in their future life. Whereas I'd been free to browse as I pleased in my father's library, the Tsarina controlled her daughters' educational curriculum and censored their reading so that they'd no access to 'unsuitable' material.

What they did share with me was growing up within a household where they were kept ignorant of the real politics of Russia. But whereas I was now rapidly learning the truth, the Tsar and Tsarina deliberately kept their children apart from the real world. They existed inside a warm bubble of isolation. For me, living in my village near Yekaterinburg, it didn't matter so much. For them, in their situation and station, this lack of knowledge was potentially ruinous. Even I could see that as members of the ruling family they should be aware, not only of the activities of their nobles, but also of the circumstances of the poorest of their subjects. Their parents' attitude was that individuals were born into their life for a purpose, and must endure whatever that position brought them. None of them had any depth of appreciation of the effect of enduring abject poverty, and how rash and volatile their subjects might become. Crucially, they also had no depth of appreciation of the universal hostility towards Rasputin, or that this had extended to the Tsarina, with the stain also spreading over the children.

But their relatives and Ministers of State had seen the danger Rasputin posed and tried to warn them. With Rasputin absent and the Tsar stationed at the Front, the extended family came to visit the Alexander Palace. Uncles and cousins and members of the nobility arrived and left. The Tsar's mother – and even the Tsarina's own sister, who'd married another member of the Romanov family – urged her to break away from Father Grigory Rasputin.

The Tsarina would come from these encounters neurotic and exhausted. She took to locking herself in her sitting room for hours on end as she tried to dispel the migraines which plagued her. Then she'd emerge with an increasing resolve that she'd been too accommodating with the Ministers of the State and the representatives of the Duma. Her belief was that Russia needed a strong hand to rule it. The Romanovs were leaders and, like responsible parents, while they loved their subjects, a degree of strictness was required. Therefore the Tsarina wouldn't listen to any talk of democracy. It was against the will of the Tsar, which meant that it was against the will of God. Any minister who demurred was sacked and replaced. As she made these pronouncements I could see her doctor shaking his head in despair.

To begin with I only spent the late evenings and nights at the Alexander Palace, travelling into Petrograd each morning to continue my work at the hospital in the Winter Palace.

Stefan was right when he said I wouldn't have to get up so early each day. The coachman, Sergei Pavlovich, drove me on my journeys between the Winter Palace and Tsarskoe Selo – but I missed the camaraderie of the bread queue. The conversations there were so much less stilted than those of the Imperial Family. When I'd first taken a turn at waiting, some women had tried to elbow me out of my place, but Vera and Duscha and other friends of Galena took me under their wing. They teased me for my country accent, for the way I tied my shawl, for my ignorance of city politics, but there was no malice in their manner. I met Vera on the Prospekt one afternoon and she laughed in disbelief as I spoke wistfully of our times together outside the bakery.

Every evening I'd call in at Dr K's house to share a meal or collect clean clothing. The weather was becoming cooler and Dmitri had sent a box of my personal property from Yekaterinburg, which included boots and a warm coat. He wrote that the harvest was excellent and the estate should have enough food and fuel for the winter. He also said that, most likely, he'd be unable to send me any more of my possessions as Viktor Ilyich, the lawyer, was making a detailed account of the contents of the house. Until he completed this inventory Dmitri was forbidden to enter any room apart from the kitchen.

'Your father's lawyer sounds as if he might be valuing the household goods in order to sell them,' Dr K said when I mentioned this at dinner one night. 'I have some savings, Nina, so if there were things of yours or your father's that you wanted in particular I'd be happy to purchase them for you.'

'There is nothing I want or need,' I replied. 'I have my mother's photograph, my father's story pamphlets, and a carved—' I broke off to curb my loose tongue. 'I lack for nothing in my present life,' I added lamely.

'I'm sure you don't,' Stefan said acidly. 'It must be a trial for you to eat this.' He spooned up a piece of the gristly meat that Galena had managed to secure to make a stew.

'I'm guessing the Romanov table is buckling under the food laid upon it each day.'

'They endure rationing,' I responded coolly, to show Stefan that I was impervious to his jibes. 'But I assure you that it is no trial for me to eat this food. Galena's stew is infinitely better than any dish made by the royal cook.'

Stefan's face coloured up – for I'd made it seem that he was criticizing Galena's cooking. I had a reckless urge to stick my tongue out at him, and I wondered how he would react. Laughter bubbled up inside me.

Dr K looked from me to Stefan and back again. 'How is the Imperial Family?' he asked me in a bemused tone.

'Despite their wealth, they are not carefree. But the children play well together – the girls especially are closely bonded.' And I told him of their secret way of communicating by interlacing their fingers. 'It's as well that they look after each other, for they carry the weight of their brother's condition and their mother's indisposition too.'

'What indisposition does the mother have?' Galena was keen to hear of the Tsarina.

'I suppose it's a frailty of temperament. A form of acute anxiety . . . almost paranoia. The Tsarina believes everyone talks badly about her.'

'She is right,' said Stefan. 'They do. And with good cause. She behaves badly – both as the leader of a nation and in her personal life.'

'Certainly her liaison with Rasputin brings her name into disrepute,' said Dr K. 'But the monk has a point regarding the war. He wants the fighting to stop because the peasants are being slaughtered in their thousands. That's something you have said, Stefan.'

'Everyone wants the fighting to stop,' said Stefan.

'Yet none dare voice that opinion,' sighed Dr K, 'lest they are accused of treason.'

'Have you met Rasputin yet?' Galena asked me.

'No,' I answered her. 'When he returns I will leave the Alexander Palace.'

'Why would anyone leave such comfort?' Stefan snorted in disbelief. He stood up from the table. 'Please excuse me.' And, lifting his dishes and cutlery, he left the room.

After the door closed behind him Galena said, 'Stefan has passed his exams at the university.'

'I am glad to hear that,' I replied stiffly. Of course I knew that they'd all passed – Stefan, Tomas, Fyodor and Eugene. Tomas had given me the news when I met him on the wards of the Winter Palace. Later that same day I'd seen Stefan, dark hair flopping over his eyes, as he read a patient's notes. I longed to go to him and congratulate him, but thought he might rebuff me with a cutting remark.

'When two strong personalities meet,' Galena said sadly, 'stubborn pride can keep them apart.'

'Indeed' – Dr K spoke directly to her – 'it's a state of affairs I'm not unfamiliar with.'

To my surprise Galena blushed and looked down at her plate.

Chapter 19

NINA

When the Tsarina first asked me to stay on until Father Grigory Rasputin returned, it was on the understanding that I fulfilled my nursing duties each day in the city, coming in the evening to Tsarskoe Selo to sit with Alexei before he went to bed.

Usually the girls would join us to listen to my stories. Their mother was often otherwise engaged. The Tsarina was in extreme agitation with the problems of government and involved in constant arguments with the ministers, who she felt were deliberately thwarting her.

'I am surrounded by enemies!' she complained to Dr Botkin, who was having breakfast with us one morning.

'Those who offer advice which conflicts with your opinion are not always your enemies,' he replied.

'Prince Yusupov has requested an audience tonight. I may refuse. Thinking about it has made my head ache already.'

'You could listen to his point of view.'

'I am already aware of Prince Yusupov's point of view.' The Tsarina plucked at her hair in distraction. 'He and his coterie of admirers hate Father Grigory. With his devotees supporting him, the Prince will ooze superficial good will while urging me to banish Father Grigory from my court.'

'That might be no bad thing. We've been managing without Grigory Rasputin this last week or so.'

'*How dare you!*'

Olga put her hand to her mouth and her sisters drew close beside her as their mother tipped into hysteria.

'How can you say that?' Every moment of worry the Tsarina had suffered in the years since the birth of her son was visible on her face. 'How can you even *think* such a thing? I have endured torture – do you hear me? *Torture* – trying to cope in his absence. My beloved husband is far away, doing his best to lead our armies to victory. My family rely on Father Grigory's healing spirit and wise words to guide us. Without his presence near, I cannot function properly.'

'You may have to.'

The Tsarina seemed unable to process the meaning of his words.

'Our constitutional crisis deepens on all fronts.' The doctor spoke cautiously. 'Your reliance on that man makes you vulnerable. If you do not cast Rasputin off, there are others who may do it for you.'

'There will be no more discussion on this matter, either now or at any time in the future,' the Tsarina said with steely determination. 'Either accept the situation or leave my employ.'

'I would never abandon you, Alexandra Fedorovna,' the doctor replied in weary resignation. 'I will stay with you and your children, even unto death.'

At this the Tsarina's eyes filled with tears and she stood up and grasped both his hands in her own. 'Thank you. I know you mean well, but you must not criticize the prop that supports me and gives me strength. I will grant Prince Yusupov an audience and I will try to listen to him. Now I must bid "good morning" to my sweet baby, Alexei.'

She left the room without having spoken to her daughters. This was not unusual. It was as if every fibre of her being was concentrated on her son and she forgot the existence of his sisters. Their currency was of lesser value. By virtue of their gender they were relegated to an inferior status, dressed up and exhibited as ornaments, used for social exchange.

Sergei, the coachman, was waiting for me so I made to leave. Whereupon Olga laid her hand on my arm. 'Is it possible that you might come earlier this evening? You could eat with us while Mama is having her meeting with Prince Yusupov.'

'Yes, do please, Nina!' said Maria; and Anastasia clapped her hands.

Olga and Tatiana stretched out to link fingers with their younger sisters in their special manner, and they formed a circle around me, laughing and teasing. 'We won't let you go until you say "yes".'

The offer was tempting. Food prices kept rising and I'd noticed that during dinner Dr K and Galena took smaller amounts from the common dishes in order to leave enough for me and Stefan. There would be more for them to eat if I had my evening meal at the Alexander Palace.

On that occasion I consented.

And the arrangement became a habit . . .

Within a week Olga reminded me that she and Tatiana did nursing work in a hospital which had been set up in the village, adding: 'Nina, it isn't necessary for you to go into the city to be a nurse. You could join Tatiana and me on the days when we tend the wounded officers at the hospital here in Tsarskoe Selo.'

'It won't be for long,' Tatiana coaxed me. 'Father Grigory will be back soon.'

The girls were keen to be with me, and I, who'd never had a sister, was appreciative of their company. I was still calling in on Dr K and Galena after my shift at the Winter Palace. They welcomed and fussed over me. But Stefan was seldom there when I visited. Galena confided in me that they were concerned he was working too hard – and spending most of his spare time at illegal political meetings.

Our paths rarely crossed in the house, but I did see Stefan regularly at the hospital, for he was often on the wards where I was stationed. Sometimes I'd think he was watching me, but whenever I glanced in his direction he'd be looking elsewhere or reading a set of patient's notes.

I knew that initially he hadn't expected me to sustain my voluntary work, for he'd been with me when I almost fainted upon first seeing the wards in the Winter Palace. The smug look on Stefan's face that day made me hold my composure. He'd expected me to pass out or vomit so I had clamped my teeth together, dug my nails into my palms and kept walking. My senses were dazed before we'd reached the far doorway. But when he offered me his handkerchief I'd ignored him, for I knew he'd take it as a sign of weakness.

Although he still clashed with me, Stefan was popular with the hospital staff, and had such rapport with patients that he could acknowledge them by name. 'Dr Stefan Petrovich!' they called to him, and he'd give them a brief wave as he passed by.

The person who most lifted my spirits when I was tending men with broken bodies and shattered minds was Stefan's friend Tomas. I looked forward to seeing him. He would ask how I was doing and make encouraging comments. His personality shone light into dark places and I found that we shared a sense of humour.

The Matron looked at me searchingly when I asked for a transfer to the military hospital at Tsarskoe Selo. 'Are you sure that this is what you want to do?'

'It's temporary,' I explained. 'For a week or so.'

'Hmmph! That's what you say, but who knows where it could lead.' She wasn't convinced. 'I'm not your parent or guardian,' she said, 'but you are a young volunteer who has been put in my charge, therefore I do feel I should give you some advice.'

I waited expectantly.

'Here.' She penned the transfer note and thrust it at me. 'Take this to the Matron at the Tsarskoe Selo hospital. But have a care, Nina. And don't forget, you'll be welcome here if you ever decide to return.'

Her last sentence made no sense to me. My intention was to return within a few weeks – when Rasputin came back to the Alexander Palace.

'I'm sorry to lose one of my best nursing assistants. Also' – she made an awkward movement with her hands – 'things are changing. The regime is shaky. I wouldn't like to see you getting caught up in any . . . unpleasantness.'

I wondered what she meant by 'unpleasantness'. Unlike the workers in the military hospital of the Winter Palace, I didn't have to queue for food. I ate filling meals, slept in a downy bed, and had Sergei to drive me backwards and forwards between the city and Tsarskoe Selo hospital. My tasks at other times were light, primarily consisting of entertaining Alexei with a story each evening to send him to sleep.

Of course I overheard gossip, and mingling with palace staff and family gave me an insight into the concerns of both. The servants at the Alexander Palace did not truly believe the Tsarina was plotting with the German government, and the Commander of the Imperial Guard respected the Tsar and Tsarina. These people would not turn against the Imperial Family.

And yet . . . Fetching a glass of hot milk for Alexei from the kitchen one night, I overheard a maid whispering:

'It's a pity that Vladimir Ulyanov is cooped up in Switzerland. He's the man to take us out of this mire.'

'Yes,' the cook muttered. 'Lenin the Leader would sweep away the whole lot of them.'

I was aghast at the change in their loyalty. Surely these mild-mannered servants would be horrified at the thought of bloodshed. They weren't revolutionaries like Fyodor, who threatened to shoot anyone who disagreed with him; or Stefan, who wouldn't be happy until the Romanovs were deposed. They liked the family they served and had a lot to lose if there was a change of regime. They were fed and clothed and kept warm . . . yet, they wanted change.

Their gossip made me uneasy. Why were they grouching? They'd less reason to be aggrieved than the workers in the city who were sending their children to bed hungry every night. The palace staff ate well. The Tsarina's instructions to be frugal for the war effort meant fewer luxury goods were used in the kitchens, but everyone's stomach was full and, when winter came, the fuel stores of the palace would be stacked high with coal and dry wood. I'd forgotten that Galena had said that the city was no more than a large village. The imperial staff kept in constant touch with family and friends there; most of them had lost relatives in battle and knew many who were being ground down by constant poverty.

Which was more than I did.

My days were busy nursing. My free time was spent chatting to Olga and her younger sisters while we sat sewing, and in the evenings I attended to Alexei. My visits to Petrograd became less frequent. I took to writing letters addressed to Galena, Dr K and Stefan. I only ever received replies from Dr K. In one of these I enquired about each of them individually. Dr K wrote back with their news, and to say that Stefan was asking how I was getting on with helping the Tsarina run the country.

I was about to replace the letter in its envelope when I noticed something written down the side in familiar handwriting. It was Stefan's! I had to take the paper to my bedside lamp and turn it sideways to decipher his scrawl:

Make sure Nina knows that I said 'run' and not 'ruin'.

It was a quip equal to any of Tomas's and it made me smile. Within my heart there was a sudden ache of longing, the like of which I had not felt since first I'd left Yekaterinburg.

That night I slept with the letter under my pillow.

The days passed like this until one evening, when I'd just begun my nightly story, the door to the sitting room was flung open abruptly. Without warning or prior announcement a voice boomed out:

'It seems that I have a rival?'

'Holy Father!' The Tsarina half rose from her chair to greet an obviously highly important visitor.

He was dressed in black trousers, of the sort that peasants wear, loosely gathered into long leather boots.

His tunic was also black: cuffed at the wrist, high-collared, with a single embroidered sash slung down diagonally from one shoulder and tied around his waist, Siberian style.

'At last! At last!' The Tsarina was almost weeping with relief and joy. 'My prayers are answered. You heard me calling upon you and you came!'

He paused, his figure framed in the doorway. He was tall with a shaggy mane of hair. Square of shoulder and long of face, the man had striking features – deep-set eyes and a distinctive nose. His gaze, roving freely, took in everything before him. Even from there his presence filled the room. He didn't need to announce himself. His identity was obvious: branded as a drunkard, a charlatan and the ruin of Russia – here was the man they called Rasputin.

I sat up, utterly stunned by the sight of him. Not by his eyes, or his wild hair, or his height, or his voice, or any part of the magnetism that emanated from this person. It was something else which held me rooted in my seat.

Tucked in the sash which crossed his chest was a dagger.

The blade was curved, the handle set with white pearls. And within their heart a ruby stone shone blood red.

Chapter 20

NINA

Rasputin's eyes fixed on me.

'I hear that the Tsarevich has a new attendant. Someone who can stave off Alexei's headaches and reduce his pain by the power of words alone.' He was smiling as he came into the room, but there was a ripple of resentment in his tone. 'And this person is also from Siberia. Perhaps the Imperial Family has no more need of Father Grigory Rasputin?'

'Never say that!' the Tsarina responded. 'I have been demented by your absence. The Tsar is at the Front and I've had no one to turn to. We are constantly pestered with aggrieved relatives and disobedient government ministers. Their incompetence is appalling and they seem incapable of following a simple order. Beleaguered on all sides, we require you here more than ever.'

'We had no one to lead us in our prayers,' said Olga. 'Father Grigory, you are our spiritual director.'

Her sisters joined in with their own exclamations of joy at seeing him again. Alexei stretched out his arms as a much younger child does, in the expectation of being lifted up by a favourite adult.

Ignoring the chorus of greetings, Rasputin made his way slowly towards me. 'I wish to introduce myself.' He indicated for me to stand up.

When I got to my feet, my head was on a level with his shoulder. I had not switched my attention from the dagger and now it was directly before me: a perfect match to the one which lay in my carved casket. How could that be?

I glanced up. Rasputin was watching me with a curious expression. Galena's warning echoed in my ears. Immediately, I looked at the floor.

Rasputin placed both his hands on the top of my head. Then he slid them down my cheeks to cup my face. Determinedly I kept my eyes downcast. His hands were cool, the skin surprisingly smooth. With long fingers he took firm hold of my chin and tilted my face up to meet his own.

I opened my eyes.

And trembled under the intensity of his gaze.

His face was very close, covering mine as the sun might do the moon. Blotting out my light with superior radiance. My head went limp in his grip.

The colour of his eyes was dark, almost black, the pupils deep pools – waxing like a spinning planet and burning with a strange inner light. A pinpoint of red which . . .

'Receive the Spirit,' he murmured, and blew gently into my face.

His breath was hot and sweet, and yet was a cool balm to my soul.

'Nina.' He spoke my name the way no other ever had. It was as if only he knew how to pronounce it, with an emphasis that drew me towards him. Like an invisible drug his personality coiled around my being.

His eyes grew larger.

I was drowning.

He took his hands from my face and placed them on my shoulders. When he moved, a glint of fiery light flashed from the dagger held in the sash across his chest. Ah! It was *not* identical to mine. This one was a mirror image! The blade of Rasputin's dagger curved in the opposite direction.

The daggers were a matched pair!

My mind, hooked by that thought, shifted from its dream-like trance to the present moment. I blinked. Time had passed. And I had no idea if it was minutes or hours.

Then I heard a bird call from outside and noises within the palace . . . and became aware of the heavy silence in the room. I looked around. The Tsarina and her children were transfixed like wooden figures in a medieval tableau. They waited, as if only by Rasputin's authority could they resume their life.

I straightened up as Rasputin dropped his hands to his side. Still he was observing me and I saw now that there was a slyness in his eyes. His hypnotic hold on me had loosened and he wanted to know why. Noticing where my attention lay, he plucked the dagger from his sash and held it up.

'Do you like beautiful ornaments?'

'Not particularly,' I answered him steadily.

'Surely jewellery has some appeal?' he cajoled. 'These pure white pearls would make a fine necklace for your pretty neck.'

I stepped back as Rasputin reached to touch my throat. Apart from him I seemed to be the only person in the room capable of independent movement. And then I recalled how, when travelling through the countryside, Papa and I had met many pilgrims trudging the roads. Some were preachers or practising faith healers and earned their living by charitable donations. They were known as *starets*. Most villagers welcomed them, but sometimes stones were thrown, or they were mocked and rough boys and dogs set upon them to chase them away.

'Often these *starets* are delusional,' Papa told me. 'And it is the worst type of delusion, for it is self-delusion. They believe themselves to be a direct channel to the spirit world. Being absolutely convinced of this aids them in convincing others that their delusions are real. They can control the minds of their followers by means of their voice and their eyes.'

I seated myself upon the sofa, spreading my skirts wide so that the monk could not sit beside me. Rasputin gave a soft laugh. Then he turned and clapped his hands. At once the children joined in, clapping and smiling.

Rasputin spent the rest of the evening regaling us all with tales of adventures he'd had, being chased by wolves and fighting a bear single-handed. At bedtime he gave each of us a cone of incense he'd brought from his retreat at the monastery of Verkhoturye. We placed them in pottery burners and lit dozens of candles. He began to pray; chanting in a mellow voice which rose and fell in a rhythm that lulled the senses. As he raised his eyes to heaven, the sound ebbed and flowed, a combination of mouth music and mystical incantation. It seemed as if he was communicating directly with the Almighty.

And . . . I was a child again, half sleeping, my head in the crook of my father's arm as we listened to a story-teller in a remote village. And suddenly the words were familiar! I came awake and alert in the present time. Where others might think Rasputin was talking in tongues, I now recognized the language as an obscure Siberian dialect.

Was this man a total trickster?

The heady smell of our offerings combined with the cosy glow of the candles to create comforting warm contentment, and before the Tsarina and her children retired for the night Rasputin blessed them individually, laying his hands upon their heads.

Chapter 21

NINA

Rasputin was waiting in the corridor outside my bedroom.

'Why are you fascinated by the dagger I carry?'

He'd blocked my way and was obviously not going to move until I answered him. We were not so far from the rooms of the other personal staff so I was not especially intimidated.

'What makes you think I am?'

Rasputin gave me a knowing look. 'I see on your face what others do not. I see beneath the skin.'

'Ye . . . es,' I responded slowly, to allow myself time to think. It was obvious that he was an observant person, and had noticed my gaze fixated on the dagger he carried. I saw only one course of action if I was ever to find out the background to the dagger Papa had kept inside the carved wooden casket. I returned his gaze steadily. 'I own a similar dagger.'

He laughed – a braying scornful sound. 'Child, you are mistaken.'

'Mine has the same design: a ruby within a setting of pearls.'

'Impossible! If you knew where this weapon came from you would understand why.' Rasputin shook his head. 'There is no dagger which exactly matches the one I carry.'

'I did not say that my dagger was exactly the same. I said that it is similar. The difference between the two daggers is that their blades curve in opposite directions.'

'No!' The change in Rasputin was frightening. His face paled, he tore at his beard and tears flowed from his eyes. 'No! No!' he repeated. 'This is an ill omen!' He beat his fist upon his chest. 'Am *I* not the one to be saved?' he cried. Incoherent ramblings poured from his lips. 'I was sent to help the Russian people. My work is not yet done.'

I cowered against the wall as he ranted, but he seemed to have forgotten my presence.

Finally he flung himself on his knees and, turning his face, damp with perspiration, upwards, he chanted over and over, 'If it is to be, then I accept my fate.'

I tried to squeeze past him to reach my room, but his hand shot out and he grasped my wrist.

'Come with me!'

I struggled silently. He was stronger than me. My throat closed over in terror, and I could not shout for help. Against my will he dragged me along the corridor and through a series of rooms until we came to a section of the palace unknown to me. They may have been state apartments, or an imperial suite, used before the family moved to their present living space. We stopped in a reception hall. The windows were unshuttered and the light of the moon spread an eerie white glow upon the floors and walls. The decoration was formal: golden paint and wallpaper, gold ornaments, with heavily gilded furniture.

Far from any other living person, no one would hear my screams.

Rasputin dropped my hand and paced about, mumbling to himself and peering at the paintings which adorned the walls. I leaned against a pillar, shaking so much I could hardly stand. The door was ajar. I willed my legs to function and tried to walk towards it.

'By the bones of St Peter!' The yell he let out caused me to freeze. He leaped across the room, grabbed me round the waist and propelled me towards a particular painting. 'Look!' he commanded. 'The figure dressed in the skin of a wolf. See what Ivan the Terrible carries in his bandolier!'

The scene depicted the very first Tsar of all the Russias. His fierce gaze stared out at us. In years past Ivan had terrorized his nobles and courtiers, committing unspeakable atrocities upon them and the peoples of the lands he subdued. The artist had drawn a portrait of a battle where Ivan the Terrible stood with his foot on the bloodied body of a vanquished enemy.

In the sashes of the bandolier which criss-crossed his chest two daggers were set: a matched pair with their handles nestling side by side. Each hilt was encrusted with pearls and centred with a single flaming ruby.

'I don't understand,' I whispered.

'These daggers are bewitched.' Rasputin had recovered his composure.

'Bewitched?' I repeated stupidly.

'When I was given my dagger,' said Rasputin, 'I was told that it was one of a pair which carried a special enchantment.'

'Who gave the dagger to you?'

He ignored my question to continue with his tale. 'Recently, an older servant here told me of this painting. He said that the daggers had once been treasures of a Siberian tribe. Forged from metal by their first ruler, each ornamented with freshwater pearls and a giant ruby stone, and prayed over by their *staret*, holy priest, the daggers carried both a blessing and a curse.' A cloud shifted across the sky and the moon's light was dimmed.

'What kind of curse?' I shivered in the darkness as Rasputin's voice rolled around the golden hall.

'The twin daggers!' Again Rasputin was working himself into a frenzied state. 'Murderous and Merciful! Alpha and Omega! The Beginning and the End!'

'What happened to the daggers after Tsar Ivan died?' I cut in with my question to divert him.

'The next Tsar kept them, and they were passed down through the Imperial Family, to the present Tsar. But they were stolen from him. They disappeared, until—' He broke off.

'Until what?' I prompted him.

'Our meeting is an ill omen!' The cloud moved on and the moon's light showed Rasputin starkly outlined like a great beaked bird of prey. 'You have been sent to warn me of my own doom!' There were flecks of spit upon his beard. He was quieter, but an undercurrent of unease hung about him like a dark cloak.

'The Tsarina simply sent for me to help with Alexei while you were away.' I strove to speak in a manner that would calm him. 'That is my purpose in being here. I do not have your faith-healing skills. All I do is tell stories at night.'

'Stories . . .' He meditated for a moment. 'Stories have power,' he said. 'A story is the most powerful weapon in the wide, wide world.'

'We both know stories are not real.'

'We both know that stories have meanings that are very real,' he countered my statement. 'They are multi-faceted and many-layered.'

I considered my reply and, while I did, I realized that in this conversation Rasputin was speaking without his mask; he'd abandoned his role of the flamboyant prophet. We were having a genuine discussion. 'They bind people together,' I said. 'Validate their culture and emotions and give the humblest a voice.'

'And stories never die,' Rasputin added.

I sensed that it would not last, but for those few minutes I glimpsed a slice of honesty in this man. This made me brave enough to speak. 'We should go,' I suggested, thinking that I'd be happier where there were folk within hailing distance.

'Where did you find your dagger?'

My guard was down and the question asked so casually that I'd begun to answer him before I saw the trap.

'In a casket among my papa's papers after he died . . .' I tailed off.

'Who was your papa?'

'An ordinary man who spent his life collecting and studying the folk tales of our native Russian peoples.'

'He must have found it somewhere on his travels?' suggested Rasputin.

'I suppose so,' I answered. I'd no intention of sharing the details of my father's death with this man.

'Your dagger has a history. Nina, you must tell me what it is.'

'I have no sure knowledge of its history,' I said. That at least was true. I held back from mentioning the weird sensations I experienced when I held the dagger in my hands.

'There is something you are not sharing with me . . .' Rasputin locked his eyes on mine. This time I did not avert my gaze but stared at him with equal intensity. A minute passed, and then another. 'Hmm,' he grunted. He tilted his head to one side, accepting that he was unable to hypnotize me.

I released my breath. My confidence was mainly bluff; but at least I'd established that he could not bend me to his will.

'I should like to see the dagger you own. Did you bring it with you to the Alexander Palace?'

I'd anticipated this question and was ready with my answer. 'I did not.'

Rasputin nodded slowly. 'I caution you to say nothing about your dagger in this palace or the Imperial Court.'

'I have never spoken of it before to anyone,' I said in complete honesty.

'Wise girl!' Rasputin laughed then – one of his loud outbursts of mirth. He slung his arm across my shoulder as he might have done with a fellow drinking companion. 'You and I are fellow-healers, Nina, and we will get along together very well. Very well indeed.'

Chapter 22

NINA

That night I could not sleep.

When I returned to my room I'd taken the casket from my travel bag but I had not opened it.

I was afraid to.

My mind was in turmoil. What was the curse these daggers carried? What had Rasputin meant when he said they were bewitched? Were his words fanciful nonsense?

In a dream-like state I arose in the early hours of the morning. Carrying the casket to the window, I opened it up. The dagger was bathed in the light of the awakening world, and a force greater than I could understand made me take it once more in my hands.

Later – how much later? – I became aware that I was shivering in my nightshift, with no idea how long I'd been caught in the web of a trance. I had seen things, battles of long ago; and I'd heard stories – old, old stories.

I'd now no recollection of what they were. But one thing I was certain of: this dagger was crafted to kill. It was made as an instrument of murder. And I knew also that I had not found the dagger.

It had found me.

Rasputin reassured the Tsarina that, apart from a short visit to the monastery at Verkhoturye, he would remain in the city for the rest of the year.

His daughter had travelled from Siberia to help him in his charitable works and she was organizing shelters for the homeless which he would fund. He was busy with these projects but telephoned early each morning to enquire how the Imperial Family had passed the night, and called in at some point during the day that he might lead them in prayer and have a philosophical discussion. When he managed to catch me alone he would quiz me about the dagger I owned.

Had I ever held it in my hand? Rasputin asked. Did I feel drawn to wear it? Had I seen or heard things when in its presence?

To all these questions I answered 'no'.

When I said this he seemed relieved, yet slightly disappointed. For every question he asked me, I asked the same of him. And I believed him when he too answered 'no'.

One night when we were in the sitting room, waiting for the family to join us, I indicated the dagger in his belt and said, 'Can you definitely state that an object might be bewitched?'

He turned his great dark eyes upon me and said, 'Can you definitely state that it might not?'

'What is this talk of bewitchment?' The Tsarina entered the room and fluttered to his side like an elegant jenny-long-legs towards the lamplight.

Rasputin beamed at her. 'The Tsarina of all the Russias is the most bewitching creature ever born.'

She made a show of protest but dimpled with delight. I withdrew to my sewing corner as their two heads bent together and she unburdened herself by relating yet another spat she'd had with a government minister.

He was now in constant communication with the Tsarina and the children, and so, as Galena pointed out to me when I visited her, there was no further reason for me to lodge full-time at the Alexander Palace.

Yet no member of the Imperial Family mentioned my leaving, and I didn't raise the subject. I'd become accustomed to my new life. It was comfortable and relatively carefree. Working in the hospital at Tsarskoe Selo with Olga and Tatiana meant that my duties were less taxing than in the Winter Palace. And the city scared and depressed me. The streets were dirty and always thronged with demonstrators. Protest meetings were broken up by the police or detachments of soldiers; street corners haunted by mothers with babies happed up in shawls, begging for food.

Autumn was fading. The trees shed their garments of gold, yellow and bronze, and poked accusing fingers heavenwards. Their stripped spindly branches mimicked the stick-like limbs of the children who gathered in the city centre at midday to gobble the bowls of hot gruel dished out in buckets by volunteers. The thought of their suffering affected my own appetite and my throat closed over when I saw the dishes of food assembled for me to eat in the Alexander Palace. Yet the younger children in the palace whined because their morning pancakes were served without butter or sugar. I became conscious of how spoiled Alexei and his sisters were, and how the Imperial Family's acts of charity and donations to good causes did not impinge on their living conditions or their way of life.

Sergei Pavlovich, who drove me to and from Dr K's house, was also Rasputin's coachman. 'The monk is a wild drunkard, of that there's no doubt,' he told me, 'but we often stop on his journey home and he hands out anything the Tsarina has given him to refugees on the road.'

With the Tsar many miles away, Father Grigory Rasputin's visits lasted longer and longer; sometimes the Tsarina delayed her appointments with Ministers of State while she accepted the monk's advice on how to deal with them. She then reported back to him and they'd confer as to what her next move should be. Only after her subsequent action was the Tsar informed, by telephone or letter. I was sufficiently detached that I could observe Rasputin's effect on the family, collectively and individually. The Tsarina and her son were totally dominated by him. She consulted with Rasputin on every aspect of her life; it seemed as if the the boy relied on him even to breathe. Olga and Tatiana were submissive and easily swayed by his suggestions. Maria had a carefree nature but I saw that he guided her, and also the youngest girl, Anastasia. I worried that, as their reliance on him increased, if anything happened to him they would collapse in confusion.

In one thing the Ministers of the State and the Councillors of the Duma were united – this man Rasputin was a malevolent influence on the Imperial Family, and the Tsarina in particular. It was now a common cause between them and the nobility. Prince Yusupov especially loathed him – seeing Rasputin as a threat to the existence of every noble family. And so it was a complete surprise for him to arrive on the same day that the Tsarina was holding a reception where certain chosen guests could meet Father Grigory.

I was curious to see the young man whose inherited fortune was greater than the Tsar's, and who had a reputation for excessive self-gratification; throwing extra-vagant parties and buying exorbitantly priced jewels to adorn his clothes. He was married to the Tsar's niece and she loved him, whereas the Tsarina and her daughters clearly did not.

I heard the Tsarina caution the Prince before he entered the salon. 'You will be respectful to Father Grigory,' she told him, 'else I will have you escorted from the palace.'

This was not the form to speak to a nobleman. I expected one of Prince Yusupov's famous peevish outbursts, but he smiled and said, 'I will obey your wishes, Your Imperial Highness.' He bent to kiss the Tsarina's hand. His smile was as smooth as butter, his tone obsequious. 'For the good of Russia, I have resolved to befriend the man.'

Felix Yusupov was thirty years old, slim, handsome and worldly-wise. Hair combed and slicked flat with scented pomade, he was dressed in stylish clothes, making him the most fashionable man in the room.

'I do believe he's wearing kohl around his eyes!' A shocked whisper from Tatiana resulted in a disapproving look from her mother.

Prince Yusupov listened, seemingly engrossed, to Rasputin's account of his time as a contemplative hermit in the Verkhoturye Monastery. He asked questions about mysticism and how a man could interpret divine purpose. I had the impression that I was watching a play. Very skilfully performed – but nonetheless a show of acting.

'Fascinating, fascinating.' Yusupov's head was nodding so often that Maria murmured she thought the Prince was turning into the puppy in the folk tale *The Dog Who Could Never Say 'No'*. 'My wife is very interested in the occult,' said Prince Yusupov. 'It is a pity she isn't here to hear your thoughts and observations.'

'Ah, your wife . . . I have heard of her beauty and her grace.' Rasputin had drunk a large amount of alcohol but was only slightly tipsy. He gave Yusupov a crafty grin. 'Perhaps I should visit her personally, in your home?'

Yusupov's mouth twisted as he tried to cope with a remark which was verging on an insult to his wife's honour.

'Prince Yusupov's wife is our cousin, Irina,' Olga said quietly to me. 'She has never taken to Father Grigory as we have, and avoids his company.'

To the astonishment of everyone in the room Prince

Yusupov replied pleasantly, 'My wife would be overjoyed if you favoured our house with your presence. Come and visit us before Christmas?'

'Shortly I intend to spend a few days in the monastery at Verkhoturye.' Rasputin waved his hand in a careless manner. 'When I come back we will exchange letters and find a date to suit us both.'

'I will send a note to Cousin Irina' – Olga spoke to me privately after the prince had left – 'to inform her of this conversation. She adores her husband, but might decide to visit their estates in the Crimea rather than stay at the Moika Palace, for she'll not want to receive Father Grigory in her home.'

'Does your cousin dislike Father Grigory?' I asked.

Olga shook her head sadly. 'Like many people, Irina does not know our friend as we do. She sees him as an uneducated oaf.'

I looked across the room to where Rasputin was greedily eating the remainder of the cake and drinking the dregs from abandoned wine glasses. In this company it was a boorish act, but in the wastes of Siberia, where starvation stalked the land, food was never left to go to waste on a plate. I had a rush of empathy with this rough peasant man so far from home. And it stirred in my subconscious that eventually my resolve would weaken and I would reveal to him all I knew of the dagger I owned. There and then I resolved not to open the casket, or look upon the dagger, until I was able to tell Dr K about it and ask his advice.

It was a resolution I failed to keep.

Chapter 23

NINA

At the beginning of November winter spread its icy hand across the land.

'Snow!' the Tsarevich Alexei cried out, and he ran to the window.

'Careful, careful,' his mother called to him.

'Careful! Careful!' he parroted back at her. 'Fetch Nagorny! We'll have a snowball fight!'

'No, no, my sweet boy. No snowball fights for you.'

'Find my sledge, then!'

'You may have your sledge, but only so that Nagorny can pull you through the gardens.'

'I want to go down the long slope of the parkland.'

'You cannot, my beloved baby.'

The boy made a rude face at his mother.

'Alexei, you really mustn't do that.'

'I *will* slide down the long slope.' Alexei stamped his foot in anger. 'I will! I will! I *will*!'

'Of course you will,' said Maria, always the sister who would join in any fun.

Over her son's head, his mother looked to Olga for support.

'Hush,' Olga told her sister. 'It is too risky for our brother to play in the snow.'

'There is another good tale about Masha,' I said, hoping I might help dissuade Alexei from going outdoors. 'She gets lost in a blizzard where the snow has covered the houses. Everyone is inside, gazing out a white nothingness, when suddenly a bear—' I tried to intrigue him by breaking off in mid-sentence. 'It is called *Masha and the Bear of the Snowy Mountains*. Might we share that story this afternoon?'

'That sounds interesting.' The Tsarina, understanding my motive, seized on my suggestion. 'I'd like to hear that tale. Wouldn't we?' she appealed to her daughters.

'Of course, Mama,' Olga and Tatiana, being more mature, agreed with their mother.

The youngest girl, Anastasia, looked longingly out of the window and said nothing.

'I will take the front place on the sledge, Mama,' said Maria. 'Nina will go behind Alexei and hold him. That way he'll be cushioned on both sides.'

Alexei squealed with pleasure. Then he turned on his best look of heart-rending sadness, hung onto his mother's hand and pleaded until she relented and said, 'So be it!

But the pathway must be prepared to smooth out the bumps and remove any stones or harmful objects.'

Brooms were fetched and the servants crawled among the snow, sifting out the tiniest pebble lest the sledge topple over.

'I love snow!' said Alexei. 'Russia has the best snow in the whole world! And it's all mine.' He looked at his mother for confirmation. 'Isn't it, Mama?'

'Of course it is, my darling boy. God has ordained it. We are his ministers here on earth. Everything and everyone in Russia belongs to the Imperial Family.'

We played outside until the light faded. More snow began to fall, the flakes thicker and wider than before, and the icy wind caught in our throats. Alexei's cheeks were pink with healthy play, but I was relieved when Olga arrived with an order for us to go inside.

Nagorny took Alexei off to prepare him for bed. The girls bathed and changed into nightclothes, wrapping themselves up in thick fleecy dressing gowns. I went with them to the family sitting room where the Tsarina was waiting for us. The smell of hot chocolate and roasting chestnuts wafted through the air.

'Nina, you may tell me that story now,' said Alexei.

'Which story is that?' I asked him.

'*Masha and the Bear of the Snowy Mountains.*'

'That is a very good choice for a winter's eve.' I was about to settle myself beside Alexei when Father Grigory entered the room. He clicked his fingers at me. I hesitated and then thought it wiser to move so that he could have the privileged place next to the Tsarevich.

I glanced outside to where the sun was singeing through the snow clouds. Molten flame spreading across the sky. Like the ruby on the dagger stuck in Rasputin's sash.

He saw me looking at the dagger, and his lips curved in a sly smile. Raising his eyes to mine, and in a direct challenge, he declared, 'Tonight *I* will tell a story. It is a tale that I was told recently by an ancient sage who lives at the monastery of Verkhoturye.'

His voice was soft but had such a sinister timbre that the Tsarina asked with a nervous laugh, 'A story suitable for children, I hope?'

Rasputin didn't acknowledge her enquiry. He spread his hands and said, 'They say that everyone has another self walking the earth, and once upon a time this dagger of mine' – he gestured to the dagger in his sash – 'had a twin.'

My breath shortened.

He cast no glance in my direction.

'Many years ago the twin daggers found their way into the possession of a certain man. This man was rich but he was also greedy. Despite everything he had, he wanted more. He wanted what he owned, and he also wanted what other people owned. And one day he saw this pair of marvellous daggers.' Rasputin drew his dagger from his sash. The pearls gleamed in the lamplight; the ruby burned like a hot cinder. 'The daggers belonged to someone else, but the greedy man had visited this person's house and saw them, and he wanted them for himself.

Now' – Rasputin paused – 'what the greedy man did not know was that the daggers carried an enchantment . . .'

Alexei gasped. 'What sort of enchantment? Who placed the enchantment upon the daggers?'

'All in good time, my dear Tsarevich. Listen to the story and you will find out. First I must tell you how the daggers came to be. It was the nights of the Wolf Moon. In January – when time itself is changing – the Old Year dying; the New Year birthing.'

Rasputin was a master storyteller. Whatever else the monk was, or was not, storytelling was his forte. He modulated his voice, caressing the words, using his breath and his body to create drama and suspense and hold his audience entranced.

'This was the moment – when ravenous wolf packs roam the land – which was chosen for the daggers to be made. The blades were forged from the stars that shine in the arching vault of the sky. Orion the Hunter, the Great Bear – the ancient constellations that swing above us each night gave of their glory to make this metal.

'The pearls were harvested from the underground river which divides our world from the next. They are the tears of those awaiting the ferryman who will come to row them to the other side and into eternity.

'The ruby is a single flame captured from the fire that burns since time began in the centre of the earth.'

Alexei stared open-mouthed at the dagger as Rasputin held it aloft and twirled it in his hand.

'The greedy man had no knowledge of the enchantment.' Rasputin flicked a glance at me. 'The daggers were made for the mighty Genghis Khan. With great ceremony and in formal procession they were brought before him, whereupon the Magi of the tribe laid a mystic incantation upon them.'

Surreptitiously, the Tsarina crossed herself.

Rasputin's eyes went back into his head so that the whites showed, and he chanted what sounded more like sorcery than a prayer:

'*One dagger to save a life! One dagger to take a life!*'

Laying the dagger flat in his left hand, with his right he made a sign across it.

'I speak the very words as spoken by the Magi over the twin daggers. One dagger blessed. One dagger cursed.

'*Cursed!*'

He repeated the word so loudly that everyone in the room jumped in fright.

'The curse is that of violent death. He who holds the cursed dagger will use it to kill!'

'Eeee!' A strangled sound escaped my lips. What trickery was this? Apart from his initial devious look, Rasputin had not glanced in my direction. Yet he wasn't just telling the story to entertain the children. This tale was designed to confuse me.

'Father Grigory.' The Tsarina too was unsettled. 'How came you by this dagger?'

'Did you steal it?' Alexei's eyes were round with a morbid curiosity.

'Of course not!'

'How *did* you get the dagger?' The children clamoured for their answer.

'It's a story,' he reassured them; 'only a story.'

But, as Rasputin himself had said, stories have enormous power. I thought of the ones circulating in the city about his relationship with the Tsarina. In his manner and actions Rasputin was over-familiar with the Imperial Family; I didn't believe anything improper had happened between them, but the pamphlets and the pictures saying otherwise had achieved an authority. I saw now why the Okhrana Secret Police confiscated these publications, punished the students and the workers and smashed their printing presses. Stories stimulate our imagination.

'And so' − Rasputin lowered his voice to a sibilant whisper − 'the greedy man waited for his opportunity and he took the daggers. He *stole* the twin daggers, and thus he possessed both the blessed dagger and the cursed dagger. But, with no knowledge of the enchantment, he was unaware that he was in the greatest danger.'

Rasputin paused and took a long drink from the glass of spiced wine that sat on the table before him.

'In this story there is another man. An honest man. He was clever and studied many things. But he had no money. Now the greedy man had a daughter. She was very beautiful, and she too was clever and she too studied many things. She met the honest man and the honest man met her. And they fell in love.'

'Like a princess in a fairy tale,' breathed Anastasia.

'The honest man came to the house of the greedy man and asked to marry his daughter. He explained that he didn't have much money, but he had enough that he and the rich man's daughter could live with food and warmth. But the greedy man said he would not allow them to marry. He considered his daughter to be his property and, as he owned her, then no one else should have her.

'The daughter pleaded with her father but he refused. He told her that from that day forth he would lock her in a high room with no windows, and there she would remain until the day she died.

'Then his daughter declared that she would not stay in the house a moment longer. The honest man promised that he would look after her and protect her for the rest of her life. And he took the hand of his beloved and they walked towards the door.

'The greedy man pulled out one of the twin daggers he'd stolen, and he threatened to kill the honest man if he did not leave immediately, without his daughter. But . . .' Rasputin paused to gather in the gaze of his audience, pointedly ignoring me. 'What the greedy man did not know was that the dagger he'd chosen was the one with the curse.'

'No!' Tatiana cried out.

Olga reached for her sister and the girls entwined their fingers together for reassurance.

'The honest man was frightened,' said Rasputin. 'Not for himself, but for the girl. He believed that if he went away the greedy man might harm his daughter. He did not want to leave her in the house alone with him. The daughter shared his fears, and said that she would go with the honest man. The honest man struck the dagger from the hand of the greedy man and it clattered to the floor.

'The greedy man was apoplectic with anger. He was not strong enough to kill the honest man but he vowed he would prevent him from taking his daughter. He ran to where the dagger lay on the floor, and he picked it up and lunged at his daughter!'

'Horror!' Maria exclaimed dramatically. 'The Princess died in a pool of her own blood in her lover's arms!'

Rasputin shook his head. 'There *was* a pool of blood. And someone *did* die. But it was not the daughter.'

'It was the honest man?' said Alexei. 'It is sad that he died, but honourable that he sacrificed himself to save the Princess who he loved.'

Again Rasputin shook his head. 'It was not the honest man who died that night.'

'Tell us!' cried Tatiana. 'Please, Father Grigory, tell us what happened.'

'The honest man struggled with the greedy man. He tried to loosen his hold on the dagger. But the greedy man would not let go and the blade twisted and plunged deep into his own body. He fell dead upon the floor. Still clutching the bloodied dagger, the honest man called upon his beloved to open up the door. And the young couple fled from the house and ran away as fast and as far as they could.'

'Where?' asked Maria. 'Where did they go?'

'That I do not know.'

'A palace,' said Anastasia. 'Princesses always live in palaces like ours. Happily ever after.'

'This is a story you constructed around the dagger you carry?' said the Tsarina.

Very deliberately Rasputin shook his head and replaced his dagger in his sash. 'That is not the story of the dagger I carry,' he said. 'It is a story told to me concerning the *other* dagger, the twin of this one.'

'What happened to that other dagger?' Alexei asked him.

Rasputin stared at the boy, and then at each of us in turn. It was only now that his gaze connected with my own. A bright light shone forth from the depths of his eyes to lock with mine, and I had to grip the arms of my chair to prevent myself from rising up and walking across the carpet to him. I sat immobile; I could not break the spell. The sounds of the room, the children breathing, the wood crackling; these faded.

Time suspended . . . like a droplet of water hanging from a dripping tap. I could hear the swish of the snow outside and far away – far, far away – the howl of a wolf.

Rasputin snapped his head towards the window. He had heard it too!

My attention came back into the room. The children and the Tsarina sat unmoving. Then Rasputin laughed. A great uproar of noise that prompted everyone to join in.

Everyone except me.

A sliver of ice remained in my heart. Rasputin had been telling part of the life story of my father and mother. Of that I was convinced. Drawing myself to my feet, I went to the window and looked out. The snow had stopped. The sun was setting: a monstrous ball of fire pouring a swathe of crimson, like blood spreading over the white land.

'I must go home,' I said.

When they realized that I would be deeply unhappy to stay even one more night, the Imperial Family allowed me to leave. Before I went I asked to speak in private with Father Grigory Rasputin.

The austerity of his room surprised me. I'd expected silken covers and cushions, but it was furnished with a small table, a single wooden chair and a plain cot bed with rough blankets. There were no wine bottles, either full or empty. But there was a cloying smell, and as Rasputin's eyes were dilated and his voice slurred I guessed he had taken some drug.

I placed the carved casket on the table and opened the lid.

'Ah!' Rasputin breathed. 'So you *do* carry the other dagger with you. Be warned, Nina. The ancient sage said that the daggers could claim the soul of the person who owned them.'

'Please,' I begged him, 'tell me everything he said.'

'When you told me of the dagger you owned, I returned to the monastery and asked the oldest and wisest monk what he knew of their history. Most of what he said made no sense, but I stitched his ramblings together and embroidered them to make a performance for the children.'

We regarded each other warily. Rasputin was with-holding something from me, as I was from him.

I pushed the casket towards him. 'I want you to have this dagger as a gift for yourself or the monastery you visit.'

'They will not accept it.' Rasputin shook his head. 'They were glad to present me with the one I have. The sage said that ever since it arrived in their midst there have been factions and fights among their community. He spoke of visions, premonitions, of an apocalypse to come.'

'Tsar Ivan, who once owned them, had fits of madness.' I spoke hesitantly, thinking of my father, who had suffered mental torment in his last hours.

'Since I've been carrying this dagger I am more troubled in my spirit,' Rasputin admitted. 'And you, Nina? He looked at me keenly. 'Are you troubled in your spirit?'

I bit my lip, and then stammered out: 'It may be that I am dreaming. In my head I see and hear . . .'

'Scenes of blood and battles?' he pressed me.

I nodded.

Rasputin murmured, 'One dagger to take a life. One dagger to save a life.'

'And I have the dagger which takes life . . .' I said miserably. 'So there was no need for you to be alarmed. Our meeting was not an ill omen for you, after all. It is my burden to bear.' I closed the lid, lifted the casket and went to the door. 'I wish you well with your dagger, Father Grigory; that it may one day save your life.'

'I fear that I myself am not due any protection this dagger might offer.' There was an immeasurable sadness in

Rasputin's eyes as he replied. 'There was a singular aspect that the ancient sage was very definite about – when this dagger saves a life, it will be a life worth saving.'

As the sleigh runners sang over the icy road towards the city, thick white flakes again began to drift from the sky.

For the soldiers at the Front, the peasants in their hovels and the workers in their squalid houses, it signalled months of cold despair.

For the inhabitants of the Alexander Palace a fresh fall of snow caused joy. Exciting games would be planned. They'd eat gingerbread and drink hot cinnamon tea. I felt no pang of envy as I thought of this. They were inside a prison. The bars were made of sugar candy sticks and the floor lined with quilts of eiderdown – but what they lived in was a cage. A cage . . . and the door was closing.

At Dr K's house I shivered as I stepped out of the carriage.

'Have this.' Sergei reached in and dragged out a fur travelling blanket and thrust it at me.

I hesitated.

'It's no loss to them,' he said. 'They have fur blankets and coats beyond counting. You'll make better use of it.' He glanced upwards and then pointed to the team of animals which drew the sleigh. 'There are few birds about, and see how the horses labour in their breathing. This winter will kill more Russians than the guns of our enemy on the battlefields.'

Chapter 24

STEFAN

Dr K and I were ripping out the shelves in the long walk-in pantry cupboard when Nina returned from her extended stay at the Alexander Palace.

Galena, who was supervising our efforts at carpentry, went to answer the doorbell. 'Look who is here!' she announced. 'I will serve tea. And we will eat cake with our soup tonight.'

Everyone's mood lightened as Nina walked into the kitchen. I nodded a greeting and continued with my work.

'What's going on?' she asked, seeing what we were doing.

'I laugh at them,' said Galena. 'One is a qualified surgeon, the other a surgeon-in-apprenticeship, yet they wield a saw and a hammer like two-year-olds. And the litter they leave! Always, always, whatever he does, Dr K makes a mess.'

'You'd best be silent, woman,' Dr K grumbled back at her, 'if you want your new bedroom finished and somewhere to lay your head before midnight.'

Galena bustled off to find some treat she'd been saving for Christmastide while Dr K hugged Nina and then asked: 'Why did you return without sending word and so late in the day? Is there something wrong?'

'No, nothing,' she answered. And then, speaking as if she had rehearsed her statement, she said, 'Father Grigory Rasputin telephones the Imperial Family every morning and visits most days or evenings. I was able to come home as that arrangement fulfils what they need.'

'What they want, perhaps,' said Dr K, 'but not what they actually need. No, definitely not what they need.'

Nina indicated the broken shelves stacked beside the coal scuttle. 'Why has Galena to sleep in the pantry cupboard?'

'Fuel is strictly rationed,' Dr K explained, 'so we will no longer heat the middle floor of the house. My bed is being moved to my study and Galena will be by the kitchen. Stefan has elected to remain in his attic eyrie. While you, my lovely lass' – he kissed her on both cheeks – 'will have the dining room.'

'Let Galena have the dining room,' said Nina.

'The pantry is handier for me,' Galena said in her 'this-argument-is-now-ended' voice, 'to slip out in the morn-ing and stake my place in the bread queue.'

'I can do that,' Nina said. 'I will fetch the bread as I did before.'

'No, Nina, you can't.' Galena shook her head. 'Since you've been away things have changed in the city. The women of the bread queues must be at the bakery before five a.m. and wait for hours to obtain the most meagre loaf. It can only be me who does this because Stefan is training in surgery under Dr K and they are both fully occupied at the City Hospital. Refugees from the fighting are flooding in and the hospitals are swamped, so it's best if you return to nursing in the Winter Palace and help with our weekly clinic here. I will go out to find food and fuel to keep the other members of this household fit and able enough to use their medical skills for the good of the people. Now' – she chucked Nina under the chin – 'we will eat.'

Nina had with her a box of foodstuffs which the Tsarina's daughters had presented to her as a parting gift. She told us this almost apologetically.

'Bringing food or no food, Nina, we are glad to see you back with us again,' said Dr K. He gave her another hug and reached out to Galena who, looping her arm through mine, drew me with her to complete our circle.

Thus I was close to Nina, and could see the wisps of hair that framed her forehead and smell the natural scent from her skin, and I recalled the day of our first outing together. It made my heart ache for a return to the spirited squabbling we'd engaged in before everything became so complicated and murky.

Increasingly I felt isolated. I was losing touch with my friends from the university. Tomas, who wanted to specialize in neurology, was working in a military hospital for officers set up in one wing of the Moika Palace of Prince Yusupov under the supervision of a Dr Lazovert. Eugene had volunteered for the Army Medical Corps, in the unit which ran the hospital trains. Fyodor was working exclusively for the Bolsheviks. We'd had a huge row when he told me of his intentions to do this. I'd been bad-tempered and said that, even if the war ended, his hero Lenin's preferred method of revolution would create plenty of work to keep the doctors busy.

Politically too our group had fragmented – Eugene believed the war was a necessary evil, and he must devote his skills to helping the wounded from the battlefield. Tomas was a pacifist, while Fyodor and I disagreed on the best way to convince people to support a revolution. We were all so occupied that we could barely keep abreast of each other's news or meet up to enjoy companionship.

While we ate, Galena relentlessly quizzed Nina about her time in the Alexander Palace. Nina obligingly supplied answers until Galena said, 'Did you meet the monk, Father Grigory Rasputin?'

'I did.'

'And?'

'Rasputin is everything everyone says of him,' she said slowly.

Her apparent reluctance to discuss Rasputin caused Galena to glance at Dr K.

'And what do *you* say of him?' Dr K smiled and offered Nina a piece of bread.

'He is not an evil man. I know he sins in certain ways and is greedy for control, but he is self-deluded and at times quite vulnerable.' Her face took on a bleak expression.

Dr K laid down his soup spoon and put his hand over hers. 'Are you quite well, Nina?'

'Yes,' she said. 'Yes. I am now.'

'And yet you are strained, and thinner than when you left us. I would have thought there were few shortages in the Alexander Palace.'

'I had more food than I could eat,' she said.

'Self-deluded mystics can infiltrate the minds of others.' Dr K looked around and spoke as if he was having a discussion with everyone at the table, but he did not let go of Nina's hand. 'Although they might not be able to make you do as they want, they can plant a thought inside your head which becomes troublesome to you. And it is hard for the person to get rid of that thought.' Dr K was behaving the way he did when trying to coax a patient to relax in order to help them – an outwardly casual conversation but one with a purpose.

'I thank you for your wise words,' Nina said gratefully. Her tension dissipated and she said, 'I remembered your good advice, Galena, and it served me well whenever I was in Rasputin's company.'

'Does he indeed have eyes that burn like two hot coals?' Galena asked.

Nina smiled and replied, 'How could I know that when you told me never to look into his face?'

'I'll warrant the Tsarina looks into his face,' I said.

'They all do.' She took my sarcasm seriously. 'It's why Rasputin has such success in controlling them. His is an overpowering presence. He half hypnotizes Alexei into believing that whatever he says is true – thus if he tells Alexei he will recover from a bout of illness, then the very act of telling the child this aids him in doing so.'

'But because everything about the child's illness is cloaked in secrecy,' said Dr K, 'the Tsarevich is being denied the best care. Britain and America are experimenting in blood transfusion. If those techniques were perfected, who knows how long the child might live?'

'And if Rasputin were a true miracle worker,' I said, 'then he would heal the boy completely.'

'I'm sure he does his best,' said Galena. 'And every bit of assistance he gives must help in some way.'

'Unfortunately, in other matters his presence is not passive or neutral,' said Dr K. 'He helps the child, but he hinders everything else.'

Nina agreed. 'Without Rasputin's advice, the Tsarina can barely decide on which clothes to wear. He has no experience of government office, yet she appoints or sacks ministers according to his opinion. She is melancholic and desperately lonely, and he gives her the attention she craves. Her only son, upon whose shoulders rests the continuance of everything they believe in, is irrevocably ill. Whatever future medical advance might be made to relieve Alexei's condition will probably come too late for him. I sense it is awful to be Alexei,' she added, 'knowing he is only needed to survive long enough to breed another heir.'

'What a burden to have that as your sole purpose in life,' said Galena.

I did not join in their collective sigh of sympathy. The Romanovs themselves were a burden on Russia.

'May the Holy Mother look benevolently upon Alexei,' said Galena as she rose from her chair to fetch a tray from the kitchen.

Out of respect for her I waited until she had left the room before saying, 'I do pity him.' I flashed a look at Nina to show that my sympathy was genuine. 'Truly I do – but it may be best that he does not live. For the good of Russia, none of them should live.'

Chapter 25

STEFAN

Despite Dr K's wise advice and Galena coaxing her to eat more, there was a veil of disquiet around Nina that was beginning to bother me.

The house was too crowded downstairs for private conversation so I volunteered for shifts at the Winter Palace in order to speak to her. But the days went past and there was never an opportunity. The ever-vigilant Matron was on the prowl and the place was too public. And . . . I was nervous in case she spurned me. I was sure she'd seen me on a few occasions, but was she deliberately ignoring me? She seemed willing to chat with Tomas, who visited occasionally. I didn't blame her. The wards had some horrible cases and Tomas was witty and funny.

Once they were by the sluice room, and she was telling him of a young patient who refused to take his medicine because it tasted vile.

'There's a simple solution to that problem,' said Tomas. 'Make a great show of swallowing some of it yourself. Ensure that the men in the nearby beds see and hear you do it. Declaim loudly that, even though you are female and young and weak, you will do this to set him an example. He'll be shamed into drinking it.'

'What a wonderful idea!' Nina exclaimed.

'If any of it touches your lips, you mustn't screw up your face like this.' Tomas contorted his face like a gargoyle.

They were laughing together. I turned away so as not to disturb them.

On my way there one day I met Fyodor. He was bursting to tell me his news. 'Lenin is asking to be allowed safe passage through Germany to return to Russia!'

'The Germans must think he'll push for peace negotiations with them, so that they can turn their forces round and overrun France.'

'Who cares about the reason? The point is, he would energize and inspire the Bolshevik Party.'

'He'd be arrested as he stepped off the train.'

'That's true.' Fyodor gave me a meaningful look. 'But if enough people joined our cause, Lenin would have his own personal guard to protect him.'

'Not for me, thank you, Fyodor,' I replied. 'I don't want to trade an international war for a civil war.'

'It will happen anyway, Stefan – with or without you.'

When I got home, I related this conversation to the others.

'I fear Fyodor may be right,' said Dr K. 'The changes that Alexander Kerensky and other Duma councillors are proposing would take a long time to have a measurable effect on people's lives. Nina' – he addressed her – 'living as you did in the Alexander Palace, where the Tsarina is pulling the strings of our puppet government, were you aware of any developments?'

'Not with any degree of accuracy,' Nina replied. 'It's difficult to explain. What happens in the city and the rest of Russia does not interfere significantly with daily life in the Alexander Palace. They eat and read and sew and entertain friends; and each week there is a music recital. Before and after State Council meetings the Tsarina prays with Father Grigory Rasputin for divine guidance, and his advice prevails. Sometimes the Tsar wavers, but she manipulates her husband, who inevitably accepts Rasputin's point of view. The concerns of ordinary people are not fully represented or heard.'

'Then he is not just an incompetent Tsar,' I said. 'He is no Tsar at all!'

'The Tsar is very conflicted. He loves her. She loves him. They both love their children. What colours everything, affects their moods and movement and lies heavy upon their hearts, is Alexei's illness.'

'Which is definitely the condition known as haemophilia,' said Dr K.

'Do you know this for sure?'

'I did some research, made enquiries. Their physician, Dr Botkin, does what he can, but he is limited because the Tsar and Tsarina wish to maintain a shroud of secrecy about it. Haemophilia is genetically prevalent in royal families. The crowned heads of Europe fear that if people realized how frail and vulnerable the royal successions actually are, then it could lead to revolution and anarchy.'

'In Russia we are more than halfway along the road to a revolution,' I said.

'What Stefan says is true,' Dr K told Nina. 'Even the Russian nobles realize it is coming. Some are making independent contact with high-placed members of the Duma. If the Tsar does not give the Duma councillors constitutional power before the end of this year, then by the end of next year they will take it from him.'

Chapter 26

STEFAN

At the beginning of November Dr K and I were doing double shifts in the City Hospital, but as we slid into December the pressure eased. An official communiqué from the Ministry of War informed us that the practicalities of warfare meant that major engagements did not take place during the winter. The field marshals and generals planned their offensives for the spring.

When Dr K read this out at a staff meeting, one of the senior orderlies commented, 'That's not what our patients are saying. They tell us that the reason there are fewer wounded is because there is a shortage of stretcher-bearers, nurses and doctors. The ambulance service is so badly organized that if soldiers fall on the battlefield there is no hope of them being rescued. The wounded lie forgotten in no-man's-land.'

'There is a truth in their remarks,' a junior doctor

agreed. 'The men tell us that at the Front they bless the colder weather. They believe that freezing to death is an easier way of dying. They prefer it to bleeding out, or lying with infected flesh festering for days, going mad for lack of water.'

But the surgical wards of the City Hospital continued to be busy and we were working long days to deal with the number of operations.

Nine days before Christmas, Dr K and I, having finished a session in theatre, were discussing the fact that patients who we thought were recovering had relapsed, requiring further surgery. We'd spent a day cutting off limbs – whole legs and arms – from soldiers who'd had a foot or a hand amputated at the Front.

'Gangrene is tracking up the muscle.' Dr K paused outside the door of his office. 'I want to prepare a report to be sent to the War Ministry. The army doctors need to be aware of the consequences of their actions upon their patients. Their methods of dealing with shattered limb bones by guillotine-style amputation and suture seals in bacteria and encourages infection to spread. With gangrene it delivers a death sentence, for it spreads into the body, and by the time we see the patient it's too late. We need someone at the battlefield instructing the medics there how to perform a more efficient amputation.'

There was a burst of laughter from behind us. 'Oh, that's funny, that is.' A grizzled soldier, a double amputee, was sitting on a pallet in the corridor. The rough bandages on the stumps of his legs above his knees were suppurating brownish pus. 'Honourable Doctor, sir,' he said, 'there are no medics to perform amputations on the ordinary soldiers of the Front Line. We do it ourselves with kitchen knives or rusty bayonets.'

Dr K wiped his hand across his face. 'Nevertheless,' he replied, 'I will personally deliver the report I write and make sure that someone in authority reads it. Even if I have to take it to Tsar Nicholas himself.'

'Then, Honourable Doctor, please oblige me, and every other conscript, by ramming it down the Tsar's throat until he chokes upon it.'

Kneeling down beside him, Dr K said gently, 'You are suffering. I will give you something to take away the pain.'

'I have watched my comrades die unspeakable deaths,' the soldier replied. 'There is nothing you can give me to take away the pain in my heart.' And this man leaned back against the wall, closed his eyes, and quite deliberately gave up his spirit; passing away in front of us.

Dr K stayed motionless.

As did I.

Seconds ticked past and still we did not move. A suffocating blanket of despair descended upon us, draining away our energy and hope.

'Sir?' A hospital porter addressed me.

'What?'

'Sir? Will I take this soldier's body to the morgue?'

I nodded dumbly and bent to help Dr K to his feet.

When I made to follow him into his office, Dr K stopped me.

'Go home, Stefan,' he said. 'Go home and eat. Eat and rest. I want to be alone for a while.'

I was leaving the building when my friend Tomas hailed me. In the circumstances I was overjoyed to see his cheerful face. 'What brings you here?' I asked him. 'Why are you slumming with ordinary folks when you've sided with the nobility and treat only the officers?'

'Dr Lazovert sent me to fetch a phial of potassium crystals from the hospital pharmacy and bring it to the Moika Palace.'

'Potassium crystals? Is your medical team so hopelessly inept that you are deliberately killing off your patients now?'

'Prince Yusupov asked him for it. He said that the household is teeming with rats and they need a strong poison to get rid of them.'

'In the city slums they are eating the rats to stay alive.'

'So they say . . . and in the weeks I've worked in the military wards at the Moika I've never seen a rat.' A frown appeared on Tomas's chubby, pleasant face.

'Why didn't Dr Lazovert obtain the potassium from the hospital pharmacy himself?'

'He said he didn't have time. The stuff was needed speedily. The Prince has refurbished his basement to host a supper party there tonight and he didn't want his guests affronted by vermin scuttling about.'

'The rats would be in good company,' I joked, 'for Yusupov's relatives and friends *are* vermin.'

As we walked along, I told Tomas of the incident in the corridor, with the soldier who'd had both legs amputated, whereupon he asked me to come and look at one of his patients at the Moika Palace whose wounds were leaking a similar red–brown fluid. He added that, as a doctor, he had access to Prince Yusupov's well-stocked kitchens and we could share a jug of beer and some food.

It was an attractive idea. Galena wasn't expecting me at any specific time and lately she'd been going to bed very early so as to rise before dawn to get a place in the bread queues. Dr K would sleep on the sofa in his office, as he frequently did when he'd had a trying day. Nina would be at home . . . If we were alone, then maybe there would be an opportunity to speak to her and ask if there was anything troubling her. But . . . it was a long time since I'd met up with my friend, and I was enjoying the easy banter of our conversation. We were still making jokes about the Russian aristocracy as we walked along the canal to the entrance of the Moika Palace.

'This way,' said Tomas, leading me to a small courtyard. 'There is a secret door here to a private staircase going down directly to the basement. This is where Dr Lazovert instructed me to deliver the poison.'

I hung back in the yard while Tomas knocked upon the door. A shaft of light spilled out on the snow as Prince Yusupov himself answered the door.

'Come in!' he said gaily.

'I have patients to attend to.' Tomas made to turn away.

'Come in, I say!' Yusupov's words were slurred. He was drunk, but not enough that he would allow what he considered a lesser mortal to disobey his command. He pulled Tomas inside, failing to close the door behind him. I could hear Tomas protesting loudly. He wouldn't want to get involved, for it might harm his career to be associated with one of Prince Yusupov's decadent entertainments.

'A fellow doctor has come with me to consult over a special case,' said Tomas. 'We are hoping to save the man's life.'

'Bring him in too! What's his name?' asked Yusupov.

There was a silence and then I heard Tomas say, 'Tobias. My friend's name is Tobias.'

Yusupov began to call, 'Tobias! Tobias!' at the top of his voice.

I went through the door and followed them down the narrow staircase. The basement room was small but lavishly furnished. Plush drapes hung upon the walls, with expensive ornaments placed in alcoves and upon the mantelpiece. In the grate, a log fire burned, which should have made a rosy glow within the room. Instead, the leaping flames seemed demonic, casting grotesque dark shapes onto the ceiling.

No one had eaten, and yet the supper table was being arranged to make it look as if several people had taken a meal. Dr Lazovert was littering the imaginary guests' plates with food selected from a central dish containing cream-filled pastries and fancy chocolate cakes. Yusupov picked up a bottle of wine and slopped irregular amounts of it into the glasses. I had never seen this man at close quarters before, but his looks confirmed his reputation as a degenerate. His lean face was faintly mottled and his eyes intense, but his hands were steady enough as he bit into a cake and set the half-eaten portion upon a plate.

A false image of normality – the aftermath of a meal eaten with friends. For what reason?

'We should leave,' Tomas tried again.

'Don't be like that,' Yusupov chided him. 'Tonight's fun is just beginning.'

'My patient—' Tomas began.

'—is a member of the Romanov family.' I finished Tomas's sentence for him with a lie, in an attempt to find a way out of here before we were implicated in whatever devilish scheme was being concocted. 'And we are concerned for his health.'

'In that case' – Yusupov pouted – 'I suppose I must let you leave to do your doctoring work. But later I'll be upstairs with my real guests. After midnight we will be celebrating with music and dance. You are welcome to join us then.'

'Sire.' I bent my head. It made my skin crawl to do it, but I saw it as the fastest way out of that room. It reeked of evil, the stench worse than the gangrenous flesh which Dr K and I had been dealing with during the day.

On the staircase I was behind Tomas. At the door I glanced back. Dr Lazovert had put on a pair of rubber gloves. He emptied the contents of the phial into a bowl, then, using a pestle, he began to grind the potassium crystals to a powder.

Chapter 27

STEFAN

We went by the courtyard, through the gardens, to reach the wing of the palace where the military hospital had been set up. It was a revelation to me to see the amount of materials this unit had obtained. Stacked at the end of the ward were boxes containing instruments, bandages and cotton wool.

'The City Hospital is constantly running short of supplies,' I said enviously.

'Prince Yusupov is the richest man in Russia,' said Tomas. 'More wealthy than the Tsar. I suppose we must give him credit for spending some of his vast fortune on this.'

'He deserves no praise,' I said. 'Yusupov was pressurized into allowing a hospital in his home as a sop to preserve his status, for it was a scandal in high society that he refused to take a commission in the army. Olga, the

Tsarina's eldest daughter, commented openly about the disgrace of it. Yusupov's wife, Irina, is cousin to the Tsar's children, and Olga reduced this woman to tears with the shame he was bringing to the family. Nina told us. She said it was a source of tension among the Romanov relatives.'

'How is Nina?' Tomas's face softened at the mention of her name.

'She is fine,' I said.

'I miss her company,' he sighed. 'It's a great opportunity for me to work here. Dr Lazovert has a lot of experience and I'm learning so much. But I shared some jolly times with Nina in the Winter Palace when we were students, and I drop in there when I can, to exchange a few words.'

'Huh! I spoke to her once when she was on the ward and the Matron threatened to have me expelled from the university!'

'Perhaps it was the way you were speaking to Nina,' said Tomas. 'You can sound dismissive, Stefan. Nina and I tried to make jokes about our work and I tell funny stories. Nobody seemed to mind – and when the staff are happy it helps the patients too.'

'Let me look at this patient of yours,' I said to change the subject, for there was a sting of truth in what my friend was saying.

We spent over an hour with the man. I explained Dr K's experimental system of wound drainage. Tomas said he would ask Dr Lazovert to speak to Prince Yusupov so that they could obtain the necessary equipment. It was galling to think that the officer class would have access to this innovation, while the ordinary soldier languished in a poorly provided hospital scarcely a mile across the city.

When we'd finished, we made our way down the staircase to the kitchens. The landing windows looked out onto the beautiful snow-covered gardens and courtyard. Below us we heard a motor engine and twin beams of light pierced the darkness.

'It's gone eleven o'clock,' said Tomas. 'One of Prince Yusupov's guests is late for his mysterious supper party.'

We paused on the landing floor. So it was that we both saw the car stop and Dr Lazovert emerge from the driver's seat to walk round to the opposite side. He opened the passenger door and offered his arm to the person inside.

A large man climbed out. Framed in the headlamps, his shirt reflecting bright white from the snowy ground, there was no mistaking the figure of Grigory Rasputin.

Chapter 28

STEFAN

'It's none of our business,' said Tomas.

'But don't you think it strange that Rasputin arrives here secretly so late at night?' I asked. We'd carried on down to the kitchens and were sitting on stools enjoying a piece of chicken washed down with some pale ale.

'Strange things go on in the Moika Palace late at night,' said Tomas. 'Prince Yusupov holds séances and Ouija board sessions. His society has an unhealthy interest in the occult. He entertains disreputable people from every walk of life and indulges in every vain pursuit that money can afford.'

It was obvious that Tomas was uncomfortable talking about his host so I decided to leave it. In any case, I was tired. Unaccustomed to having my stomach so full of food, and woozy with the beer, I wanted to go home and sleep.

As I got up Tomas said, 'Please let Nina know that I was enquiring after her health.'

'I will,' I said, 'although she pays scant attention to anything I say.'

'That's not true, Stefan. When we'd converse she was forever quoting your opinion on subjects. Things you said around your dinner table.'

'Really?' I replied. 'I never thought that she paid any heed—' I was interrupted by a sudden sharp noise. 'What was that?'

'It sounded like a gun going off.' Tomas went to the kitchen door and opened it a crack. 'It came from Yusupov's private apartments.'

'I thought Yusupov didn't like guns,' I said. 'Isn't that why he didn't enlist in the army?'

'Should we investigate in case anyone is hurt?'

'If they kill each other off it will save the Bolsheviks the bother,' I said.

'But we are doctors . . .' Tomas said.

'Oh, very well.' I gave in to his kind heart. 'I'll come with you. It's worth the price of a jug of ale. But let's be cautious. They might think that having finished our work we want to join their party.'

We went to the main door of the palace and rang the bell. Faintly we heard a gramophone record playing music with a lively tune.

'They can't hear us,' said Tomas. 'Let us go down to the kitchens again and into the gardens to the courtyard.'

We'd just stepped outside when there was the sound

of another muffled explosion. This time the noise was unmistakable. It was definitely a firearm going off.

'I'm not sure that we should interfere.' I stepped hastily behind a pillar and Tomas came with me.

On the other side of the gardens a door crashed open.

Rasputin staggered out. He was foaming at the mouth and bellowing with the full power of his lungs. 'Help me!' he howled. 'For Mother Russia! Someone hear me and help me!' Roaring and screaming, he flailed his arms wildly.

A figure appeared at the door he had come through. Silhouetted from behind, it was hard to tell who it was. Not tall enough for the doctor, yet too broad to be Yusupov.

He raised a gun in his hand. Took aim and fired.

Rasputin fell down – the red blood from his body a sharp contrast on the white snow-covered ground. He got onto all fours and clawed his way along a few more paces.

The man approached him, step by determined step. This assassin kicked the body, which was squirming at his feet. Not once, but several times. Then he lifted his foot to stamp upon the defenceless man's head.

I started forward, but Tomas held me in a neck lock. 'Nothing we can do!' he sobbed in my ear. 'Nothing we can do. Stefan, listen to me. If they know we are here, we are dead men.'

The man bent over and grasped Rasputin by the collar of his coat. He heaved the body round so that it faced upwards. Then he leaned over and, placing the gun to Rasputin's forehead, fired a single shot.

Tomas dragged me to a side gate and out into a lane. We

tottered towards the river, where both of us were violently sick. I chipped some ice and put it in my mouth to swill away the spew and rid myself of the taste on my tongue.

Tomas spat into our foul-smelling vomit. 'Waste of good beer,' he said.

We were crouched so low that the car was almost upon us before we noticed it, the engine purring as it inched along the road. We flattened ourselves into the gutter.

'Yusupov's car,' Tomas groaned. 'Are they searching for us?'

I risked a peek. The driver was facing straight ahead, concentrating on the road. 'I don't think so,' I said hoarsely. 'He's driving like that to be as quiet as possible. Perhaps they're getting rid of the corpse before morning.'

Instinctively we began to follow them. They drove so slowly that we were able to keep them in our sights. The car stopped at the parapet of the Bolshoy Petrovsky Bridge. It was a night of high cloud, with the moon luminescent amid a multitude of stars. When we reached the bridge, one of the men was on the riverbank with a hammer in his hand, trying to batter a hole in the frozen surface.

'Here!' he cried out in muted tones.

The other two manoeuvred a bulky object from the car. It was weighted with chains, which clanked as they towed the body of Rasputin down the slope. They pushed him off the bank and guided the corpse to the hole in the ice. Below, the current of the river would be moving and breaking up ice into floes downstream.

They hefted the body through and it plunged into the depths.

I was hardly aware of them getting into the car and driving off. My eyes were fixed on the long streak of blood smeared across the surface of the frozen river.

'We must never speak of what we have seen this night, Stefan. Stefan!' Tomas was shouting at me. 'Are you paying attention? Stefan!'

'Yes. Yes,' I said. My head was spinning; my breath coming in great ragged lumps, the scientific part of my brain trying to deduce whether I was taking in too much oxygen or not enough.

We separated – both of us heading for home by a circuitous route via back streets and alleys. I crept silently into Dr K's house. There was a light shining from under the door of the dining room. Without thinking I brushed my fingers upon the wooden panels.

'Come in.'

Nina was sitting up reading a book. In the glow from the bedside lamp, her hair gleamed gold as it cascaded around her shoulders. 'Stefan!' she said in surprise. 'I thought it was Galena knocking.' She paused. 'Is there something I can help you with?'

I didn't speak.

She peered closer. Then she dropped the book, scrambled out of bed and came towards me. 'What is wrong? Tell me! Why are you so distraught?'

I couldn't form the words on my tongue. I gulped and gasped and then managed to say: 'Tonight I witnessed a murder.'

Chapter 29

NINA

'Murder!'

In disbelief I repeated what Stefan had said. 'Witness to a murder? Who has been murdered?'

He couldn't reply, just stood, unable to move – as if saying those words had sent him into shock. From this rigid state he went into a fit of shaking. I ran to Dr K's study and poured a measure of brandy. I led Stefan to my bed, made him sit down and then held the glass, which knocked against his clenched teeth.

'Drink it!' I said in my firmest nursing voice.

But he was trapped in a state of terror. He cast his glance about the room as if there were monsters lurking in the corners. As if beasts might leap out at any moment and rip him apart.

'Shot in front of me,' he said. 'Shot right in front of

my eyes. Falling down in the snow. Blood spilling out, staining the snow red.'

'Who?' I asked him. 'Who fell down in the snow?'

'Mama.' He spoke in the voice of a lost child. 'My mama fell down in the snow. Her eyes are open, but she cannot see me. I can see her. But she cannot see me.'

My heart trembled. 'Your mama is not here, Stefan.'

He looked at me with an air of bewilderment.

'I'd like you to drink this,' I said, offering the brandy glass again.

'Where is my mama?'

'She is not here. But I am,' I said. 'I am Nina, and I am here.'

'Yes,' he said. 'You are Nina.'

'I am Nina and I would like you to drink this brandy.' I coaxed the glass to his lips.

'I'm cold,' he said. 'So very cold.'

I set down the brandy. Taking my green and purple shawl which was draped over my shoulders, I wrapped it around his, and pulled it tight to try to bring some warmth to his body. I reached for the glass again. 'Stefan, please drink the brandy,' I whispered.

His teeth parted and the liquid burned his throat. He spluttered, and I patted his back with the flat of my hand as nurses do to ease a patient's racking cough. The shaking stopped and he shook his head a few times, as if beginning to be conscious of where he actually was.

'Nina . . .' He turned to me.

His eyes were on a level with my mine. Deepening

pools of amber. His breath was on my face. And the next moment he was in my arms, and . . . and . . . I'd no idea that a kiss from a man could be like that, to send a wild fire coursing—

'What am I doing!' Stefan drew back and jumped up from the bed. 'I didn't mean to take advantage of you. My behaviour is appalling. I regret what has happened here. Nina, I am very sorry.'

I looked up at him. Penitent – like a small boy caught in a misdemeanour, his black hair tousled. Colour rising in his handsome face.

A range of emotions was surging through me but the one thing I did not feel was regret.

For what had just happened, I was not sorry at all!

Chapter 30

NINA

'Who do you think has been murdered?' I steadied my voice as best I could.

'Rasputin.'

'Father Grigory Rasputin?'

Stefan nodded.

I was astounded. I expected him to say that on his way home he'd run into some street brawl and inadvertently got himself involved in it.

'How can you possibly know this? Were you in his company?'

'I met Tomas coming from the hospital. He was on his way back to the Moika Palace, having been on an errand for Dr Lazovert to collect some potassium crystals from the pharmacy— Oh!' Stefan broke off, looking at me in horror. 'Tomas and I are so stupid! The plan was to poison Rasputin! I saw the doctor grinding up the crystals into a powder. No doubt they sprinkled it on the cakes and pastries. It's why they arranged the table as if people had already eaten some of the food – so Rasputin wouldn't be suspicious. The intention wasn't to shoot him. That's why it turned into such a chaotic mess.'

'Whose plan was it to poison Rasputin? What mess are you talking about?'

And then Stefan told me what had happened in the Moika Palace and afterwards at the river. I was silent as the full wickedness of the events was related.

'Is Father Grigory definitely dead?'

'Yes,' said Stefan.

'You are absolutely sure of this?'

'I am. By now Rasputin is more dead than any corpse I've ever seen. They pushed him below the ice on the Neva. If he was not dead when he entered the water, then he most certainly is now.'

'This is a tragedy. For the poor man himself, and for his wife and children.'

'Yes,' said Stefan. 'I thought him a selfish shyster, but no one deserves to die in such a manner.'

'His relatives will have no body to pray over, no grave to visit,' I said. 'That will be a heartache.'

'It won't be long before his absence is noticed,' said Stefan, 'and his family will report it to the police.'

I knew that there was another family who would take note of his absence. In the Alexander Palace the Tsarina and her children would build their anxiety to a crisis. And then another thought struck me. One that caused my throat to constrict in fear. 'Did anyone see you or Tomas? Were you followed here?'

'I can't be sure, but I don't think so.'

'I'll look outside.'

The street was empty, but the Okhrana had spies every-where.

'I should go to my attic,' Stefan said. 'Galena will be getting up soon. If she found me in your room like this she'd horsewhip me.'

'Horsewhip you!' I scoffed. 'Galena adores you. You are the son she never had.'

'If I hold the position of son, then you are the daughter of this house.'

I smiled. 'Is it sibling rivalry then, that we so often clash?'

'Earlier tonight Tomas told me that I spoke to you in a dismissive manner.'

I raised my eyebrows and waited. I wasn't going to make it easy for him.

Stefan bit his lip, striving to overcome the obstacle of his pride. 'It isn't done intentionally to offend you.'

I was so glad that he'd admitted this that I decided to be merciful and change the subject. 'Speaking of Galena,' I said, 'we shouldn't tell her or Dr K what you saw tonight.'

'There's no point,' Stefan agreed.

'What has happened . . . has happened,' I said. 'If the assassins didn't see you or Tomas, then it's safer that no one else knows you were there.'

'The body may never be found,' said Stefan. 'It is weighted with chains. The current should drag it towards the sea.'

But the aura of malevolence which surrounded Rasputin would not dissipate with his death.

We looked at each other. We both knew that the body of Rasputin *would* be found.

Chapter 31

NINA

Two days elapsed before a policeman patrolling the bank of the River Neva noticed an object wedged in the frozen surface.

'It took them twenty minutes to cut through the ice to get to him,' Galena told us at dinner that night. 'A woman in the bread queue is married to a fireman in the Nevsky Brigade.' She lowered her voice. 'It wasn't an accident. Rasputin didn't fall down in a drunken stupor. The body was weighted with chains. This woman says he was found lying on his back with his hands up, fingers curved, as if he was trying to claw his way out from under the ice. Rasputin must have been alive when they threw him in.'

'He couldn't have been alive when he was put in the river!' In an immediate reaction, the unguarded words flew from Stefan's mouth.

'What makes you say that?' Dr K looked searchingly at him.

'If Rasputin's body was tied with chains,' I said quickly, 'then it's most likely he was dead.'

'Yes,' said Stefan. 'Obviously.'

'Maybe not,' said Galena.

'Grigory Rasputin was without doubt dead before he entered the river.' Dr K spoke very deliberately. 'His body was brought to the morgue at the City Hospital for a preliminary examination before being impounded by the Secret Police.'

'Did you see him?' Galena asked.

'Briefly. To ascertain that there was no sign of life. The post mortem will be done by a police surgeon, with forensic tests and a full pathology report.'

'If you only saw him for a short time, how can you know that he didn't drown, or wasn't suffocated under the ice?' Galena was not giving up her quest for more details.

Dr K hesitated. 'This information must not be shared with the ladies of the bread queue, or indeed anywhere else.'

'Of course not!' Galena said indignantly. 'What do you take me for? A common gossip? Over the years I have kept silent about many things I've seen and heard in this house.'

'Forgive me.' Dr K stretched out his hand to her. In response Galena tossed her head. 'I apologize,' he said. 'To everyone at this table,' he added. 'I'm trying to protect you. These are dangerous days and I fear the consequences of this murder will echo around the world and never be forgotten.'

'Well then, tell us.' Galena smiled at him to show he was forgiven. 'What makes you say that Rasputin was dead before going under the ice?'

'He'd been shot in the forehead. There were other serious injuries which would have killed him more slowly. But the bullet in the brain was the one which rapidly terminated his life.'

I murmured what I thought was an appropriate response, while Stefan bent his head and focused on eating his food. I sensed that Dr K was observing both of us. Galena chatted on, telling us of the situation on the streets, where factories were running out of coal and the owners were refusing to pay the workers even though it wasn't their fault that they couldn't work – until, nearing the end of the meal, the front doorbell rang.

'I'll wash up the dishes,' I said as Galena rose to answer the door.

'And I'll help Nina, if you have work to do,' Stefan said to Dr K.

The doctor quirked an eyebrow, but went in the direction of his study.

'Now they have found Rasputin's body, we must be careful what we say,' Stefan whispered to me.

'It was you who spoke out of turn,' I reminded him.

We heard Galena exchange a warm greeting as she opened the front door. 'Tomas!' she exclaimed. 'I haven't seen you since you graduated!'

Stefan dropped the plate he was holding and it shattered on the floor. 'Tomas is here!' he said to me in fright. 'Something has happened at the Moika Palace. Please don't let him know that I told you we witnessed Rasputin's murder. He made me swear that we'd never share it with anyone else. For shame I broke my vow to him.'

'Don't be ashamed.' I collected the broken pieces of crockery. 'You were distressed and in shock.'

'My upset is not important.' Stefan put his hands on my shoulders. 'It is *you* I am concerned about. If the Okhrana are questioning people, Nina, say you know nothing. I will deny I ever spoke to you.'

'Come inside.' Galena was bringing Tomas through the house. 'Stefan is in the kitchen with Nina.'

'It is not Stefan I came to see,' we heard Tomas reply. 'I was hoping to have some time with Dr K.'

'You are lucky you've caught him at home,' said Galena. 'He spends most days and evenings at the hospital.'

'Not luck,' said Tomas. 'I've been waiting for hours at the end of the street to ensure he was at home, and that you had finished dinner.'

'Have a care the Okhrana don't recruit you,' Galena joked. 'Come along with me to his study. Don't look so scared. Dr K doesn't bite.'

A few minutes later Dr K came to the kitchen door. 'Nina.' He beckoned, and led me to his study, where Tomas was standing, shifting nervously from foot to foot.

'I will leave you young people,' he said. 'Please take as much time as you need for your discussion.'

'What discussion?' I asked when we were alone.

'I will explain.' Tomas's face became sober. 'As your parents are dead I spoke to Dr K – he is your nearest living relative.'

'You were speaking about me?' I asked, relief in my voice that it could have nothing to do with the death of Rasputin.

'Yes. Nina . . .' Tomas's face went red. 'I, em, I wondered if – if . . .'

'Tomas!' I smiled. 'Whatever is the matter?'

'I asked Dr K whether he would consent to us being married.' The words came tumbling from his mouth in a rush.

'I beg your pardon?' I was completely taken aback.

'Nina –' Tomas took my hand in his – 'I would be so happy if you would become my wife.'

In all the time we'd spent in each other's company, not for one moment had it occurred to me that this was in Tomas's mind.

'We get along very amiably together,' he went on. 'There is no shortage of conversation between us, and when I am with you I feel light-hearted. I've spoken to my parents and they've made no objection. They know the reputation Dr K has and how well-respected he is in the city, and I'm sure they would like you personally.'

'I . . . I . . .' My thoughts scrambled in confusion.

'Would you consider it, Nina? Could I make you as happy as you would me?'

It was the sweetest and loveliest proposal a girl could

have. Tomas was right. We did make each other laugh, and had lots of things to talk about.

'I will not press you for an answer,' he continued. 'But I will tell you my thoughts. I want to quit the city. I'm not suited to the work at the Moika Palace. The conditions there have become . . . untenable. My parents have a house in Moscow, where my father has a friend who has said that I could practise medicine with him, with a view to partnership. I'll be arranging transport to go to Moscow and explore the options. Most likely we will not see each other until the spring. But if everything is suitable and you are agreeable, then we could be married, move to Moscow and begin a new life.' He looked at me for a response.

'This is unexpected,' I managed to stammer out. 'I . . . don't know what to say.'

'You have not immediately said "no". So for the moment I am content.' Tomas relaxed and grinned at me in the way he used to do when we were working together in the Winter Palace.

I too relaxed and smiled at him.

'May I kiss you?'

I hesitated.

'I understand if you would rather not.'

He looked so crestfallen that I stepped forward, raised my face to his and closed my eyes. His lips were light and soft on mine. I opened my eyes. His face was suffused with pleasure.

'I am ecstatic,' he whispered.

'Tomas—' I began.

'That one kiss will sustain me for the months we are apart.'

'I need time to think.' I said this reluctantly, unwilling to crush him.

'Of course. Of course.' Tomas nodded as we walked towards the door. 'But you have given me hope.'

I left Dr K's study in a daze. Stefan was on the stairs. Swaddled in a warm blanket and armed with hot-water bottles, he was on his way to his own rooms.

'I have asked Nina to marry me!' Tomas burst out with his news.

'Oh!' Stefan looked down at us. 'Oh! Oh, indeed,' he said. 'Congratulations. Yes. You are . . . suited to each other. I hope you will be happy.'

I looked at him. His face was pulled in an expression I could not read. Annoyance or disappointment?

We stood like that, saying nothing, until Galena came hurrying from the kitchen – for Tomas had gone ahead to tell her of his proposal. 'Is it true?' she asked me. 'Are you to marry Tomas?'

'I-I-I said I would think about it.'

'Oh, you must think about it very carefully,' she said, and swept her glance over me to linger on Stefan. 'Everyone should think about it very carefully.'

PETROGRAD
(ST PETERSBURG)

1917

Chapter 32

NINA

In the streets of the city and throughout Russia there was rejoicing over the death of Rasputin.

When the house was quieter I went to my room and unlocked the carved casket. The dagger seemed unnaturally still. But the stillness was not a quietness of spirit. It was more a shadow, waiting. A malignant thing, creeping in the darkness. I looked to the corners of room where Stefan had glanced nervously on the night of Rasputin's murder.

Rasputin . . . The dagger he owned had not saved his life. Therefore it was a fraud.

And if it were a fraud, then so too was this dagger.

Thus I need not fear it.

Yet I did.

Galena's footstep was in the hall. She would be bringing me my hot-water bottle. I snapped down the casket lid.

I dreamed of wolves that night. Howling at the moon. Packs of them ravaging the land, leaving a trail of blood over the snow.

When I awoke unrested, I resolved to pray for the soul of Father Grigory. In my mind was the holy image of the Mother of God with the Christ child on her knee which hung in my father's study. And I thought of the candle I'd lit before I left my home.

I knew that in the Alexander Palace a thousand candles would burn in memory of their dear friend. The Imperial Family would be heartbroken. The girls would weep for days, but at least they had the comfort of their sisterhood. I imagined Alexei becoming sullen and rebelling even more against the rules imposed by poor Dr Botkin. But it was the health of the Tsarina which would take the biggest blow. By her own admission this woman could barely function with Rasputin gone for only a few days. The news of his permanent passing could cause a total breakdown of her mental faculties.

She was to be pitied, and I said as much when the others were once again discussing his death.

'Rasputin may have been a scoundrel,' said Galena, 'but one would not wish such a death on anyone. The Tsarina and her children will mourn him deeply.'

'I mourn Rasputin too.' I felt compelled to speak up, for I believed that Father Grigory Rasputin did have deep empathy with suffering. It was what caused him to try to ease Alexei's pain and to donate sums of money to feed the starving refugees. He was deeply flawed and egotistical.

Yet I could understand why he craved alcohol to blot out reality.

'You genuinely mourn the passing of Rasputin?' Stefan said in surprise.

'He thought that sending our soldiers to the battlefields was causing the annihilation of the Russian people. Rasputin said it was a crime against humanity, and that the war should be stopped, regardless of the price to be paid.'

'Halting the war without considered negotiation is not a viable solution,' said Dr K.

'Rasputin didn't think deeply on any subject. In many ways he was a shallow man who lived from day to day. It was his undoing and' – I paused as I considered the possible further consequences of his death – 'perhaps that of the Romanovs too.'

'That would be a good result from his death,' said Stefan. 'To have the Romanovs removed.'

Stefan said this so often that it had become his mantra. His bitterness hung around his neck like the giant stone collar that former serfs were made to wear as punishment for trying to escape. And, like them, for Stefan there was no escape. He claimed that with the Romanovs as leaders Russia could neither prosper nor move on. But a country needs someone to rule it. The Imperial Family were pleasant, well-meaning people. Who would replace them if the Tsar was forced to abdicate?

A major complaint against the Tsar and Tsarina concerned their inability to make decisions and lack of clear action. But in the matter of Rasputin's death, the Tsarina was not just deranged – she was vengeful, and determined. Following rapid investigation, the forces of the law made their way to the door of the Moika Palace.

Prince Yusupov's clumsy attempts at concealment failed. Bloodstains were found on the doorstep and firearms confiscated. The police gathered witness statements from the gatekeeper and others who had seen Rasputin enter the courtyard and never leave. And the Prince had boasted to his friends about what he termed his 'noble deed'. The evidence mounted up so that it could not be ignored.

It gave me two reasons to be glad that Tomas had left for Moscow. Firstly and most importantly, it meant that he was safely out of the city and away from the wrath of the Imperial Family should his connection to the murder ever be discovered. Prince Yusupov and his fellow conspirators were banished from the city. While publicly denying the charge, privately Prince Yusupov was unrepentant – claiming that he'd done the monarchy and the country a favour. If Tomas's role in fetching the poison had come out, then, being of a lower class, he might have received a harsher sentence.

The other reason why I was happy to see Tomas go was that it gave me time to think about his marriage proposal. I had no doubt that with little effort on my part he would be a contented husband. But would I be a contented wife? He would love me and indulge me and make me smile. Was that enough to enable two people to spend the rest of their lives together? I had no experience of a happy marriage.

I knew that my parents had adored each other, but I'd not witnessed how they lived and got along day by day.

As the year ended and a new one began, Tomas's letters arrived. When he wrote of how he was settling into his medical position in Moscow and into the appropriate society for someone of his rank and status, I realized that there was an overriding reason why I couldn't agree to be his wife. I was the child of an unwed couple. If we were officially engaged, his parents would investigate my background. They would soon find out that my present name as the familial niece of Dr K was false, and that my original name had no legitimacy. They would never accept a union with me for their son. I could not marry Tomas – even if I wanted to.

Father Grigory Rasputin was buried on the estate at Tsarskoe Selo in a funeral service arranged by the Imperial Family. I wasn't totally surprised when, some weeks into the new year, I received an invitation from the Alexander Palace to attend a private service in his memory.

'They will use this opportunity to emotionally black-mail you into staying on with them,' Dr K said. He and Galena were adamant that I should refuse.

But what Sergei delivered was not just the official invitation on embossed card; it included a handwritten note from Olga – the eldest daughter, with whom I'd been most friendly.

Prince Yusupov has left the city, Olga wrote, *to be with his wife, our cousin Irina, in the Crimea. We are starved of company, Nina, and would like to see you and talk of happier times.*

'It's about what *they* want.' Stefan shook his head as I read it out. He looked at me intently. 'You should not go there.'

Of course I went – to the disapproval of everyone in the house, and also of Sergei, who collected me.

'Young lady,' he said, 'the royal estate at Tsarskoe Selo is not a place where you should dally for long.'

The girls were there to welcome me, and after the memorial service Olga linked my arm with hers and said, 'You must stay with us until tomorrow at least. The sun goes down so early at this time of the year and the coachmen hate driving the roads at night.'

And so I stayed, and that night became two, and three . . . No letter came from Dr K to ask how I was, or to urge me to come home, and I slipped easily back into that semi-dream world, coddled in a cocoon of royal privilege.

Each evening as they ate supper they talked incessantly of Father Grigory.

'We knew that there was something wrong,' said Maria. 'I had a nightmare and awoke the next day with a feeling of dread.'

'His habit was to telephone every morning and speak to Mama and ask how Alexei had slept,' said Tatiana. 'He'd reassure them that he kept them in his prayers and so, if he was unable to call in on any day, they were content that he was always watching over them.'

'Mama is bereft without him,' Olga confided in me. 'Most days she keeps to her room and doesn't speak to us

226

directly – only Alexei is allowed in. We can hear her praying and constantly calling out for Father Grigory to guide her thoughts. He used to advise her on many things, Nina, even matters of State. She'd tell him which minister was doing what and ask his advice . . .'

There was doubt in her tone. And I saw that Olga was old enough to appreciate that this might not have been a good idea. She was the eldest child, and although she cared for her mother she was closer to her father. I suspected that she longed for the uncomplicated days of her youth – before her brother was born, before the workers began to make demands; when the Russian people did not blame their Tsar for their misery and her father had more time to dote on his children.

For now the Tsar was fenced in with increasing problems. The Prime Minister, who'd been only appointed last November, was gone by the new year, and in January 1917 yet another took up the position. In a show of bravado the Tsar declared that the Spring Offensive would provide victory in the war. I knew that Eugene had written to Stefan to tell him that what was happening at the Front was a massacre. Many of the soldiers had no guns! But I didn't mention this. Instead, I sank into their dumb complicity of denial.

Then a telegram arrived to say that Tsar Nicholas would come for a short visit. Servants spent the day scurrying about to prepare for his arrival. The Tsarina roused herself to order the dusting of already immaculate furniture, and the preparation of special dishes to tempt his appetite. Alexei insisted on wearing his sailor suit, while the girls and the Tsarina spent hours dressing and having their hair arranged. I'd no expectation of meeting the Tsar, but thought it best to change into a fresh nursing uniform. It was fortunate that I did, for members of the Imperial Family's personal staff were summoned to the hall as his carriage approached.

Arms outstretched, the Tsarina greeted her husband as he entered the palace – as though they might actually embrace in public! The Tsar was shorter in height than I'd expected and looked tired. Upon seeing his wife, the slight figure in military uniform straightened up and seemed to grow in stature.

'Imperial Highness.' The Tsarina spoke formally to her husband and took his arm.

His face glowed with affection and he allowed himself to be led through the hall to his children and then past the personal staff. He greeted each person courteously by name, and the next moment he was before me. I bowed my head as the others had done.

'This is Nurse Nina,' said Alexei. 'I wrote to you about her.'

'The storyteller' – the Tsar's eyes twinkled and he stroked his moustache – 'of whom my son speaks so highly?'

I stuttered a reply. I didn't hate the Romanovs as Stefan did, but nor did I consider myself a dedicated monarchist like Galena. Yet my breath quickened in the presence of the man millions believed to be God's representative in Russia.

However, in the relaxed seclusion of his family home, the Tsar of all the Russias behaved with his children like every doting papa. He chatted and played with them, but signs of nervous exhaustion became apparent when matters of State were brought to his attention. Reports of differing opinions among his ministers appeared daily. These caused him to fret and pace the rooms of the apartments, endlessly talking to himself – as if he could not come to a conclusion, far less a decision, regarding the direction of his government.

The Tsarina, still shattered by the loss of Rasputin, did her best to soothe and protect him. When he reminded his family that he would have to go back to the Front, they swarmed around him, hugging and kissing him so much that the Tsar himself was reduced to tears. He broke away to walk to the window and compose himself.

He breathed upon the glass and, with a finger, drew the outline of his face, his hair, his eyes and his fine moustaches.

'You are as handsome as when we first met.' The Tsarina, admiring his impromptu portrait, stepped near to her husband. 'Must you leave us so soon?'

With a hopeless gesture the Tsar replied, 'It is my duty to be with our troops.' He took her hand, and together they turned towards where their children sat.

Behind them, on the window, the condensation melted, causing the lines of the drawing to disintegrate. The Tsar's image trickled down the pane; the moustaches drooped on either side of his mouth, the contours about his eyes morphing to heavy bags, his face instantly ageing.

Chapter 33

NINA

A day or so later I was in the kitchen fetching a glass of warm milk for Alexei when Sergei appeared in the outside vestibule.

'Be off with you!' a maid said cheekily. 'The cook will belt me if I let you in here with your snow-covered boots.'

'I have no intention of coming inside.' He waved his hand and I went into the vestibule, where he handed me a folded note. 'The person who gave that to me said I must wait while you read it and then take it from you.'

I opened out the sheet of paper. It was in a handwriting that was unfamiliar.

I send you this as a friend because letters sent to you previously by your uncle telling you to go home have not reached you. You must leave the Alexander Palace AT ONCE. Please do as instructed by the person who delivers this message.

'Do you know what this note contains?' I asked the coachman.

'I do.' He turned his face away from the kitchen door as he spoke. 'You should heed the warning. When I go into the city tonight I won't be coming back to Tsarskoe Selo. Not ever.'

A chill went through me, and not because I was standing on the stone floor of the vestibule. 'I am to obey your instructions?' I said.

'First we destroy the note.' He took the paper and flung it into the stove where, within seconds, it curled into ash. 'When the Tsarevich has drunk his milk and you have finished your storytelling, then, like the others, you must go to your bedroom. Dress warmly in outdoor clothes. Just before midnight, come along the ground-floor corridors to the other wing of the palace, where you will find the Golden Hall.'

A shiver ran through me. It was to this place that Rasputin had taken me when he'd shown me the portrait of Ivan the Terrible.

'Unlock the terraced window of the Golden Hall at midnight. This will be dangerous for me, so you may have to wait a while. Tell no one else. *No one,*' he repeated, 'lest you risk the lives of others. You must not say goodbye to anyone.' He paused as if he knew it would be difficult for me to do this. 'Their papa is home. Let the children enjoy the company of their parents by themselves for a while.'

At a quarter to midnight I left the Royal Apartments and crept through the palace and along empty passages until I reached the Golden Hall. I went to the window, undid the bolt and looked out. Some distance away the palace guards were sitting around a bonfire. Not spaced at intervals, standing on sentry duty – but grouped together, chatting and drinking. Part of their conversation came to me: complaints about less pay and short rations and the brutality of their commanding officers in punishing simple offences.

Half the night I waited there until, cramped by inaction and the cold, I began to walk about to keep warm. Inevitably I was drawn to the painting of Tsar Ivan wearing the twin daggers in his bandoliers. Like malevolent red eyes the ruby stones stared out at me.

I went closer to the painting and looked at the figure of the Tsar, with the pelt of the wolf encasing his upper body. A shadow slid across the surface of the canvas and the sigh of the snow falling outside was a whispering voice:

One dagger to take a life.

It was as if Rasputin was in the room with me.

The shadow grew larger and the whisper louder:

One dagger to . . .

Mesmerized, I stared into the eyes of Ivan the Terrible. His gaze met mine.

'*Nina.*'

A noise behind me. I turned round. A figure outlined against the window pane . . .

Rasputin?

'Holy Mother!' I raised my hands to shield my face.

'Hush!' Sergei came in the terrace door.

So shocked was I that I couldn't move.

'What ails you?' He walked forward. 'You look as if you've seen a ghost.'

'I did. The figure in the painting looked out at me. I saw it. I heard . . .' I gabbled on about Rasputin and daggers, and Tsar Ivan and curses. 'The monk told me the story of this painting,' I finally gulped to a halt.

'It was me who told the story to the monk,' said Sergei. 'When he returned to the palace and I saw that he was carrying the dagger I advised him to give it away, but he didn't listen.'

'You!' I said. 'Then you know the origin of the daggers and where they went.'

'I know neither of those things,' he replied. 'The daggers are centuries old, and where they went is a mystery.'

'What *do* you know then?'

'The legend of their power was common currency among the servants. The saying was: "One dagger to take a life. One dagger to save a life." When I was a young stable lad the twin daggers were kept here, in the Golden Hall, inside a display case positioned below the painting of Ivan the Terrible. One January, at the time of the Wolf Moon, there was a reception in the Golden Hall. The room was crowded. Titled people from Russia and beyond

233

came to eat and dance, to gossip and gamble and conduct romances. The next morning the daggers were gone. They searched the servant quarters. Nothing was found.

'It must have been a guest who took the daggers,' Sergei went on. 'A servant would never steal such things. There would be no way one of us could hide them or sell them without being found out. Servants do steal, yes – but mainly food; a nibble here and there, a piece of fruit, perhaps a lace handkerchief, no more than petty pilfering – never silverware or goods like that.

'But they weren't believed. The footmen on duty in the Golden Hall that night were horsewhipped anyway – in the main courtyard, as an example to the rest – and they and their families thrown off the estate to starve and die.'

'That is a terrible tale,' I said.

'It is,' said Sergei. 'But better that these daggers are lost, for where they are, death and destruction follow on.'

When we reached the city I said goodbye to Sergei and thanked him and wished him luck.

Before he drove away he called out to me, 'Do not think any more about the Rasputin dagger,' he said. 'It is gone from history as he has – for ever.'

I entered via the back gate, knocking quietly on the scullery door as I knew Galena would already be awake and on her way out to join the bread queue. She was in raptures to see me.

'I'm so glad you are home, Nina!' She wrapped her arms around my waist in a bone-crushing hug. 'We've been frantic for news of you! The price of milk and potatoes has risen again and children are dying from the cold. There are rumours that some ruffians will try to seize the Tsar and his family and burn down the Alexander Palace. I hope their guards are fully armed and can fight hard.'

I thought it best not to mention the soldiers I'd seen lounging around their braziers, and only said, 'Then it's as well you sent the note to tell me to leave the Palace at once.'

Galena paused in the act of tying her snood. 'I never sent you any note.'

'I assumed it was you,' I said, 'for I would have recognized the handwriting of Dr K or Stefan.'

She turned away from my direct gaze. 'It wasn't me,' she said. 'No, it definitely was not me. But' – she smiled – 'I am grateful for whoever wrote it, for Dr K guessed that his letters weren't reaching you and he was determined to ride out to Tsarskoe Selo today to fetch you himself.'

'You needn't worry any more,' I said. 'I will not go there again until at least the war has ended.'

'The city was quiet last night,' Galena went on. 'But it's the silence before a storm. Vera and Duscha are saying that it's time the women showed the men what to do. But whether there is trouble today or not, your life may change soon anyway, Nina.' She looked at me archly. 'Have you decided to accept the marriage proposal from Tomas?'

'Not yet,' I replied.

'Good,' she said, and off she clumped down the path in her big boots.

Chapter 34

STEFAN

The sound of a sleigh in the street woke me and I went to the window and watched Nina dismount onto the pavement and go round the side of the house. Wrapping myself in a blanket, I went downstairs.

My heart hiccupped when I reached the step where, weeks ago, I had looked down to see Nina coming out of Dr K's study, where Tomas had proposed to her. I'd thought she'd noticed me on the stairs and that was why she was smiling. And then Tomas was close behind her, and he touched her on the shoulder and she twisted her head, and I realized that the smile was for him. I guessed by the expression on his face that he'd just kissed her.

They looked natural in each other's company – as if they belonged together.

Why was I even thinking about it?

About her.

Tomas was a good friend. Cheered me up when I was low. So I was glad for him; glad he'd found someone he wanted to share his life with. It was one pleasant thing in the sea of sewage that was our modern life. When he left for Moscow he'd shaken my hand and made me promise to take care of Nina. He'd write often and return in the spring, when he hoped they would be married.

What happened to Nina didn't make any difference to me.

And yet . . .

My mind kept going back to the night I'd come into the house after Rasputin's murder.

How close we'd been.

She was a pretty girl. I knew many pretty girls in the city.

She was clever. I met lots of clever young women in the university. And ones that were both pretty and clever.

But . . . when I was in an abstract mood it was Nina's face swimming across my vision. Her I heard voicing her fractious objections to my statements, which forced me – not always successfully – to justify my own opinions.

I opened the kitchen and overheard the exchange between Galena and Nina.

She hadn't yet agreed to marry Tomas! And now she was home – but this time she had no fur blankets or boxes of food with her. Dishevelled, and with an unhealthy pallor, she stood by the stove, trying to get warm.

A superior remark was forming in my head. But instead of voicing it, I draped the blanket from my bed over her shoulders.

'Thank you, Stefan.' She didn't use my name often, but when she did she had a way of emphasizing the first and last letters, which made it sound different yet familiar.

'Tea?'

She nodded.

I brought two stools nearer the stove and she sank gratefully onto hers. 'Don't tell.' I handed her a biscuit. Her eyelashes fluttered a question. 'I know where Galena hides the Treat Tin,' I explained.

'She will have counted the biscuits and see that one is missing.'

'Two,' I said. I sat down beside her and began to eat my own biscuit. 'We share the blame.'

She held her glass of hot tea and I watched the colour seep back into her face. We sat there for a bit, not speaking. But the silence wasn't awkward.

'Glory be!' Dr K swept in and gathered Nina up in a massive embrace. 'Listen, young lady!' He set her away from him with a hand on each shoulder. 'You must never go to Tsarskoe Selo again.'

'I've already made that promise to Galena,' she said. 'I will not visit the Imperial Family until after the war is ended.'

'What is happening on our battlefields is not a war,' I said. 'Eugene's letters tell me it is mass slaughter. Disaster follows disaster. Often the common soldier carries just one round of ammunition. Essentially they are fodder for the cannon of our enemies. They say the German soldiers break down and weep as they shovel Russian corpses away from the front of their trenches. But it isn't the German army which is responsible for this crime against our people. It is those who govern us who are murdering our fellow Russians in their tens of thousands. Is it any wonder that the conscripts are deserting?'

'The mood of the Imperial Guard at the Alexander Palace has changed,' said Nina, and she told us of the sentries sitting chatting when they should have been on duty.

'Fyodor says that the Bolsheviks will make their own army. I suggested they call themselves the Red Guard.'

'When did you meet Fyodor?' she asked. 'How is he?'

'I spoke to him yesterday. He asked how you were, but he's as mad as ever. I *told* him he was making a catastrophic mistake joining that party. The Bolsheviks have given him a gun, may the Saints preserve us!' I said in mock prayer. 'He'll probably rush to the Alexander Palace and shoot the lot of them. Not that I would object to that,' I added.

'How are the Imperial Family?' Dr K asked Nina.

'I don't expect they commemorated the anniversary of Bloody Sunday?' I commented sarcastically.

'Bloody Sunday?'

'The twenty-second of January 1905,' I answered her. 'Unarmed civilians walking to the Winter Palace to ask for food and fair working conditions were gunned down by the military.'

Dr K put his hands on the table. 'You should know, Nina, that it was on that day that Stefan's mother died.

I met them both by chance as we marched to hand in a petition to the Tsar. Without warning the army fired upon the crowd. To save his life Stefan's mother ran in front of him and she was shot.'

'I had no idea . . .' Nina's voice faltered.

'You've never spoken of it, Stefan,' said Dr K. 'Perhaps this is a time for you to do so?'

But I didn't want sympathy. The ocean of bitterness that slopped about inside me wanted payment, not pity, for that life lost. 'There is nothing to say,' I replied. 'The people went to speak to the Tsar. The army stopped them and murdered hundreds. The Tsar refused to discipline the officers responsible. Afterwards he said he'd allow a Duma Council of the People to have a say in the running of the country, but he doesn't give it any power. And now we are where we are.'

'Do you recall anything about that day?'

'No. Nothing.' I rejected Dr K's attempt at therapeutic counselling.

'Nothing at all?'

He wasn't going to be put off so easily. I would have to give him something so that he would leave me alone. 'I was trying to get to the front of the crowd. At the side of the road there was a water fountain. I thought I might climb up there and actually see the Tsar if he came out onto the balcony to greet us. He didn't listen then.' My voice began to crack with stress. 'He's not listening now.'

'Stefan is correct in what he says.' Sensing that I was on the verge of tears, Nina moved her stool closer to mine and angled her body to give me a semi-private space. 'The Tsar is not listening. He seems incapable of paying attention and absorbing information. Let me tell you what happens within the private apartments of the Alexander Palace.'

She began to speak in a steady voice. And I felt the bond between us strengthen as I realized that Nina was deliberately drawing attention away from me in order that I might have time to recover myself.

Chapter 35

STEFAN

We were eating our watery porridge when Galena came hurrying into the house empty-handed.

'The bakery is shut down,' she said. 'They say there is no more bread.'

'No bread?' I repeated in disbelief.

'None at all.' She shook her head. 'There is no flour in the city.'

'If that is the case, then there will be a riot,' said Dr K.

'Not a riot,' said Galena. 'A protest with a purpose. The women from the bread queues are meeting up and taking to the streets. We are going to find the government grain stores and batter down the doors. I'm just here for extra clothing.' She went into her pantry bedroom and came out carrying a bundle of blankets. 'There are those who do not own a coat and we will be outside the whole day,' she explained.

Dr K ran out of the room and returned almost immediately. 'I have locked the house. I forbid you to leave, Galena.' He positioned himself at the entrance to the scullery and was holding the back-door key in his hand.

'You can't forbid it.' Galena crammed the blankets into a bag which she slung over her shoulder.

'There will be trouble on the streets today.'

'There is always trouble on the streets.'

'Not like this. This is special.'

'I know exactly how special it is.' Galena held out her hand for him to give her the door key.

'You are my housekeeper.'

She laughed in his face.

'I employ you to follow my orders.'

'So sack me!'

I had never heard them row like this before.

'Your place is to be in this house and – and to look after things . . . wash and iron, cook and – and such-like.'

'My place is on the streets with the rest of the women.'

'There are official orders banning large meetings. This means that the police and the army are free to use any force to curb illegal gatherings. Even though you are peaceful women they might bring out the Cossacks, for the authorities will think the protest has been organized by revolutionaries. The Bolsheviks will welcome the conflict and won't care who is shot or trampled to death. Lenin and his like see it as a necessary sacrifice to create anarchy.'

'We have to show that we will not sit meekly at home and watch our children starve. The world needs to know the truth.'

'Who knows the truth of anything?'

'Women,' Galena replied at once. 'They are the ones who wait in the bread queues. That's where the real truth is.'

The doctor bowed his head. 'That in itself is a truth.'

During their heated exchange Nina had left the kitchen to change into a heavier coat. She'd wound her green and purple Siberian shawl around her head and shoulders, crossed it over and tied it at the waist. The tip of her nose peeped out among the swaddling of snood and scarf.

Dr K looked at Galena in disbelief. 'Not Nina too!'

My heart began to beat very fast. As a boy I had stood in front of a company of Cossacks. Half a lifetime ago – but I'd never forgotten it. The line of riders waiting for their order to charge. The sound of steel on steel as curved sabres were drawn. The thunder of horses' hooves. The pounding of my own feet as, covered in a sweat of terror, we ran for our lives. Nina would be crushed like a butterfly.

'Galena! Please!' Dr K was begging. 'We have a duty of care. You must not take Nina with you.'

'No one is *taking* me anywhere.' Nina's voice came, muffled but resolute, from amongst her coverings. 'I go where I please. I too am a bread-queue woman, and today I will join with my fellow women.'

Galena nodded. 'We are Russian women. It is our duty to take part in this protest. We will walk together.'

'We must keep Nina here!'

'How do you propose to do that?'

Dr K threw the keys onto the kitchen table, stamped off into his study and slammed the door. I went in the opposite direction, towards the scullery.

'Stand out of my way, Stefan.' Galena was using her 'no-further-argument' voice. 'Do not try to stop us.'

'I have no intention of trying to stop you.' I lifted my coat from its peg. 'I am coming with you.'

Chapter 36

STEFAN

We linked arms.

Galena in the middle, with Nina on one side of her and me on the other. I was glad of the bulk of Galena's body as my anchor. Fear was rising from my stomach like a physical sickness. The twelve-year-old child inside me was crying to go home.

We heard the noise before we reached the main road. A babble of voices; shouts and cries of pent-up frustration rose into the air in a caterwauling of desperation. From houses and huts, wynds and walkways, shops and schools, the women of Petrograd were streaming onto the streets. The world was black with moving figures, gathering together, then swirling apart in a restless tide.

We swung onto the Nevsky Prospekt. There were crowds of women in the middle of the road; blocking the traffic and looking as if they might overturn any carriage which attempted to pass. Some soldiers from the fortress of Saints Peter and Paul were trying to encourage them to return to the pavement. The women were having none of it.

As I approached I heard their officer say, 'Your cause is just. But for the moment would you please clear the road?' His tone was light and unaggressive.

When a woman asked about the bread situation the soldiers shrugged and said, 'We heard there was a consignment of flour due in at the railway station tonight.'

'How will I feed my children today?' the woman replied piteously.

'You must ask the Minister of the Interior,' the officer replied, 'whoever that may be this morning. The Tsarina might have demoted him and appointed another since yesterday.'

'I expect the Tsarina's children have full stomachs while mine are whimpering with hunger.'

The crowd clapped in support of this statement.

'Take this, Mother.' The youngest of the soldiers found a coin in his pocket and handed it to her. 'It's all I have.'

'Bless you.' She kissed the coin. 'But if there is no bread to buy, then my baby will be dead within a week.'

The soldiers looked at each other. The young one took off his uniform hat and tunic and threw it upon the cobblestones. 'There!' he said. 'I'm done with this. A soldier is meant to protect our citizens – not do them harm.'

A silence fell over the group as they waited to see how the officer would react.

'Boy,' he said, 'put on your clothes, else you might get yourself shot, for losing your uniform is a court-martial offence.' There was a growl of dissension from the women. Several of them bent to pick up stones and clods of dirt. The officer was hemmed in. And he knew it. With a grand flourish he waved his hands and announced: 'Ladies! The street is yours. Roam where you will. My men will not stop you.'

A roar of approval. The soldiers were hoisted high and carried along as the women marshalled themselves into a procession which headed for the government storage facilities. And as we went the numbers swelled, the women from the clothing factories and other work places leaving their posts and spilling onto the streets.

'No bread?' From mouth to mouth the question became a statement. 'There's no bread!'

Then a demand:

'Give us bread!

And eventually a battle cry: 'Bread! Bread!'

In buoyant mood we marched to the outskirts of the city. The security guards at the storage depot fled in the face of our advance. We broke open the gates.

The grain silos were empty.

The crowd turned in confusion. Hundreds of armed policemen appeared and tried to split the mass of people into sections and disperse us. A good number of soldiers had joined the march. Fights broke out between them and the police.

Shots were fired. Then all was chaos. Screaming. Running. Galena and I were wrenched apart and a policeman's baton struck her in the face.

Before me, in slow motion, she keeled over.

'Galena!' I shrieked.

My world twisted away from me, my mind dropping into a chasm. In the absence of my mother, throughout my adult life, Galena had been my rock. I had never seen her lying down. Not ever. Blood was pouring from a wound on her forehead.

'Get up! Galena!' I pleaded. 'Get up! Get up!'

Nina stretched herself across Galena's body, trying to protect her from the thudding boots.

'Galena!' I fell on my knees beside her. 'Galena!' I sobbed. 'Don't die! Please don't die!'

'Think like a doctor!' Nina's face was right up against mine. 'Stefan! You are a doctor. The best way you can help Galena is to *be* a doctor right now!'

'Yes. Yes.' I probed with my fingers as Nina wiped the blood from Galena's face. 'Surface wound. Concussion. Cheek swelling. Eye undamaged. Nose not broken.'

'That's good.' Nina's voice was reassuring.

'Get her to the hospital,' I said. I put my arms under Galena's shoulders.

'Let's wait.' Nina looked up. 'The women are being herded off in sections. When it's quieter we'll ask some of the soldiers to help us carry Galena there.'

★

In the hospital I cleaned and dressed Galena's wound, placing an eyepad over the cut side of her face. She was still unconscious, so Nina said she would wait with her while I fetched Dr K. On my way home I had to pass by the university, where a rally in support of the women was taking place. Fyodor was perched on a statue in the square and was haranguing people to join what he referred to as the 'Red Brigade'.

'Workers of the world must unite!' His face was flushed; his eyes sparkled in frenzy. 'We can take this city! We can take this country! We can stop the war! We can stop all wars!'

When he paused for breath I caught at his sleeve. 'Get down from there, you hothead!'

He pulled away from me. 'Lenin is returning to Russia! Stefan, I must motivate the workers. Don't you see? This is our chance. The revolution is happening!'

Local women had fetched pots and pans and were clanging on them with spoons and sticks. A group of students began to sing a bawdy ballad about the Tsarina that had become popular in the city's drinking dens. Children ran among them waving makeshift red flags and shouting slogans. But among them were citizens of a different category, and something more alarming was taking place on the outskirts of the crowd.

'What is happening,' I shouted in his ear, 'is that truck-loads of Secret Police are blocking off the exits to this square. It's time to leave, my friend.'

'I'm not a coward!' Fyodor cried, struggling against me

as I hauled him into a doorway and through to another courtyard. 'I will not desert my people!'

'If you are referring to those folk in the square we have just left, half of them are police spies. The army is refusing to act against the women so they've brought in the Okhrana to subdue us. The jails will be full tonight, but those like you whom they consider a serious threat will simply disappear.' I bundled Fyodor down an alley. Instead of being grateful he was beside himself with rage. As soon as we were clear he turned on me, kicking and punching.

'You always think you know better than anyone else, don't you, Stefan? High-handed and arrogant beyond belief!' He flung the insult over his shoulder as he went down a wynd by the river.

Galena was awake when I arrived back at the hospital with Dr K, and was in the process of discharging herself. 'Not a word,' she warned him. 'If you say a single word to me about this you will have to find yourself another housekeeper.' She refused any offer of help, and we were left behind as she stomped off ahead of us out of the hospital.

Then Dr K drew his brows together in a comical face of frustration. Nina giggled, I smiled at her, and we ran to catch up with Galena.

That night Dr K was called to yet another emergency meeting of Duma councillors. He came home weary, and the four of us sat at the kitchen table, almost too tired to talk.

'Has the Duma any suggestions for solving this crisis?' Galena asked him.

'Once again Alexander Kerensky has said that the Tsar should be removed from his position as Head of State.'

'The last time he made that suggestion the Tsarina said Kerensky should be hanged,' I pointed out.

'The official Ministers of State are beginning to ignore the Tsarina . . . and indeed the Tsar,' said Dr K. 'They are approaching the Duma privately for advice.'

'Who would take the Tsar's place?' asked Nina.

'His younger brother,' said Galena. 'The Grand Duke Mikhail Alexandrovich. With the Tsarevich being too young to rule, he is the closest male relative.'

'In the name of fortune! Why should we have another Tsar?' The question exploded from my lips.

'The country requires a leader.' Galena looked bewildered.

'But it doesn't have to be one of *them*!' I was too incensed to censor my words. Facing reality was overdue in this house. 'The Romanovs are parasites! And incompetent ones at that. An ordinary person could do it. My God, Galena. *You* could do it! A lot better than any Romanov.'

She thought I was joking so she laughed. I was glad to see her laugh, even though the eyepad and bruised face gave her an absurd appearance.

'I would vote for you,' said Dr K with unusual tenderness in his tone.

'Don't say such silly things,' she upbraided him, but you could tell that she was flattered.

'Anyone would be better than Mister Vladimir Ulyanov Lenin.'

'Huh!' said Galena. 'With one hand you give a compliment and with the other you take it away again.'

Nina and I exchanged a smile, happy to see them back in their habitual way of speaking to each other.

'Fyodor was inciting a crowd while standing on a statue in the square at the university,' I said. 'He says Lenin is returning to the city.'

'If Lenin ever takes charge,' said Dr K, 'we may replace one autocrat with another.'

Chapter 37

STEFAN

The next day, after breakfast, Nina prepared herself to go out.

Galena said, 'I will rest this morning. I am too dizzy to walk without falling and I don't want to endure yesterday's shame of being carried by soldiers through the streets like a sack of coal.'

'Even though one of them was very handsome?' Nina asked with an impish smile. She continued tying up her shawl.

'I recommend that you remain at home too,' said Dr K.

'The women are assembling again,' Nina replied. 'They hope that the male workers will join them today.'

'I heard a rumour yesterday that the Bolsheviks were happy that the women could not find the secret grain stores,' Dr K went on. 'They want to stoke the fires of rebellion even if it builds to an explosion of violence. If the male workers join, it will mean hundreds, possibly thousands, on the streets. They will bring the city to a standstill. The Government will send in the elite forces.'

I knew what the words 'elite forces' meant. *Cossacks!*

'All we are asking for is bread for the children,' Nina replied. 'They have no one to speak for them.' She left the house without another word said.

Dr K and Galena turned to look at me.

'I'm going, I'm going.' I grabbed my coat and cap and headed for the door.

This morning the women were better prepared. They were in organized groups – some carrying banners which read FEED THE CHILDREN and BREAD FOR ALL.

We were mingling with Galena's friends from the bread queue when Nina pointed to a figure standing on the steps of a block of offices. 'Look!' she said. 'It's Fyodor.' She skipped off through the throng, leaving me to trail in her wake.

Fyodor's normally dour face broke into a smile when he saw her. 'Nina! I should have known you would be here. You are so brave and principled.'

Resentment rose in me at his familiar way of speaking to her.

'Will you walk with us today?' she asked him.

I glowered at both of them and resolved to go home at once if he joined us. But Galena would not let me in the house if I returned without Nina.

'I can't,' he said, 'much as I'd like to. My task today is to try to persuade the white-collar workers to come out on strike. I'm to speak to the clerks in this building. The Bolshevik Party has the names of those who favour our cause, and' – he spoke more ominously – 'the names of the ones who do not.'

'We should go,' I said to Nina. 'Your bread-queue friends are beginning to move.'

'Which direction are you headed?' Fyodor asked.

'The railway station, I think,' said Nina. 'We will search for flour in the goods yards.'

Fyodor looked about him furtively. 'Listen.' He bent his head close to hers. 'Try the garages in the street behind the nail works. But be warned,' he called after her: 'that the area will be well guarded.'

'So there is a kind heart beating under that hard exterior.' I tried to banter with him.

'Comrade!' He saluted, and with a bitter look turned away from me.

Even without the efforts of Fyodor and his fellow Bolsheviks it was obvious that a huge number of office workers had not reported for work that day. The women ran here and there, kissing and hugging them and each other and anyone who'd let them.

Then I saw Professor Kirichenko in a group of academics surrounded by a host of students. And as we walked on through the university district, the cafés where the writers and artists gathered closed their doors, and staff and customers merged with the masses.

Chatting and chanting our slogans.

Snow began to fall. Undeterred, we went on under the swinging banners.

I'd made my own banner . . .

People around us burst into song.

We were singing as we marched along. Flags were waving, and the clamour grew louder, rising into the bitterly cold air.

'We only want bread to stop us starving.'

My heart was beating to the sound of the singing and tramp of shoes on snow.

The mood was high and hopeful.

Soldiers were waiting in the square. Cossacks and Hussars – with rifles ready.

They were waiting for us today. By the nail works: armed policemen on either side of the street. And lined up, facing us . . .

Cossacks.

The whisper went through the people like the wind across the steppe.

'*Cossacks!*'

I felt my gut melt and my legs shook so that I could hardly stand. Nina was by my side. I moved forward to place myself in front of her.

She stepped up and put her arm through mine. 'Beside you, Stefan,' she whispered. 'I stand beside you.'

'*Cossacks!*'

Behind us the crowd solidified as the message was passed back. Today the bread-queue women would not disperse.

The horsemen gathered and formed ranks.

Drew their sabres.

I braced myself.

They trotted forward. Slowly. Deliberately. The distance diminished. Now we could hear the jingle of the harnesses; see the puffing breath of the animals.

Too close to us now to start a full gallop.

Did they think we would stand like sheep and allow ourselves to be butchered? It wasn't a terrified boy who was facing them today. I was a grown man who could at least try to defend himself. I would grab the stirrup of the officer's horse. A few more paces and I'd bring him down. Even if he killed me while I was doing it.

Our eyes met.

Flat, almond-shaped. Too dark to read an expression.

Suddenly the woman to whom the soldier had given a coin the day before rushed forward. 'Take this blood money!' She flung it at the Cossack. 'My baby is dead now for want of bread, and I have no need of it!'

He blinked. An almost imperceptible inclination of his head. Thrust his sabre in the air and shouted an order.

The crowd moaned and swayed like wheat in a field. But we held the line, determined to keep ownership of our city.

The officer kissed the blade of his sword. He swiped it across his body in a formal salute to the people. Then he and his company of men swung their horses round and trotted off.

A ragged cheer went up as it became apparent that the way was free for us to progress.

With the Cossacks no longer in our path, we began to move up the street. But on either side the police kept their position. Their Commander put his rifle to his shoulder to start the attack. The Cossack officer sheathed his sword, changed direction and raised his fist. With one blow to the head he brought down the police Commander. Bending in a smooth movement as he swept past, he collected the fallen weapon. Then he reined his horse and tossed the rifle to the nearest striker. The man grabbed it and rapidly fired off a few rounds. The remainder of the police dropped their guns and ran.

Fyodor was right.

The revolution was happening.

Chapter 38

STEFAN

Early the next morning Nina and I crept out of the house. The results of the women's action were reverberating throughout the city and we wanted to take an active part in the making of our history.

When news of the Cossacks' defection to the side of the people spread, then so did the strikes. Without fear of execution or punishment, practically every worker left their place of employment and the city ground to a halt. No transport moved, no smoke plumed from factory chimneys, and the smelting furnaces burned empty. The shops closed and shuttered their windows, and knots of soldiers were seen with no officer accompanying them. An outpouring of hope and expectation and promise flowed through the streets. It was a tangible atmosphere that seeped into your skin and infected your mind so that people smiled a greeting as they passed each other.

'I'm so glad you agreed to come with me, Stefan,' said Nina. 'I do believe if you hadn't, then Dr K might have tied me to a chair to prevent me from leaving the house.'

Quite naturally I linked arms with her and we wandered towards the university quarter. Snow had fallen during the night and cast a clean white covering over the smashed glass and debris that littered the streets. Lights blazed from the university buildings and the quadrangle was filled with students and academics debating various courses of action.

There was a likelihood that the army regiments who hadn't joined the people would stage a counter-revolution, so students and academics were volunteering to enrol in a militia to hold the city. Fyodor was on his statue again, holding forth about the imminent arrival of Lenin.

'The Bolsheviks will defend the workers to the death!' he shouted above the din. 'We are forming Soviet Committees from the workforce and the armed services. From now on the workers and the enlisted men will make the decisions, not the employers or the officers.' He jumped down from his position and, catching Nina round the waist, lifted her up. 'A glorious day!' he cried. 'Largely due to the women of the bread queue!'

She made him a curtsey and laughed as he was carried off on the shoulders of his supporters.

Fyodor's enthusiasm was infectious. Everywhere in the streets people were congratulating each other.

'A new beginning!'

'The power of the people!'

★

But the power had yet to be wrested from those who clung onto it.

'Is it true,' I asked Dr K the next evening, 'that the Tsar is on his way to Tsarskoe Selo from the Front and has sent an order suspending the Duma?'

'He could have sent twenty orders with the same effect,' he answered, 'but no one is prepared to enforce them. His train was halted in a station while the Duma councillors held a meeting anyway and elected a committee to provide Provisional Government.'

'The councillors of the Provisional Government have moved into the other wing of the Winter Palace,' said Nina. 'But another group of councillors has also moved in there – the Soviets of Workers and Soldiers Committee, to represent the armed forces and working men and women.'

'What is the Provisional Government doing about that situation?' I asked.

'Alexander Kerensky is a member of both committees,' Dr K told us, 'and they have made a joint decision to arrest the Tsar's Council of Ministers.'

'The women of the bread queue say that some of the Imperial Government officials wanted to be arrested for their own safety,' Galena told us.

'They may need protection.' Dr K watched Galena's face as he spoke his next words. 'A delegation from the new Provisional Government is going to meet the Tsar in his royal train. They will inform the Tsar that he must abdicate.'

'Tsar Nicholas the Second is a proud man,' said Galena. 'He will refuse.'

'Galena.' Dr K spoke candidly. 'Entire regiments have switched their allegiance to the Provisional Government. Some of the commanding officers are relatives of the Tsar. This means that they will no longer take orders from him. Nicholas Romanov hasn't enough soldiers to support him. He will sign the abdication papers. He has no choice.'

Galena began to clear the table, smacking the dishes against each other as she did so. 'Have you any other bad news for us?' she snapped.

'The Provisional Government has declared loyalty to the Allies and plans to launch a new offensive.'

'But that's crazy!' I interrupted. 'A million men have already gone to war, never to return. Poultry keepers, shepherds, farmers, harvesters – that's why there is no food. Don't they understand that?'

'Kerensky believes it's necessary for Russia's international status and our national pride.'

'Let me tell you what Eugene has written to me!' I took a sheet of paper from my pocket. '*Implore our new Provisional Government to make peace at any price. If they say the country's pride will not allow us to surrender, tell them the pride of Russia has bled to death upon the battlefields.*'

'That is of no consequence,' Dr K said sardonically. 'Winter has passed, so the generals are obliged to make an attack somewhere. The hope is that one more splendid assault will drive the enemy from our borders, and Russia will win the war.'

Nina shook her head sadly. 'No matter the outcome; in the Winter Palace and the City Hospital we will see the dire consequences of this decision.'

'If this assault fails,' I said, 'the people will not stand for it. The Provisional Government will fall.'

By the time the Spring Offensive petered out, with another hideous toll of dead bodies, Lenin was in the city, promising bread, land, peace and freedom.

'Isn't he magnificent!' Fyodor had persuaded Nina and me to go along to a Bolshevik Rally and he was intoxicated with the rhetoric.

'Compelling, yes,' I had to admit. Truthfully, Lenin wasn't the best of orators: his voice had little resonance and his figure was dwarfed by the red flags on either side of the wooden platform. But what he lacked in physical attributes he made up for in passion. Here was a man who utterly believed in the righteousness of his cause.

'*Russia leads the way! The people have thrown off their yoke! The whole world is with us!*'

'Listen to him!' Fyodor was almost dancing with glee. 'We cannot fail with Lenin as our leader.'

'Lenin the Leader!' repeated an old man who was standing beside us. 'My father was a serf. He was born with nothing. And he died with nothing. We lived like animals, scratching food from the soil with our bare hands. My own sons, who went into the factories, are no better off – the owners increase the hours and reduce the wages as they please. The Government made those workers army conscripts so they can be shot if they walk out. But now my children's children will not live as I did. So I will follow a leader like Lenin.'

'See how they admire him!' Fyodor indicated the crowds who were listening avidly to every word. 'Lenin is the rise of hope over despair. He is the dawn of new life to replace the darkness of the old.'

'*This war shows us that Capitalism is finished! Communism will triumph! We will give you Peace! We will give you Land! We will give you Bread!*'

'Lenin makes it seem so simple,' I said.

'That's because it *is* simple,' said Fyodor. 'It's all people want.'

'I don't think that's all people want, Fyodor. Lenin acts as though these things are his gift to give. But it was us who risked our lives on the street to spark the revolt, and we want more.'

'What else would you have him say?'

'We want a liberated press. The right to openly criticize our leaders and bring them to task if necessary. Democratic elections, with any candidate, and voting rights for every citizen by secret ballot. That's what freedom is. Do you lack the intellectual depth to see that?'

Fyodor's face went red. Nina glanced from him to me and back again. 'I know what *I* see,' she said. 'An urn of hot soup is being set up in that corner and I want to be there before a queue builds up.' She linked her arm in Fyodor's and guided him in the direction of the mobile soup kitchen.

I drove my fist into my hand. I hadn't meant to be so rude to Fyodor, but it frustrated me that those besotted with Lenin the Leader and his comrades could not see that we must have an assurance of future democracy.

Chapter 39

STEFAN

After he signed the abdication papers the Tsar was allowed to return to his family. They, along with Dr Botkin and their closest servants, were placed under house arrest at the Alexander Palace. Nina spoke about her sorrow for the Imperial Family, and I heard Dr K saying to Galena that he was going to tell her not to visit them.

'Such a wise and experienced doctor you are,' Galena replied, 'yet you know nothing of the female mind. Nina is not a girl you can order about. She must be spoken to in a more subtle way. I will deal with this.'

I was curious to know what Galena would do. That evening I invented an excuse to be in the scullery when she and Nina were ironing and folding bed linen in the kitchen.

'I'm relieved that our Tsar is reunited with his family and they have the opportunity to enjoy each other's company.' Galena began the conversation in a pleasant tone.

'I am too,' Nina replied. 'Despite his faults I don't think he is a bad man.'

'Nor do I,' said Galena. 'So I hope he may have some privacy, with just his wife and children around him.'

Nina tilted her head and, smiling at Galena, said, 'My job at the Winter Palace so occupies my time that I have no intention of visiting them . . . at the moment.'

The question of whether Nina would or would not visit the Alexander Palace was settled in August. With the Bolsheviks and other factions causing rising unrest in the city, for their own security the Tsar and his family were moved to Tobolsk in Siberia.

'I'd like to see them safe,' said Galena. 'Going east means there might be a better escape route for them. Supporters of the Imperial Government are gathering beyond the Ural mountains.'

'I do believe Kerensky would rejoice if they were rescued and removed from Russian soil,' said Dr K. 'He is stretched to the limit controlling rival factions and believes the army commanders who are still loyal to the Tsar might try to seize the city and hold the Provisional Government hostage in the Winter Palace.'

Of course Fyodor was aware of the movement of the Imperial Family, and Kerensky's problems. 'Kerensky knows that Lenin has been busy forming our Red Guard militia from the members of the Workers and Soldiers

Soviets,' he told me. 'He is willing to arm the Soviets if they promise to help defend the city.'

'Doesn't Kerensky realize that the Soviets are becoming the military arm of the Bolsheviks? It's the equivalent of a chicken handing an axe to a cook!'

'The offer is made on condition that the military equipment is returned when the danger is over,' Fyodor added.

'But as far as the Bolsheviks are concerned,' I said, 'the danger will never be over until they hold complete authority.'

'That might be what is best for Russia,' said Fyodor with finality, and he walked away from me.

The threat to the city from the army commanders subsided. Lenin continued his rousing speeches promising Land, Bread and Peace while the Provisional Government continued to send men and supplies to the Front. Although the bakeries had reopened, people became disenchanted that there was no respite from the heavy losses and shortages – which could not now be blamed on the Tsar, his wife or his ministers.

Towards the end of October I was awakened by Galena shaking my shoulder. 'I went to get our bread,' she said, 'but many of the streets are closed off by the Bolsheviks. The members of the Provisional Government are having a meeting and the Red Guard is set on deposing them. They are going to storm the Winter Palace!'

'At least it will make Fyodor happy if Lenin finally takes charge.' I sat up in bed. 'Does Dr K know about this?'

'When I returned he'd already left for the City Hospital.'

'Please tell Nina,' I said. 'I know she is obstinate, but even she must see it's wiser to stay at home today.'

'Stefen' – Galena's voice throbbed with fear – 'Nina went into work early this morning.'

I was out of the attic and taking the stairs three at a time to reach the kitchen. Galena had my outdoor clothes warming at the stove.

'There's food in the pockets!' she shouted after me as I threw them on and ran out of the door.

Hordes of people were flocking towards the city centre. Their mood was one of anger, but it was hard to judge whether it was at the Provisional Government's ineptitude or at the Bolsheviks' attempt to oust them by force. They attempted to push through the blocked-off routes. Scuffles broke out between them and the Bolshevik supporters. I went by the lanes and wynds of the canals via passageways I'd known as a child, and came out close to the Neva where it flowed behind the Winter Palace. There was a biting wind coming in off the Baltic but it hadn't deterred the rioters in the square. With strong ropes they had lassoed the protruding stonework of the great double-headed eagle – the emblem of the hated Romanov dynasty – and were straining on these with all their might.

A foolhardy soul climbed the front of the building and proceeded to hammer off chunks of masonry, which tumbled down to smash into smithereens on the frozen ground. The crowd howled their approval and began to sing out a tune in the manner of an old sea shanty, as if they were sailors hauling ropes on a ship:

'Hey! Hey!'

Bang!

Whoops of triumph while lumps of plaster fell to earth.

'Hey! Hey! Hey!'

And then they scattered as the entire edifice cracked apart and toppled at their feet.

My own heart soared when I saw the symbol of the Romanov dynasty lying in ruins. They were gone – never to return to rule Russia.

We were free!

Chapter 40

STEFAN

The defenders of the Winter Palace had erected barricades of wood and furniture to hold off the mass of Red Guards and citizens who were mobilizing before the entrance gates.

And here was revealed Kerensky's foolishness in arming the Soviets – for obviously they'd refused to give up their weapons once the threat from the Tsarist supporters was over. And so the Red Guard carried Government-issued rifles loaded with Government-issued bullets – which they were shooting at the windows of the building, where the members of the Government sheltered.

The Winter Palace soldiers' answering volley found their mark among the ranks of the Bolsheviks.

'This isn't worth the deaths of our comrades!' someone shouted.

'Let's leave them to rot in there!' another chimed in.

'No!' declared a voice I recognized. Fyodor had become a member of the Military Revolutionary Committee and was now in command of a section of the Red Guard. 'It is symbolic to take the Winter Palace and we must capture the councillors of the Provisional Government. In the face of their rifle fire let us go forward together!'

'We didn't get rid of stupid Tsarist officers to take orders from a stupid Bolshevik one!' someone heckled in response.

'Seize the man who said those words!' Fyodor yelled. 'He is a traitor to the people! He is a traitor to Russia!'

Sickened by the sight of the militia converging on this unfortunate fellow, I withdrew. I went to the side entrance on the river, where I used to come and go when I was a medical student. The soldier on duty there looked terrified.

'What's happening?' he asked me.

'The Red Guard militia – with citizens and deserters from the army – are in the square,' I said, 'with the intention of arresting the Provisional Government and establishing the Bolsheviks as the ruling party. They're dithering over whether to launch a frontal attack, while snipers inside pick them off as they argue.'

'Only cadet units and some royal staff are holding the palace,' he told me. 'They will be easily overcome.'

'The Red Guard don't know that though, so I have time to find the person I'm looking for.'

'I heard the Bolsheviks supplied shells for the cannon

273

of the ship moored in the river. They will blow the walls apart if the Provisional Government doesn't surrender.'

No sooner had he said this when there was an almighty thunderclap, and part of the side wall on the embankment collapsed into the river.

The soldier leaped in the air and a let loose a series of swear words. 'That's coming from the fortress at Saints Peter and Paul! They have trained their artillery on the palace!' He threw his rifle on the ground and scooted off.

I went inside. I wasn't especially worried about Nina's safety. The Winter Palace was enormous and the military hospital a good distance from the Malachite Room where the Provisional Government held their meetings. But I hurried along, for I couldn't guarantee the accuracy of the aim of the gunners – on either side.

For once the Matron was sympathetic to me. She'd heard the ruckus outside and, assuming it was a riot, was occupied in keeping staff and patients away from the windows. She told me that Alexander Kerensky had come by yesterday and asked for a casualty report, which she'd prepared and given to Nina to take to him this morning.

'Where did Kerensky say he would be?' I asked, experiencing a dropping feeling in my gut.

'In the other wing of the palace,' said the Matron. 'He said to deliver it to the Malachite Room.'

It was my turn to let loose some swear words. And as the Matron started to rebuke me I shouted at her, 'That's the part they're shelling! It's where the Bolsheviks are trying to break in!' I left her open-mouthed and ran for the staircase which overlooked the square.

From my vantage point I could see a wave of armed men rush forward to climb the gates. Sporadic fire hailed down upon them, but most got over. The sentry must have been right – the few hundred of the palace garrison were not sufficient to drive back the people who advanced now, without pause. Heaving against the gates, they broke them open. Under the archway they went, red flags flying.

'Nina!' I ran as fast as my legs would carry me along corridors, through room after room, shouting her name.

The Malachite Room was empty. The council table was jumbled with papers – signs that the meeting had been hastily abandoned. Some councillors had taken refuge in an adjacent chamber. There was no sign of Alexander Kerensky.

'Kerensky is gone,' they told me. 'He said he would try to rally forces sympathetic to the Provisional Government.'

Which way would Kerensky go? Would he have taken Nina with him? Had she even delivered the report?

On I went, searching the maze of corridors . . .

'Looter!' The collar of my coat was grasped in a mighty fist and I was hoisted into the air.

'Not me!' I gasped.

I'd been grabbed by a giant of a man and he spun me round to face him. Broken teeth, foul breath; he covered my face in spit as he bawled at me, 'You're a spy!'

'No,' I protested. 'I hated the Okhrana as much as anyone.'

He spat on the floor at the mention of the State Secret

Police. 'The Okhrana are no more. We are setting up our own secret police squads to torture the truth out of the likes of you.'

'Please!' I was crying in fear. 'I am a revolutionary, like you.'

'You're not a Bolshevik and you're not a starving peasant. You're a member of the Provisional Government. Or a Tsarist sympathizer.'

'I'm here to find one of the hospital nurses who got lost!' My brain was swimming as I struggled for oxygen. 'I'm a doctor. I worked in the other wing, in the military hospital. I fixed up many soldiers when they were wounded in battle.'

He took his gun from his hip holster. 'A single bullet is all it takes to spatter your brains across the wall. Let's see if you can fix that up . . . *Doctor!*'

His comrades snorted with mirth. 'An execution by the people for the people!'

'Wait! Wait!' An older man stepped forward. 'I recognize him. Dr Stefan Petrovich?'

'Yes!' I gulped. 'Yes, I am.'

'Huh! No sport with you.' The giant dropped me with a thud. 'Let's see if we can find any traitors in this rabbit warren of rooms.'

He strode away, leaving me to crawl, gagging and choking, upon the floor.

The soldier who'd identified me helped me to sit up. 'They've broken into the wine cellars,' he explained. 'Everyone is as drunk as a despot. But I've been through most of the rooms. The nurse you're looking for isn't in this side of the palace. She probably went straight home to get away from the fighting.'

Of course! I should have worked that out myself. If she couldn't get back to the hospital side, Nina had sense enough to leave the building. By glancing from the window she would have seen what was happening. With the help of the soldier who'd saved my life I made my way outside. Only the ragtail remnants of the invaders were there. The main body of them were inside, attempting to organize their new regime. As I crossed the square I glanced towards the water fountain.

And saw a familiar coloured shawl!

Nina stood holding a bunch of evergreen in her hand.

'What are you doing here?' I demanded, torn between relief that she was safe and bad temper at seeing her so unperturbed.

'I wanted to pay my respects to your mama.'

'Why? You never knew her.'

'When I heard the story of Bloody Sunday, it helped me to understand . . . things . . . to understand . . . you.'

'How can that be?' My laugh was without humour. '*I* don't even understand me.'

'I meant I understand you better, Stefan. It hurts to lose someone we love, but it can help to speak about the person. It eased the pain of my grief when Dr K shared his memories of my papa.'

'I don't know if I agree with that point of view,' I said.

She didn't reply, but went on tying the evergreen branches to the fountain.

And I found myself telling her more . . .

'It was my birthday, my twelfth birthday. I think I might have believed that I could have cake with the Tsar. My father had been dead for many years, but although I wanted to start work and we needed the money, my mother made me take school lessons. So the day of the march was a break from the boredom of studying. I'd no sense of danger. In fact, I was thrilled at being there. We went along with everyone else. As we neared the Winter Palace we were beside Dr K, and he spoke to us.'

My throat was closing over, for I was reliving memories which I'd suppressed for years.

'When I heard that those at the head of the procession might meet the Tsar, I ran away. I pulled free of my mother's hand and I burrowed through the crowd to get to the front. It didn't worry me when I saw the soldiers. I may even have thought they were our escort.

'They didn't call out to us to halt. They fired no warning shots above our head.

'I heard her calling my name . . .

'There.' I pointed to the spot where my mama had fallen. 'She stopped the bullet that would have killed me.'

'How brave and selfless of her! Why do you act as though your mama gave you a burden rather than a blessing?'

'What do you mean?'

'In Siberia they say that if someone loses their life to save yours, then thereafter you must live the joy of two people.'

'How can I be joyful when my mother is not here?'

'Stefan.' Tears welled up in Nina's eyes. 'Had she not died *you* would not be here. You have become a doctor. She would be so proud of you.'

It was so cold that her tears were almost freezing on her cheeks. It touched me that she should cry. For I had never once wept for my mother. Not then, nor any time in the days and months and years that followed.

I reached to brush them away at the same moment she reached to brush away mine. And I realized that I was crying too, and that tears weren't a thing of shame or weakness.

And we were in each other's arms.

And I realized that I loved Nina and probably had done since the moment I met her . . .

Chapter 41

STEFAN

Within ten days the Bolsheviks had taken command of the city, and of Russia.

I met Fyodor strutting about the Nevsky Prospekt as if he had personally conquered the country. 'We have the telegraph stations and government buildings. We control the bridges. This is the real revolution!' he crowed.

'I congratulate you,' I said. 'Where do I go to claim my piece of land?'

'Stefan, in the past you yourself said that the Duma Council was uselessly slow and badly organized. The self-elected Provisional Government was no better. We have worked so hard and waited so long for this – can't you rejoice that Russia will have a democracy at last?'

It seemed churlish to throw cold water on his high hopes. Yet I was upset by the indiscriminate violence that had accompanied the seizure of power.

Fyodor viewed this as regrettable but said it was out-weighed by the greater good of the result. 'Lenin has said he will honour the Provisional Government's pledge to hold democratic elections. The result will prove that we are the party chosen by Russians to lead Russia.'

His arguments were persuasive. If I'd not been in-volved in the conversations at Dr K's dinner table, then perhaps I would have been as blinkered as any other Bolshevik.

'Lenin knows that if the country isn't given the free elections promised by the Provisional Government then the people might rise against him,' said Dr K. 'But if the Bolsheviks are so confident of their universal support why then are they forming their own secret police force?'

'These Cheka men wear a special uniform,' Galena scoffed. 'For a secret police, that does not make them very secret.'

'There are more of them, and they are more active than the Okhrana,' said Dr K. 'One of their commissars came to the City Hospital to check the names of both staff and patients. He took away a dying man for execution, and refused to listen when I pointed out that if they waited another day they'd save themselves the expense of a bullet.'

'You will need to be careful,' said Galena, 'for you were connected to the Duma and the Provisional Govern-ment.'

'I was never a member of either,' he replied.

'But everyone knows that you were a close adviser. They seldom held a meeting without you there.'

'My consultations were to do with providing a health service. I was speaking up on behalf of hospital patients and those who are unwell in the community.'

'And it is because you speak up that you will become a target. Until things settle down you must stay at home and not go out on any business.'

'Woman, when this trouble first began I told you not to leave this house, but you mocked and disobeyed me. Are you saying that I am supposed to meekly do as you order me now?'

'Yes,' said Galena. 'That's precisely what I am saying.' And she went to the sink and began to wash up the dishes.

Dr K gave a snort of impatience, but he worked from his study that day and for a few days afterwards.

'I am going to the railway station to enquire about train tickets,' Galena told Nina and me. 'I'll find out what is available. Dr K would be better out of the city for a while.' She looked at us both. 'And I'd be happier if you two went with him.'

'Would you be prepared to go away?' Nina asked me when Galena had left the house.

'I might,' I replied, 'but I don't know where. At least you have a definite place where you would be made welcome.'

'No I don't,' she said. 'My home in Siberia has been taken from me.'

It pained me to do it – for I'd rather we weren't parted – but I felt obliged to mention Tomas. 'You and Tomas regularly exchange letters,' I pointed out. 'He'd probably be able to find you accommodation in Moscow while you prepare to be married.'

Nina looked at me steadily and then said, 'I intend to write to Tomas to tell him that I cannot marry him.'

'Why can't you marry Tomas?' My heart contracted as I waited for her reply.

'You may as well know.' Her chin was high, and she spoke defiantly. 'I am illegitimate.'

'Illegitimate?' I repeated. 'I don't know what you mean.'

'My father and mother were not married.'

'Oh,' I said, taken aback. When she'd first arrived I'd thought Nina to be quite snobbish, but perhaps that had been her defence against this secret she carried. 'How unfortunate. Still, I don't see why that means that you cannot marry Tomas.'

'There is the stigma of my birth.'

'What's that got to do with anything?'

'Society looks down upon someone in my position, and—'

'For goodness' sake!' I cut in. 'Our "society" is a collection of narcissistic individuals who gather at events for the purpose of self-adulation.'

'His parents would not approve.'

'You are not marrying his parents!' I raised my voice. 'You're marrying Tomas. Don't insult my friend by crediting him with such a shallow character. He is a staunch ally and a good man.'

She gaped at me like a cod on the slab of a fishmonger. Yet her honourable intentions impressed me. I acknowledged that, really, everything about Nina impressed me. And I asked myself: Why was I making a case for Tomas?

'Tell Tomas the truth,' I went on, 'and see what he thinks. If he says that the nature of your birth means that he cannot marry you, then he doesn't deserve you as his wife.'

Chapter 42

NINA

So eloquently was Stefan arguing the case for Tomas that it was obvious he was not concerned that I should wed another.

I was watching his face as he spoke, but he turned his head to the side and I could not read the expression in his eyes. At the end he'd stumbled over the word 'wife'. Stefan said that if his friend saw my being illegitimate as a barrier then Tomas didn't deserve me as his wife – Tomas didn't deserve *me*. Did that mean that Stefan considered me a worthy wife for his friend? And if so, in what way? Did he think me clever or kind or wise? I tormented myself with these questions until, through the maelstrom of my frazzled thoughts, a stark fact emerged. Stefan did not seem to care that I might consent to marry his friend.

But why this should upset me so much I did not know.

This winter was not as intensely cold as the previous one, but severe enough that, to cope with shortage of fuel, we removed the doors from the rooms on the second floor of the house and then, piece by piece, the upstairs flooring.

'I often wondered what it might be like to be a vandal,' Stefan said as carried a pile of wood in the yard and laid it at my feet. 'There's a definite satisfaction in ripping things apart.'

He gave a sudden grin as he took in my appearance. With my hair plaited and coiled on each side of my head and wearing an old apron of Galena's, I was using an axe to reduce the wood lengths to a suitable size for burning. I was very pleased with myself because at last I'd discovered a practical talent that contributed to the running of the household. Dmitri had never allowed me to invade his kitchen domain, but Papa had taught me how to chop kindling for the fire.

'Stay away from Nina!' Stefan warned Galena, who was sweeping up after him while muttering about the mess. 'She is wielding an axe, and is dangerous to approach.' He went into the house, whistling.

From the scullery door Galena winked at me.

Dr K refused to be downhearted as we reduced the fittings of his home to lumber, merely saying, 'We must be scientific in how we do this, lest the ceiling fall in upon us as we eat and sleep downstairs.'

Stefan kept to his attic, even though he had to climb over holes in the landing floor to reach his staircase.

We sustained our good humour within the house, but the Bolsheviks were encountering opposition to some aspects of their administration, and the spirit of the city changed. It became clear that the peace they were negotiating with Germany was at a price: the displacement of millions of people and the surrendering of coal and iron deposits . . . and vast tracts of land.

The discontent began.

Galena reported back from the bread queue what was being said in the city:

'How can Lenin keep his promise for us to own land if he gives so much of it away to our enemies?'

And: *'This is not the peace we wanted!'*

'How quickly they forget,' said Stefan, 'that their sons and brothers were massacred in a futile war.'

'It's because of their loss that they complain.' I could see the women's point of view. 'We've still to queue for bread and the children are still underfed. They worry that there won't be enough land to grow crops or raise cattle to feed the population. They think that those lives were sacrificed for nothing.'

'But the killing will stop!' Stefan was too exasperated to empathize.

And the two of us were off again, robustly debating the issue.

Galena had obtained a list of possible destinations to where trains were running. Dr K rejected all of them. 'You are a stubborn man,' she berated him. 'If you delay much longer there will be fewer tickets available.'

'I *have* been considering moving to a less turbulent location,' Dr K replied. 'But I wanted to see how honest a leader Comrade Lenin actually is. Possibly I am being too cynical and Russia will be reborn. Let us wait for the outcome of our promised democratic election, then we will make our plans.'

'Let's make them soon,' said Galena, 'lest someday we find an unknown and unwelcome visitor at our door.'

Not long after that an unwelcome visitor *did* come to the door of Dr K. But this man was not unknown to me.

There was no one but me in the house when the doorbell rang. As I opened the door, the lawyer Viktor Ilyich Volkov raised his hands and pushed his way into the hall.

'There!' He closed the front door. 'Now any cries of protest you make will not be heard. I have been watching this house and know that you are alone.'

'If you touch me,' I cried, 'I will scratch your eyes out!'

'You are not so beautiful as to be so desirable,' he said nastily. 'It has taken me months and months to trace you. I have come for the thing you stole from the house in Siberia that belongs to me.'

'I took nothing of any worth. Some clothes, and a photograph of my mother in a silver frame.'

'There is some value attached to those things, but I will overlook that if you return to me the other object.'

'What other object?'

'There was a casket. An oblong carved casket.'

Viktor Ilyich knew about the dagger! I shook my head. But, unconsciously, my fingers strayed to my neck.

'Ah!' He caught sight of the chain with the tiny golden key. His eyes glistened with that same hunger which I'd noticed on the last day we parted. And I realized now that it hadn't been with desire for me. What motivated this man was the greed for money.

'I don't understand,' I said.

'You cannot deny its existence and I know that you have it. You must hand it over. It belongs to me.'

'I will not. My father gave me special charge of it.'

I braced myself for his anger. Instead he tried a different tack. 'Nina . . .' His tone was wheedling. 'I realize that my offer of marriage may have come as a shock. You are a plain girl with no sophistication and I sense I frightened you into running away. And for that . . . I am' – he hesitated as if the word stuck in his throat – 'sorry.'

I remained silent even though I suspected that Viktor Ilyich was waiting for me to accept his apology.

'I have no wish to pursue you against your will, and so I will promise not to bother you again if you hand over that casket.'

I stared at him with contempt.

He gritted his teeth. 'Don't you pine for your family home? It must be grim living in this city. There is food and fuel a-plenty in Siberia. Why don't you come back with me? The house is wide enough to be split into two halves. We'd create a separate entrance for you. I would leave you to live your own independent life.'

I thought of the fresh smell of the country air and the sweet sound of the birds and the wind in the trees. I'd lived in complete peace in Papa's house, my life bound in a rainbow ribbon which had unravelled since I'd left Yekaterinburg.

'I know!' He clicked his fingers. 'You could be my estate manager. It would give you an independent income. Albeit quite small,' he added swiftly. 'And, truthfully, I believe that Dmitri and the rest of the peasants would be happier if you returned. They would work better with you in charge.'

I thought of the servants and estate workers and I knew what he said was true. He must have sensed my thoughts for his manner became more confident. Yet I was not so naïve that I couldn't see that this was subtle manipulation.

As I pondered the situation, the lawyer opened his hands and said, 'I declare you may have the house as your own. I will remain in the village and we will only meet when required to do so by business matters.'

Perhaps this was the best option, the most favourable offer I could hope for. I would have a home and an income and the freedom to come and go as I pleased.

'I had a great affection for your father and I know he would have wanted me to look after you,' Viktor Ilyich went on. 'Here is a suggestion. Why don't we agree that you give me the casket and its contents in exchange for the house? We can have an independent lawyer draw up a settlement right here in Petrograd. You give me the casket, and the house will belong to you for ever.'

I thought about it. If I owned the house I could sell some of the furniture and send the money to Dr K and visit Petrograd whenever I chose. And . . .

The dagger repelled me. Its history was tainted with blood and despair. If it did have some strange power, then better I gave it away. It would no longer haunt my dreams.

I hesitated.

'It is the best offer you will ever get. You should take it. Let me at least have the key.'

I reached for the chain around my neck.

At that moment the front door opened and Dr K entered the house. 'We have a guest!' he said in surprise.

The lawyer chewed at his lip in frustration.

'Come into my study, please, and sit down,' said Dr K when I introduced them to each other. 'So fortunate that I finished early at the hospital today.' He nudged me as he set out some chairs. 'You were Nina's lawyer, Viktor Ilyich?' Dr K's use of the past tense hung in the air. 'I assume you are here to settle the misunderstanding of her inheritance? It is good of you to travel so far to assure her that she now owns her father's house and lands.'

'I regret to say that the house and the estate were used as security for a loan to Nina's father which was unpaid at his death. By the terms of our contract all his goods are mine.'

'You must have rich clients and high earnings,' observed Dr K, 'to have been able to lend that amount of money.'

'I have various means,' Viktor Ilyich replied.

'By what means has a country lawyer the ability to lend sufficient money to feed the folk and livestock on an estate over many months?' Dr K asked the question with a quiet insistence.

'I fail to see how this is any of your business.'

'It is my business in as much as I am Nina's godfather, a position I take very seriously. I was also her father's friend, and have correspondence from him entrusting her to my care if anything should happen to him.'

The lawyer gave him a sly look. 'It is good that your friend recognized this girl as his own but, inconveniently, there is nothing to prove that she is indeed his child.'

I turned my face away – that Viktor Ilyich should mention this so brazenly was humiliating.

Dr K laid his hand upon my arm and spoke to the lawyer. 'I was there just after Nina Ivanovna was born. Sadly, too late to save her mother, but I am a reliable witness to my friend claiming her as his own.'

'I am relieved to hear that,' said the lawyer. He rose to leave. 'Nina and I have made an agreement and I must go and prepare papers for her to sign.'

Dr K remained seated. 'You have not yet answered my question. By what means has a country lawyer the ability to lend sufficient money to feed the folk and livestock on an estate over many months?'

'One finds ways to help a friend.' Viktor Ilyich was at the door. 'When I return I will bring a contract wherein I will gift the house and all its goods to Nina Ivanovna in perpetuity. I think you'll acknowledge that is a generous settlement.'

'When Nina arrived here I made enquiries at the Ministry of War regarding the requisitioning of supplies,' said Dr K. 'It appears that payments were made to the estate of my friend in compensation for the materials taken for the war. They have details of the transactions for horses and grain in exchange for allowances paid to maintain the estate.'

'These papers never arrived.'

'And yet the money was withdrawn . . .?'

'There is some mistake in their accounts,' Viktor Ilyich blustered. 'Corruption was rife in the Tsarist Government.'

'So it would seem,' said Dr K. 'However, to take money from the War Office for personal gain is an act of treason. In the old days, for a treasonable offence you would have been tried and hanged.'

'Possibly. Possibly not.' The lawyer was unperturbed. 'There is always someone to bribe. Everyone has a price.'

'Often this is the case,' said Dr K. 'I myself do not think you will be tried and hanged.'

'I'm glad that we can agree on that at least,' said the lawyer.

'Indeed,' Dr K replied. 'The Bolsheviks who now run the government departments have a different way of dealing with people like you. They have issued a directive that in some circumstances a person can be executed without trial. Those tiresome court procedures waste too much time. They'll take you out into a yard and shoot you in the head.'

Viktor Ilyich threw me a venomous look. 'This is not over,' he said.

'On the contrary; it is.' Dr K stood up to indicate that the lawyer should leave. 'I will write to Dmitri, the steward, to say that you are not allowed further entry to the house. When the weather improves Nina Ivanovna will return to Yekaterinburg to claim her rightful inheritance.'

Chapter 43

NINA

'Nina.' Dr K went to the window to watch the lawyer walk down the street. 'Does the agreement Viktor Ilyich Volkov was referring to mean that you were considering marrying him?'

'Absolutely not!'

'That is a relief,' Dr K said dryly. 'I have yet to accommodate the idea of Tomas as a possible godson-in-law. The thought of being in a situation where I might have to welcome that odious lawyer into our family would have been a step too far.'

'I would *never* willingly marry Viktor Ilyich.'

'I applaud your decision. What was the agreement he mentioned?'

'That he would let me have ownership of my papa's house. And I thought if I owned the house I could sell the furniture and send you the money.'

'Or transport it here and use it for fuel,' the doctor said with humour. 'But I know that type of man. He does not give in willingly. What did he want in exchange?'

'Among my father's papers I found a casket,' I said. 'A carved wooden casket.'

'The lawyer pursued you far across Russia in winter for a casket? It must have some monetary value.'

'I will fetch it,' I said.

Dr K was seated at his desk when I returned and placed it before him. 'Of what worth is that?' he mused. 'Unless . . . does the casket contain some precious object?'

I handed him the key and he unlocked it and opened the lid.

'Oh!' Such was his shock that he stood up.

'Have you seen it before?' I asked him.

'Never.'

'Where would my papa get such a thing?'

'Perhaps . . .' Dr K was staring at the dagger as if mesmerized. 'It might have been part of a dowry. No . . . I do not know. Did he speak of it to you?'

'Never, except . . . on his deathbed he was raving about all sorts of things . . . He said he and his best friend had danced at a ball in the Winter Palace, and it was one of the happiest days of his life.'

'Ivan said that?' There was a catch of grief in the doctor's voice.

'In amongst other nonsense,' I said. I decided not to mention Papa's last confession. I didn't believe it to be true, and it would upset Dr K.

'This dagger is . . . unusual.'

Not so unusual, I thought. Should I tell him that Rasputin had once carried a similar dagger in his sash?

'Its value must be immense,' said Dr K. 'The ruby alone is priceless . . . and the pearls too . . .'

'Would someone give it to my father as a gift?'

'I – I'm not sure. There is one place where that might have come from—' He broke off. 'And it can never go back there.'

'I know where it came from,' I said.

'You do?' The colour drained from the doctor's face.

'From the Alexander Palace,' I said.

'At Tsarskoe Selo?' He seemed confused. 'What makes you think it was in the Alexander Palace?'

I told him the coachman's story of the theft.

'That could be true.' Dr K nodded. 'But wherever it came from and however it came into your possession, I think you would be better rid of it.'

'We could sell it,' I said. 'And give the money to the hospital?'

'Absolutely not.' He shook his head vehemently. 'There is no way to sell this without attracting attention. The kind of attention that has fatal consequences.' He pursed his lips and blew out a long breath. 'Has the lawyer seen it?'

'I think he must have caught a glimpse of it at some time in the past.'

'So he knows that there is a precious object inside the carved casket, which is why he wanted your agreement for an exchange. This dagger is worth more than your house, the estate and everything on it.'

'It sounds ridiculous but I think my father thought it cursed.'

'My friend Ivan had a lively mind. He thought there were forces other than human inhabiting our world.'

'Do you believe in spiritual things?'

The doctor shrugged. '"There are more things in Heaven and Earth . . ." than we might imagine. Cursed or not, men would kill for this. It may be that you should fling it in the Neva.' He closed the lid of the casket and handed it to me.

'Thank you, Godfather-Uncle,' I said, 'for exposing the fraud of Viktor Ilyich.'

'My dear child, I didn't investigate anything. I assessed the lawyer's character and made a correct guess as to his working methods. I knew your papa very well. He would never have left you destitute and in that man's power. And,' he went on, 'be assured that your parents were indeed married. I was your father's groomsman.'

'Do you have a copy of the marriage certificate? If you do, then I would like to see it.'

'There is no need for you to see a marriage certificate.' Dr K's answer was swift and explicit. 'I give you my solemn word that your parents were officially married. Afterwards, they decided to travel. They both loved the countryside and horses, and Ivan was interested in the peoples of Russia. He wanted to make a written record of their languages before they were lost.'

'Why did I not find a marriage certificate among Papa's papers?'

'Ah' – Dr K paused – 'perhaps the lawyer stole it so that he could have leverage over you to give him the dagger?'

Even though Viktor Ilyich was a thief and a bully, that explanation didn't quite fit. It was more that he believed my parents weren't married and tried to exploit the fact. When I'd mentioned the subject to Dmitri he'd been uncomfortable. And then there was the reaction of Professor Kirichenko at the university when I had told him my real name.

So I said, 'In the church where my parents were married, the priest would have recorded the ceremony. I could go there and see the certificate for myself.'

Dr K didn't reply but dropped his eyes to focus on the work piled up on his desk.

'Where were they married?' I persisted.

'Oh, a chapel somewhere. I can't recall the name.' Usually Dr K was a forthright man, but he was dissembling now.

I couldn't understand how the doctor could have forgotten the name of the church. Why was he reluctant to tell me where it was? Maybe it made him sad to think of his two friends, now dead. But I didn't have the opportunity to question him further, for the next moment Galena sounded the gong for dinner.

'Ah!' Dr K spoke fast. 'I'm hungry. Are you? While we eat I'll tell you of some of the escapades your father and I got involved in when we were students together.'

PETROGRAD
(ST PETERSBURG)

1918

Chapter 44

NINA

On the fifth of January 1918, the results of the first free election in the history of Russia brought over seven hundred men and women to Petrograd as our elected representatives.

This initial meeting of our fledgling democracy was to convene as an Assembly of Constituents in the Tauride, a magnificent palace built by Catherine the Great. Dr K had secured four seats for us in the high gallery. Galena, stalwart in her winter coat and heavy boots, fished in her bag for a handkerchief to dab her eyes.

'May I ask an Imperialist woman if she is shedding tears of joy that finally the people have a voice?' Dr K teased her.

'I am,' she admitted. 'Although I would prefer it if the Tsar were here to officially open the proceedings.'

Dr K dug Stefan in the ribs to stop him saying anything to spoil Galena's day. But Stefan was leaning far forward, his arms along the barrier rail, to get a better view.

'I am shaking with tension,' he confided in me.

'As am I,' I replied, stretching towards the rail. I was aware how close we were to each other. I could feel his breath on my cheek. Unbidden, into my head came an image of us sitting on my bed the night Rasputin was murdered.

'Nina,' Stefan whispered, 'isn't it amazing to be here?'

I turned to look at him. Even in profile he had a handsome intensity. 'Amazing,' I whispered back. 'At this moment there's nowhere else in the world I'd want to be.'

He grinned at me, his face alive with expectation. 'That's exactly how I feel!'

In the vast hall below us chairs had been set out in a semicircle facing a central podium. There were more than twenty political parties with varying ideologies, but since the election the majority Socialist Party had fallen out and split into two. The Bolsheviks had seized on this and tried to argue that these two parties were no longer valid representatives of the people.

Most of the day was taken up with swearing in the people's elected representatives. The political parties were diverse, from high conservative to extreme left wing. It wasn't until after four p.m. that we realized that the Bolsheviks didn't have an overall majority.

'Ho!' said Stefan. 'I wonder how Fyodor will greet that outcome?'

Dr K's brow furrowed. 'The Bolsheviks will have

had their spies at the polling stations, so Lenin must already be aware of the make-up of this Assembly.'

Different delegates got up to speak. The Bolsheviks insisted that the two main Socialist parties did not represent the people. They put forward a motion to declare the Bolsheviks as the governing party. When the vote was taken, the other parties united against them – with the result that the Bolsheviks were defeated in the count.

'This will not go well,' said Dr K, and he put his head in his hands.

From below we heard a ruckus.

'What is the commotion?' asked Galena.

'The Bolsheviks are walking out!' said Stefan.

'Good riddance!' said Galena. 'It is better that Russia lets them go.'

'But they will not let Russia go,' said Dr K. 'There will be repercussions. Perhaps we too should leave?' he suggested.

'I want to see what happens next,' I said, and Stefan agreed with me.

'I fear it has already been decided what will happen next.' Dr K pointed to the doors of the Assembly Hall, where soldiers of the Red Guard were taking up positions. 'There are the wolves who will tear the heart out of Russia.'

A uniformed man strode onto the podium.

'Fyodor!' cried Stefan.

'You will disperse at once!' Fyodor announced. 'This

meeting has been deemed illegal. The Soviets are a higher form of democracy than this Assembly of Constituents. The Bolshevik Party will not allow the hard-won power of the Soviets of the Workers and Soldiers to be usurped by a spurious bourgeois elite! We speak on behalf of Russia!'

Stefan was out of his seat and clambering over the gallery benches to get to the stairs. I chased after him as he caught up with Fyodor, who was overseeing his soldiers in harrying the members of the Assembly out of the hall.

'What are you doing?' Stefan grabbed Fyodor by the sleeve.

'Protecting the Revolution!' Fyodor replied. 'We know the true needs of the proletariat.'

'Fyodor,' I said. 'It was the various Soviets — those of the Workers, and the Soldiers and the Peasants — who directly elected these people.'

Fyodor stared back at me. '*We* are the people,' he said. 'The Soviets will do as we say.'

When we got home Galena spoke again to Dr K about moving out of the city.

'Why don't you come to Yekaterinburg?' I suggested. 'I would love to welcome you all there. Now that my Godfather-Uncle has spoken to the lawyer I can claim Papa's house as my own.'

'When did you speak to the lawyer?' Galena asked Dr K.

'Weeks ago. He came to the house to bully Nina. Fortunately I arrived home unexpectedly and was able to . . . em . . . persuade him to change his mind regarding his claim on her property.'

'Why didn't you tell me that man was in the house?' Galena rounded on Dr K. 'I would have had harsh words to say to him.'

'For that very reason, woman,' he replied. 'I didn't want you chasing him down the street with a broom in your hand.' Then, addressing Stefan and Galena, Dr K asked, 'Perhaps Siberia is too far away?' Neither of them replied, so he said to me, 'But you should go, Nina. I'll buy you a train ticket at the earliest opportunity.'

'I don't want to go on my own,' I said. 'I want to be here.'

'Do you mean with us, wherever we go, or "here" in the city?'

'With you.' My face went pink. 'With all of you.' I avoided Stefan's eyes.

Dr K smiled at me. 'What do you think, Galena?'

'For weeks now I have been nagging you to leave,' she said. 'I am sure the house is being watched, especially on clinic day, when any stranger can enter the shed in our back garden. I've told you to be selective of your patients.'

'My patients are whoever turns up and needs medical aid.'

Galena sniffed. 'It's risky for you to treat former Imperialists.'

'May I remind you that you are a former Imperialist. Should I not treat you if you become unwell?'

'I'm not a former Imperialist,' she declared. 'I am a *present* Imperialist. The Tsar had bad advisers. That is why things turned out the way they did.' She lowered her voice. 'The women in the bread queue say there is a force called the White Army who are going to rescue and reinstate him.'

Stefan groaned.

'Yekaterinburg was a safe haven for my good friend Ivan,' said Dr K. 'It has the advantage of being far away from this city, and Moscow. Perhaps we should consider Nina's invitation? I'm sure doctors would find work in Siberia, and we might return when the political situation is more stable.'

'Oh, yes!' I said. 'Please do come.' An image came into my head of me showing Stefan the paddock and the horses, the orchard and the meadows of spring flowers.

'It will give us a rest, and Nina can ensure that this crooked lawyer has registered the title deeds of the house in her name.' Dr K looked again at Galena and Stefan. 'Does everyone agree?'

'I do,' said Galena. 'Anything to get you to a safer place.'

'Stefan?' Dr K asked.

Stefan was looking into the middle distance and Dr K had to repeat his name before he refocused his attention and replied, 'Siberia sounds like a safe haven.'

Galena put her hand over his where it lay on the table. 'We will come back, I promise. And things will be the same again.'

Stefan got up. He paused at the door to look around the room before saying, 'Things will never be the same again.'

It could be weeks before we obtained train tickets, but before we left the city there was something I had to do.

I took the carved casket from my travel bag but I did not open it. Dr K was right. The dagger was dangerous. Not just because of its great value but because of the aura that surrounded it. Every time I looked upon it or touched it, my mind was infested with fanciful thoughts. Someone like Viktor Ilyich should never be given charge of it. If the dagger was gone, then it could bring no harm to anyone.

The next morning I volunteered to queue for our bread. On my way there I walked by the Neva. There was a strong current. The water, although sluggish with snow, was moving purposefully downstream. I leaned over and let the casket slide from my hand.

I experienced a deep sense of release as I dropped it into the inky water. Now it was under the ice but, unlike Rasputin, this dagger would not rise to the surface.

Chapter 45

NINA

The Bolshevik Party made a pronouncement that any people or organizations who disagreed with their views were enemies of the State.

Recognized opposition parties were branded, along with Tsarist sympathizers, as 'Counter-Revolutionaries'. Lenin accused them of subversion and treason, destroyed their printing presses and suspended the rule of law. The Bolsheviks' special armed police force, the Cheka, placed agents and informers inside academic institutions, offices and factories. Protests were ruthlessly quashed by the Red Guard. A new type of fear stalked the streets – that of suspicion and intimidation. It was clear that Lenin did not fully trust the Petrograd Soviets, for the city had a reputation for free-thinking and independence of spirit. He decided that the Russian capital was now to be

Moscow; a Soviet Government would be set up within the Kremlin.

'Not a government,' said Stefan. 'A dictatorship.'

We took turns to wait in day-long queues at the railway station to buy tickets. It took over a week to secure the four that we needed. But, before we could rejoice at our achievement, the regime issued a directive to say that special passes were needed to travel by train – special passes that could only be issued by personal application at party headquarters. I remembered Papa's friend, the stationmaster, saying that whoever seized control of the railway system would hold all the winning cards.

'I refuse to talk to them,' said Stefan.

'It would be unwise for any of us to do that,' said Dr K. 'We would be subjected to investigation.'

'I will write to Dmitri, our family steward,' I said, 'and ask him to speak to the stationmaster at Yekaterinburg.'

The thaw had set in, and I began to dream of Siberia in the springtime. I promised them that they would love my village, and I described my house with the paddock and the orchard, and the meadows full of wild flowers. Talking about this was an antidote to what was happening in the city and elsewhere. A resistance organized by Alexander Kerensky crumbled and he had to flee the country. The Bolsheviks then orchestrated a purge of what they termed 'terrorist elements' – in reality, it was aimed at rooting out dissenters. Workers and soldiers, students and professors, ordinary housewives, the old and the young were rounded up – to disappear in the torture cells or be executed.

One clinic morning, when we were drinking our early morning tea, Galena came from the front door with a slip of paper in her hand. Her face white, she stood at the entrance to the kitchen.

'What's amiss with you?' Dr K was on his feet so fast that his chair overturned. 'Come, lean on me.' He helped Galena sit down.

'What's wrong?' Stefan too jumped up from his stool.

'This was in our letterbox. It must have been put there during the night.' Galena placed the note on the table:

> Dr K should leave the city AT ONCE. The Cheka have his name. Burn this note after reading it.

'What?' Dr K forced a laugh as Galena read it out in a shaking voice. 'Is that what's alarming you? Put it in the stove. Pay no heed to anonymous letters.'

'I wouldn't laugh about the Cheka,' Stefan said. 'The Bolshevik Secret Police are building a worse reputation than the Okhrana. They are an execution squad in all but name.'

We were sitting close enough that I could see the paper and a shiver passed through me. 'It is the same handwriting as the note which warned me to leave the Alexander Palace.'

'And it was a timely warning,' said Galena, her voice stronger now that she'd got over her initial fright. 'If

Nina had not left when she did, she might have been detained under house arrest with the Imperial Family.'

'Did the coachman tell you who wrote the note?' Stefan asked me.

'He would say nothing except that it must be burned. I supposed he'd been bribed, but I also think he was frightened of whoever had handed him the message.'

'Let us follow both the example of the coachman and the last instruction in this letter.' Dr K lifted the piece of paper and dropped it into the stove.

'You should think seriously about what was written in that note,' said Galena. 'If not for our sakes, then for theirs.' She indicated Stefan and me.

'My dear Galena' – Dr K gazed at her with an expression of thoughtful admiration – 'in all our years together you have never given me bad advice.' He stood up and walked to the kitchen window. 'There is already a queue of patients waiting to be seen.' He sighed heavily. 'I think we should open as usual so as not to attract attention. Immediately afterwards, I will depart from the house without carrying any luggage, and walk to the City Hospital. I'll go in but leave by a side door and find somewhere to stay.' He held up his hand to forestall any interruption. 'I won't say where. That means if you are questioned you can tell them nothing. I'll find a way of contacting you so that when Nina receives our railway passes we can set out for Yekaterinburg.'

Galena's shoulders slumped in relief but she rallied enough to say, 'My dear Dr K, in all the years I've given you good advice, you have rarely taken it. I am glad that you're making an exception today.'

When we'd finished the clinic session, Stefan went into the kitchen to help Galena set out our breakfast. Dr K sat down to write up his notes while I wiped the work surfaces and benches.

He picked up his pen. 'It's strange to think that it might be months before I sit here——'

He was interrupted by the shed door opening. Two men in the uniform of the new Bolshevik Secret Police stood there.

'Is this the clinic of the surgeon who works at the City Hospital, the man known as Dr K?'

I drew in my breath, but Dr K answered them before I could speak. 'Come in, please' – he stood up to greet them – 'and tell me what is wrong with you.'

'There is nothing wrong with *us*.' One of the men walked into the shed. 'I am a commissar of the Commission for Combating Counter-Revolution, and I say it is you who are doing wrong here.'

'In what way?' Dr K put down his pen and faced the Cheka officer.

'Has this clinic been officially registered with the Petrograd Soviet Council?'

'I don't believe it has,' Dr K replied. 'I was unaware that it was necessary.'

'Being unaware does not absolve you of responsibility.'

'That is true. I am closing up now and will go to the Council offices immediately and register it.'

Dr K's answer did not satisfy this policeman. He picked up some strips of bandages. 'Did you steal these from the City Hospital where you work?'

'They were not stolen. We make them ourselves from the fabric of our own bedsheets.'

The Cheka commissar dropped the bandages and opened a drawer which contained a pair of scissors and some cotton wool. 'You have supplies here which could be better used elsewhere.'

'They are kept for the poorest who cannot afford doctors' bills,' Dr K explained.

'It is for us to decide who receives aid, not you. There might be more deserving cases than the ones you choose to treat.'

'We treat everyone. This clinic has always been open to everyone.'

'And what does that mean, exactly . . . "open to everyone"?'

'It means that anyone who is unwell or requires medical aid, but cannot afford the fee, may come here and I will attend to them.'

'Anyone at all?'

Dr K waited a moment and then he said, 'Yes. Anyone at all.'

'So if a former Grand Duke or Duchess or some other enemy of the State came here, then you would help them?'

Dr K said nothing.

'I have asked you a question.' The commissar pulled his handgun from its holster. 'Answer me at once!'

'Doctors take an ancient oath to help those in need.' Dr K spoke carefully. 'We ask patients about their symptoms, not their politics.'

'That sounds like treason to me,' said the policeman who was guarding the door. 'Which makes you a traitor.'

'Traitors get a bullet to the body.' And without saying anything further the Cheka commissar raised his weapon – and shot Dr K in the chest!

The two policemen exchanged a look and a nod, and then left the shed and the garden. I watched in shock and horror as Dr K gave a dreadful moan and crumpled to the floor. He tried to get up but failed.

'Stefan!' I screamed. 'Stefan! Help. Stefan! Stefan!'

Galena came running from the kitchen, Stefan overtaking her on the path.

We carried Dr K into the house and laid him on his bed in his study. His shirt was soaking red.

'Galena! Fetch his medical bag!' Stefan cried.

'Don't go.' Dr K reached out and clasped at Galena's apron. 'There is no point. I recognize arterial blood when I see it. Stay here and see me through this.'

'Let Stefan try to stem the flow,' she said.

'Woman, will you not even obey this last order that I give you,' he said.

'Konstantin! Konstantin!' Galena lamented as she knelt

down beside him. 'Time and again I told you that your recklessness would lead to ruin.'

'Hush, hush.' He brushed her cheek with his hand. 'I am not worth your grief. One last favour I ask. Be strong for the children and it will make my passing the easier.'

'I will.' She took his fingertips to her lips. 'I will.'

Dr K switched his gaze to Stefan and me. 'I've never told anyone before, but I asked this woman to marry me. Every day for a year I proposed, and she refused. Said that the daughter of a washerwoman could not marry a surgeon. Can you believe it?'

I shook my head, not trusting myself to speak, for my eyes were aching with unshed tears.

'But she agreed to be my housekeeper. That way she could scold me perpetually as any wife might do. And I had her company more than any husband.' He coughed and a great clot of blood landed on the coverlet.

'Messy to the end,' said Galena.

'To the end,' the good doctor murmured, and he closed his eyes and breathed his last.

Chapter 46

NINA

They came from every corner of the city to attend the funeral of Dr Konstantin. The streets were lined with people. Workers removed their caps and women knelt in the snow as his cortege passed. The steel makers had sent a special carriage for his coffin to rest on. They did not forget that as a young, newly qualified doctor he'd gone into the foundry to care for the men burned when a vat of molten metal had exploded.

Everyone had a story to tell.

'My son's leg was broken. The other doctors wanted to amputate from the hip. He'd never have had any chance of work. But Dr K splinted it and found him a hospital bed while the bones healed.'

'I was dying from blood poisoning. I couldn't afford treatment. He found the abscess and lanced it and I am well again.'

'He gave us bread from his own table when we were starving.'

Fyodor arrived at the house an hour before we were due to leave to express his condolences, and with an offer of a dozen Red Guards as an escort for the cortege.

'Hypocrite!' Stefan had followed Galena to answer the front bell. 'That you dare to show your face at this door!'

'Stefan—' Fyodor began.

'Betrayer of the Revolution!' Stefan raged. And he cursed Fyodor and Lenin and their whole party as liars and cheats. 'Where now the rousing speeches on the rights of the people to self-determination? What happened to the high-minded ideals of wise government?'

Fyodor staggered back under this onslaught.

Galena pushed Stefan inside the house and spoke to Fyodor. 'We thank you for your offer,' she said diplomatically. 'Dr K was a pacifist, so a military escort of any type is not appropriate.'

'Why don't Fyodor's men line up along this street and see us off?' I suggested. 'It would be a prudent move, and it means that they are not with us all the way.'

Stefan was outraged. 'The effrontery of Fyodor to come here and offer sympathy when he represents everything Dr K fought against!'

'The Red Guard are not the Cheka,' I said. 'They are workers who became soldiers to fight for their human rights. Come, let us walk with Galena and give her the support she needs today.'

∗

I thought Galena would want to rest after the funeral, but when we returned to the house she took off her coat and put on her apron. 'There are things we have to do,' she said. 'And they must be done right away.'

'What kind of things?' Stefan asked her.

'You saw the turn-out for his funeral?' she said. 'I knew Konstantin was popular but I didn't appreciate how much.'

'I think he was more than popular,' I said. 'I think he was loved.'

'Exactly,' said Galena. She had fetched a hessian sack from the scullery and was going about the kitchen popping small ornaments into it. 'That made him dangerous, and now the memory of him is doubly dangerous.' She hurried off into Dr's K's study and began selecting items to go into her sack. 'Other than Lenin, the Bolsheviks do not want the people to love or respect any single person ever again. They fear the rise of a leader that the people would listen to and follow.'

'Dr K is dead,' said Stefan with a break in his voice.

'So they cannot allow him to become a martyr. At the graveside I heard murmurings against his murderers. The Cheka will have heard them too. They will ransack this house to try to find anything to incriminate him as a traitor and justify his death as a valid execution. And they'll confiscate everything of any value so that we are left destitute and powerless. Here' – she shoved the sack at Stefan – 'dig a hole in the garden and bury this stuff. We can retrieve it at a later date. I dare not hide too much in case they suspect what I've done and search more thoroughly.'

Stefan stood holding the sack. 'Do you really think this is necessary?'

'I do,' said Galena. 'And so did Konstantin, for I am following the instructions he gave me in the event of anything happening to him. Nina and I will search through his papers and burn what we think could be misinterpreted as actions against the State.'

Galena went and sat at Dr K's desk and picked up a sheaf of papers. 'He did treat people of all classes,' she said. 'We must destroy the files of any of the nobility or members of the Duma or the Provisional Government. Go!' she said to Stefan. 'Hurry! They will strike shortly, while they think we are in mourning and unprepared for their visit.'

As soon as Stefan left the room Galena stood up. 'Sit here, Nina' – she indicated the doctor's chair – 'and check the paperwork. It is my secret and a source of shame to me that I can neither read nor write well enough to perform this task.'

We worked into the evening to sort the house and Dr K's study to Galena's satisfaction. One item of interest which I did find I neither returned to the files nor gave up to be burned. Instead, I folded the paper and slipped it into the pocket of my skirt so that I might study it later.

Scarcely had we sat down to eat when Stefan pushed his plate away from him and got up. 'Please excuse me. I find I am not hungry.'

Galena bent her head to weep as Stefan left the room and we heard him climb the stairs to the attic. I too felt tears stinging my eyes. And I realized it wasn't just for my own sadness; I was upset for the grief that Stefan was suffering. Galena placed Stefan's dinner on the stove and we forced ourselves to finish our meal. I heated some water and filled the hot-water bottles. Before Galena went to her pantry bedroom she indicated Stefan's plate. 'I doubt if he'll come back down tonight and my legs are too old to climb to the third floor of the house. Yet he needs to eat . . .'

'I'll take it up to him.' I picked up the plate, went upstairs to the attic and knocked on his door.

'Yes?' The voice from inside was thin and dejected.

Stefan was lying on top of his bedcovers, still wearing his clothes and house shoes. No lamp burned in the room but the moon shone bright through the uncurtained window.

'Oh. It's you,' he said.

'Indeed, it is me,' I replied. I thought how, months ago, I might have been offended by his tone, but I realized the flatness in his voice came from his lack of interest in life. 'Galena asked me to bring you this food.'

He turned his face to look out of the window. 'How can I eat when I have lost the only father I ever knew?'

'Denying yourself sustenance serves no purpose.' I recalled the words Dmitri had used to comfort me after the death of my father. 'The passing of a person you love leaves a hole in your life. But we must allow that space to be filled with the memory of their wisdom, and act in a manner that shows we are living in the light of their spirit.'

'You are quoting someone,' he said.

'Dmitri,' I replied. 'My father's steward. He comforted me after Papa died.'

'What else did he say?'

'I don't know.' My voice was wobbling, for I was reliving the days of dark despair after Papa passed away. 'Dmitri encouraged me to focus on what the person might have wanted you to do. Which,' I added, 'would have included being sensible and eating, even if you do not feel hungry.'

'You are blackmailing me.' Stefan struggled half upright in the bed.

'I also think that it's good to take time to talk about the person, remember times of laughter and of arguments too.'

'We had plenty of those,' said Stefan. 'Arguments, I mean.'

'I believe Dr K enjoyed the arguments. In a world of lies the truth was spoken around our dinner table.' I thought of the first meal I'd eaten in this house. 'I found it very . . . refreshing.'

'Is that your honest opinion?' Stefan gave me a quizzical smile. 'That our arguments are "refreshing"?'

'Of course!' I smiled in return.

As Stefan reached out to take the plate from me, his hand covered my own. And he left it there for more than a moment. I felt its warmth. I saw the depth of feeling in his eyes.

And, like a physical blow, love filled my heart and soul.

Chapter 47

NINA

I'd never totally believed that Dr Konstantin had forgotten the name of the church where my parents were married.

After Viktor Ilyich had left the house that day, the only other information which Dr K had let slip was that it was small, more of a chapel than a church. Since that conversation I'd traversed the city, visiting every chapel I could find. And in every one I would say a special prayer, in the hope that it might be the one where Papa and Mama had pledged their lives to each other.

Until now I'd had no real hope of identifying the actual church. But a few days after the funeral I smoothed out the sheet of paper I'd taken from an old file of the doctor's and I read the address that was written upon it. And so it was that I opened the door of a tiny chapel near the university.

The interior was dark but there was enough light from the sanctuary lamp for me to see that directly in front of me hung an icon of the *Strastnaya*.

'Mama!' I whispered. The image was identical to the icon in my father's study in Siberia – my mother's favourite religious painting, before which I'd knelt to pray on the day I'd left my childhood home.

Heart hammering inside my chest, I went forward. The background of gold leaf glowed upon the surface of walnut wood. And I knew, for certain, that my mother had stood before this image. There was the crimson robe of Mary covered by the veil of a dark blue and gold maphorion. My fingers reached to touch the child's foot – his little sandal with the loose strap which was falling—

'Daughter, may I help you?'

I turned. An old priest, heavily bearded, stood beside me.

'I don't know,' I whispered.

'It is a sad image.' He indicated the two angels on either side of the main figures. 'They hold the instruments of the Christ's Passion; hence the name given to the icon.'

'I never saw it as such,' I replied. 'When I was growing up I liked the fact that the little boy's sandal was falling off.' I explained how I used to run barefoot among meadow flowers.

'Where did you grow up?'

'Siberia, near Yekaterinburg.'

'That is very far from here.' His voice was guarded. 'May I ask why you have come to the city?'

I looked at him as he looked at me, both of us searching

the other's face for the real reason for this meeting. From my lips came tumbling my life story and my ignorance of my parents' history.

The priest led me to a private room. There he sat me down and told me what I needed to know.

'Your mother's father would never have allowed her to wed your papa, or indeed anyone. But I recognized the depth of their love, the goodness in the woman and the honesty of the man, so I agreed to perform the ceremony. I will bring you proof that your parents were married.'

I unrolled the marriage certificate he gave me. There, in plain scholarly script, my father had signed his name:

Given name: *Ivan*
Family name: *Izmailov*

Alongside it I saw my mother's elegant handwriting:

Given name: *Valentina*
Family name: *Romanov*

Chapter 48

NINA

Romanov.

I am a Romanov.

My name is Romanov.

My name is Romanov.

Beating in my head.

The hated name. Romanov. Detested by Stefan. Despised in the city I'd come to love.

Romanov. Romanov.

I ran home and flung myself, weeping, onto my bed.

Galena was by my side in seconds. 'What's amiss? Were you attacked in the street? Tell me.'

'I know who I really am,' I sobbed. 'I found the church where Mama and Papa were married. The priest showed me their marriage certificate.'

'Ah, that . . .'

'You knew?' I sat up in bed to look at her.

'No secrets can be kept from a housekeeper,' she said. 'But I knew your parents from when we were young together. My mother was a washerwoman. We lived near the apartments where the university students lodged and the lads would tease me as I took the laundry baskets backwards and forwards to the houses of the dons and the professors. Your papa and Konstantin were never rude to me as they passed the time of day. An unusual friendship developed – in that they were students and I could scarcely read or write.'

Galena paused and her lips curved in a smile at some private memory. 'But I could bake, and they both liked cake. So it went on until, in the week of their graduation, for a dare, they decided they would try to infiltrate a grand ball that was being held in the Winter Palace.'

'I thought Papa was delirious when he told me that!' I exclaimed. 'He said he'd danced in the ballroom of the Winter Palace.'

'They both did.' Galena smiled again. 'My part in their plan was to "borrow" appropriate suits from my mother's customers. So handsome they both looked,' she sighed, 'so very handsome.

'They walked in, as bold as bears, and larked about. Then your papa saw a girl in an alcove who was reading a book. At first she refused to dance with him, so he sat down beside her and they discussed the story. Konstantin was bored and went home. The next day Ivan told us he was in love with Valentina.' Galena snapped her fingers. 'Like that.'

'And she loved him too?'

'She did. But her father was a wicked man, corrupt and cruel. He was a cousin of the Tsar's own father, but was banned from the royal palaces because precious objects went missing whenever he visited. He always said he'd kill his daughter if she ever tried to leave him.

'They found a sympathetic priest and were married and met up secretly. For a long while that went well, until everything changed.'

'My mother became pregnant?'

Galena nodded. 'Valentina's father knew that she was hiding something from him. He locked her in her room and said he would beat her every day until she told him. Ivan thought her father might accept him if he explained how much they loved each other. Your papa was not without means – he'd inherited money from his parents, and had hopes of a professorship and a prestigious academic career.

'When he went to the house, though, Valentina's father attacked him, and her too. And, well . . . we never knew every detail, because when they came to us for help she was distraught and Ivan would not speak of it. Only to say that there had been struggle and Valentina's father had died after being stabbed by a dagger. But, Nina, I swear on my soul that your papa was an honourable man, and if he did the deed, it was to protect his wife and unborn child.'

'This is why they made their home in Siberia?' I asked.

'Yes. Valentina and Ivan had to flee at once. It was a

blood feud. Valentina's brothers were as vicious as their father and, whether she was pregnant or not, they would have killed their sister and her husband.'

This was why Papa had warned me on his deathbed: *Do not ever leave our family home, Nina. If you do, then your life will be in peril!*

'Your father found a remote place many days' journey from Valentina's brothers and the affluent lives they lived,' Galena went on. 'He was able to purchase a house and a small estate which would support his family. Somewhere they could live happily together.'

'And they did,' I said. 'Dmitri says they were besotted with one another.'

'When they went away Konstantin and I were bereft.'

'Did you love Konstantin?' I asked her.

'How could anyone *not* love Konstantin? He had the courage of a lion and the compassion of a saint. So, yes, I did love him,' said Galena, 'but as a true friend – not in the way he loved me. Of course, a woman is flattered when a man declares his love and asks her to marry him. If he is a good man and easy to live with, then it's tempting to accept the proposal. You know that you would be comforted and indulged, and, to begin with, you would make him happy. But I think that man's happiness would shrivel when he eventually realized that you hadn't the same kind of love for him that he had for you.' Galena wiped her face with the edge of her apron and said, 'I couldn't do that to Konstantin. But he refused to seek another bride and no one else appealed to me, so we agreed on this arrangement and I think our lives were more contented like this.'

Galena made me drink some hot milk laced with brandy and left me to rest.

I couldn't sleep. My parents' life story and a thousand other thoughts revolved round and round in my head. I thought of Tomas, and knew that Galena's wisdom in not marrying Dr K was good guidance for me. I resolved to write to Tomas and honestly tell him why I could not accept his proposal. I loved him as a friend, not as a future husband. My letter would let him get on with his life.

I would not mention the main reason why I could not marry him.

I loved Stefan.

And then the enormity of the discovery I'd made today struck me, and I was heartbroken. I curled myself into a ball and cried and cried. I knew that the happiness of love was beyond my reach. Stefan detested the Romanovs. For the death of his mother and for the ruin of Russia. Along with the Bolsheviks, he blamed them for the murder of Dr K, for had they ruled Russia wisely, then anarchy would not now be stalking through the land.

I was a Romanov and Stefan hated all Romanovs.

For ever.

Dmitri's reply arrived. He wrote to say that he was overjoyed that I was coming home. Inside the envelope were four train passes.

I had collected the letter from the post office at the end of my shift and opened it on my way home. Excited that I was the bearer of such good tidings, I hastened along the street, only to be brought up short when I saw the door of our house standing open and pieces of crockery strewn down the front steps. From the direction of Dr K's study came a racket: raised voices and furniture being smashed.

I ran inside.

Three grim-faced men were rampaging through the room, throwing precious ornaments onto the floor and tearing photographs and paintings from the walls.

'Don't you dare touch his university degree!' Galena screeched as one of them laid his hands on the framed certificate.

For answer the man broke the glass across the corner of the desk and threw it at her.

As Galena bent to pick it up, he knocked her aside, saying, 'We should visit this famous clinic where your traitor doctor tended to enemies of the Revolution.'

'Vandals!' Galena made to follow them.

Fearing for her life, I tried to restrain her. She struggled against me, and I was losing my grip when a pair of stronger arms fastened themselves around both of us.

'Best not to watch.' Stefan's voice spoke with authority. 'Hush, hush,' he murmured as Galena and I broke down in tears. 'Hush now; we are strong enough to withstand this.'

And we held onto each other then as if we would never let go.

'We should leave it as it is.' When the men had gone it was Stefan who made the most sensible suggestion regarding the chaotic state of the study and the clinic. 'Otherwise they'll only come back and do it all over again.'

'Nobody will attend the clinic now anyway,' I said. 'People are terrified that if they do they'll be reported to the Cheka.'

'I am glad Konstantin is not alive to witness this,' Galena stated resolutely. 'But I know that he would be glad that we are alive to start afresh elsewhere.'

The day before we were due to set out for Yekaterinburg, while I was in the scullery packing food for our journey, Galena came to speak to me.

'There's a woman at the front door who wishes to see the person known as Nina who lives at this address,' said Galena. 'You must go to her for she has refused to enter the house.'

The woman had on a coat with a patterned shawl about her shoulders, crossed over her chest and wrapped around her waist. By the distinctive design and the way it was worn I knew she was Siberian.

'You are Nina?' she asked me.

'I am. Please come inside. It's a cold day.'

'I have a gift for you.' She handed me a parcel bundled up in old newspaper and tied with rough string, then turned to leave.

'Wait!' I said. 'What is this gift and who is it from?'

'I do not know what is inside the parcel,' she replied. 'I am following the instructions of my father. He left a note among his possessions to say that when he died this should be delivered to the one whose life is worth saving. I was charged with taking it to the house of Dr Konstantin and giving it to the person called Nina who looked after the boy child of Tsar Nicholas Romanov. I am sorry it has taken me so long to bring this to you, but during last year my family have been hounded and imprisoned by the Bolsheviks. The chest containing my father's personal things was hidden by a friend and only just returned to us. I have no other information to give you.'

By this time the woman was on the bottom step of the staircase.

'Did I know your father?' I called out.

'Everyone knew of my father,' she said, before hurrying off down the street. 'His name was Grigory Rasputin.'

I went to my room and with trembling hands I untied the knots of the string. I peeled back the sheets of paper to reveal the embroidered white sash which Rasputin had worn on the day we met. My brain closed down. I didn't want to unwrap this parcel any further. I didn't want to see the object I knew lay hidden among its folds.

My unwilling fingers probed deeper. I felt the curve of the blade, the shape of the handle, the beads of the pearls, and the outline of the jewel within their centre.

I drew the dagger to my breast.

The ruby's light exploded in my mind.

Fiery red.

And instantly there was sound there too. Bursts of firecracker noises.

Voices – insistent . . . pleading . . . A rattling, clatter-ing . . . The howling of a wolf which changed eerily into a thin, distant, high-pitched scream.

'Nina?' Galena was standing at the door of my room. 'I was watching from the window. What did that woman give you?'

'This!' I hastily pushed the dagger under my pillow and lifted just the sash to show her.

'That's fine embroidery work,' said Galena. 'Was she delivering it as a present from an admirer?'

'Not really.' I swallowed and wiped away the hot tears that had formed in my eyes. 'It once belonged to her father . . . Rasputin.'

'I thought I recognized her face! After he died there were photographs of his children in the newspapers. Why would she give this to you?'

'When we met at the Alexander Palace Rasputin referred to me as a "fellow healer". He said that I was worthy of respect.'

'Worthy of more respect than he was,' said Galena stoutly.

I thought about this enigmatic man, Grigory Rasputin, and his tales of the twin daggers. *One dagger to take a life. One dagger to save a life.* He'd believed there was some hidden meaning in our meeting each other. That our paths had crossed for a purpose. The ancient sage had said that the life Rasputin's dagger would save must be a life worth saving. I knew that Rasputin considered himself to be unworthy.

From beyond the tomb, had Rasputin sent his dagger to keep me safe?

The next day the three of us boarded the train. After securing us seats and stowing our bags away, Stefan picked up his own and spoke. 'Now we must say goodbye.'

'What?' Galena swayed with the shock of his announcement.

My own heart turned over. Had Stefan found out my family name? I searched his face for the answer. 'You don't want to travel in my company?' I asked him.

'Nina,' he replied, 'you have no idea how happy I'd be to travel with both of you, but I am going in a different direction. Now I must tell you something very sad. Eugene is dead. He was killed some weeks ago, before Dr K died. I didn't mention it because I didn't want to cast a mood of melancholy over the household. Do not try to dissuade me, for my mind is made up. I am going to take Eugene's place on the ambulance trains.'

'Beloved boy!' Galena enfolded him in her arms.

He allowed her to shower him with kisses. Then, by almost lifting her bodily from the floor, he set her back a pace.

'Nina.' He kissed me swiftly and lightly on both cheeks. 'I'll miss our conversations.'

I couldn't speak. I stared at him, trying to memorize his features, the flop of dark hair over his forehead, his amber eyes, his mouth . . .

Stefan stepped down from the train and saluted us both. 'Look after her,' he said.

SIBERIA

YEKATERINBURG

1918

Chapter 49

NINA

I burst into tears when I saw Dmitri standing on the station platform at Yekaterinburg.

'Nina! Nina!' He was crying too, and holding me and kissing me, on both cheeks and on my forehead and my hair and on both cheeks again and again. 'You have grown. Ah! You are as tall as I am! How can that be? But so thin. And pale, too pale. Never mind, we will feed you up. How was your journey? Was it exhausting? You must be hungry. Are you hungry?' He broke off listing his questions and, looking around, said, 'Were not four of you supposed to be travelling together?'

I hugged Dmitri tightly and tried to answer him, between great rending sobs which I couldn't control. I told him of the death of the good doctor and explained the absence of Stefan.

The stationmaster produced a large handkerchief from

his pocket and offered it to me. He rubbed a tear from his own eye so I gave him a hug too.

'Enough! Enough!' Dmitri called us to order. 'I have a cart for you and your luggage. No carriage, I'm afraid. That went long ago.'

'A cart is very fine,' I told him. With a pang I realized that it was the same cart Papa and I had used to travel about the countryside. I introduced him to Galena, who had been standing silently looking at a company of the Red Guard assembling outside the station.

Dmitri took Galena's bag from her hand. 'Follow me, lady,' he said.

'Mr Dmitri,' Galena replied. 'You should not call me "lady". The Bolsheviks have abolished all titles.'

'They cannot abolish good manners,' said Dmitri.

As we went along the road I began to feel a sense of belonging. I pulled off my shawl so that the wind might blow through my hair and I breathed in sweet, clear air that I'd not tasted for almost two years.

Dmitri flicked the reins and clicked his tongue to encourage the horse. He grinned at me. 'When we say "Siberia is beautiful" the rest of Russia laughs. But there is nowhere like it on earth.'

'Beautiful,' I repeated as the rooftops of my family home appeared on the horizon. And I couldn't speak another word until I was on the porch and wandering through the house. My bedroom was as I'd left it; my father's study tidier than it had ever been.

'I had to rearrange your father's books and papers

because the lawyer, Viktor Ilyich Volkov, made a mess of them.' Dmitri looked at me attentively as he told me this. 'He was searching for something . . .'

'Thank you, Dmitri,' I replied, ignoring the unspoken question. 'Dr Konstantin ensured that the lawyer won't trouble us again.'

In typical fashion, the first thing Galena did was put on her apron and go straight to the kitchen. I found her there, standing in the middle of the floor, and could see that she was unsettled in her new surroundings.

'I hope everything is to your satisfaction.' Dmitri smiled at her. 'We have food in this part of Russia – which I think you will agree is a good thing to have.'

'You also appear to have the Red Army stationed in Yekaterinburg.' Galena was not to be won over so easily.

'Unfortunately . . . yes,' Dmitri spoke with mock sadness. 'However' – he smiled mischievously – 'we also have the White Army and every other colour of army and anti-Bolshevik faction closing in on us – including a Czech army who arrived from I know not where.'

Galena gave him a level look. 'Your friend the station-master was wearing a red armband. As were you – on the coat which you have since taken off.'

'Everyone wears them,' Dmitri said. 'It is the latest fashion in Yekaterinburg.'

They regarded each other for a moment.

'I should explain,' said Dmitri. 'Without a red armband no shop will serve you. No food tokens are given out. No business transaction is possible. So yes,' he said, 'in order to keep this estate running, the workers fed, and enough produce to fill the bellies of our villagers and their children, I will wear a red armband.' He spread his hands expansively on either side of his body. 'I will wear a dozen red armbands.'

'If I have been crass, then I apologize,' said Galena. 'I make these enquires because I am here to protect Nina.'

'There is no need to apologize,' said Dmitri. 'I understand perfectly. I felt exactly the same when I put her on the train for St Petersburg.'

A smile curved Galena's lips. It was the first I'd seen her smile since the death of Dr K. She indicated the apron she was now wearing. 'I have come ready to work,' she said.

'You are a guest,' said Dmitri. 'I cook meals.'

'I will not interfere in the running of anyone's kitchen,' she said. 'I can clean as well as cook.'

'Oh, no!' said Dmitri. 'A lady like yourself should not be sweeping up after a peasant like me. The floors here are cleaned and polished to my high standards.'

'So there is no way I can contribute to the smooth running of this household?' There was a note of resigned sadness in her voice.

'Unless . . .' he said.

'Yes?'

'I can manage the stew, but the dumplings I find challenging.'

'If you will permit me?' And Galena began to open cupboards and assemble utensils and ingredients.

Behind her back Dmitri put his fingers to his lips to warn me to say nothing. His dumplings were as good as any I'd tasted, but he understood that Galena would be happier cooking than having a meal served to her.

It was Dmitri's turn to be surprised when I began to take plates and cutlery from the drawers to set the table.

'You must eat with us,' I told him when the meal was ready. He shook his head. 'It is their custom,' I whispered to him. 'An insult if you do not.'

Galena flashed a sharp look at him when he clumsily lifted a fork in his large hands. 'Nina,' she said, 'you forgot to lay out spoons when you set the table.'

With relief Dmitri took the spoon she handed him and began to eat his food. 'Is St Petersburg as mad and bad as we hear it is?' he asked. 'Tell me all the news. Your letters can't have covered everything. What about Moscow? Are those crazy Bolsheviks holed up in the Kremlin yet? Did you stop there?'

'My friend Tomas met our train at the station and we chatted during the stopover,' I told him. 'Our new Soviet Government is worried because the White Army and those who support it are banding together as you said.'

'The combined forces are heading towards Yekaterinburg. That is why you saw Red Guards there this morning. I have stockpiled enough supplies that we seldom need to visit the town. Let the world get on with its own business and we will live quietly here.'

Chapter 50

NINA

For a while we did live quietly.

I ate and slept and wandered through the meadows, and even rode the few older horses that were left on the estate after the army requisitions. I lit candles before my mother's icon and prayed that Stefan would not come to harm. I also wrote several letters.

I wrote to Eugene's parents, sending them my condolences and telling them of the times I'd spent with their son and how much I'd respected his decision to serve his country. I wrote to Tomas, thanking him for being so kind and understanding when we'd met up in Moscow, and I had told him that I could not accept his marriage proposal.

And I wrote to Stefan.

I told him that even though I'd discovered that I wasn't illegitimate, I had now refused Tomas's proposal. In addition, I wrote of pleasant things – how healthy Galena looked and how she and Dmitri were becoming fond of each other. He wrote back to both of us, saying that his unit was to be reassigned and he intended to go home. I walked around the estate with his letter in my hand, reading and rereading it.

Stefan was going home.

I remembered the evening when he'd said, 'Things will never be the same again.' He'd known then that Eugene was dead and had been under the impression that I might marry Tomas. He would be aware that Petrograd was too dangerous a place for him now as the Bolsheviks associated his name with Dr K.

So where might he go?

That night I sat down and wrote a second letter to Stefan. And I knew what my first words must be:

I am a Romanov.

And I told him my life story, and I told him the reason why I was not going to marry Tomas.

I told him that I loved him.

Stefan did not reply.

I contained my sorrow and did not discuss it with anyone else. I'd made it clear that I would understand if he wished to have no more contact of any kind with me. So now I had to accept his decision.

Galena and Dmitri were sensitive to my mood and vied with each other in producing elaborate meals to raise my spirits.

But then, at the end of April, there was news which

meant that the business of the world intruded upon us, and we could ignore it no longer.

The Imperial Family – the Tsar and the Tsarina with their five children – had arrived in Yekaterinburg to be kept as prisoners in a merchant's house in the town.

'It must be because the White Army is advancing,' said Dmitri. 'The talk is that Lenin and his Bolsheviks are beginning to panic at the amount of ground they are losing to the supporters of the Tsar. Even in Yekaterinburg you can hear the rumble of distant guns.'

'I hope and pray the Tsar and his family will be rescued,' said Galena. 'I wish we had something of value to smuggle in to them that they might bribe their guards to help them escape.'

Over two months passed and no rescue was attempted.

'They are miserable in their harsh captivity,' Dmitri reported from one of his rare visits to Yekaterinburg. 'A single visitor is allowed per week, usually the town priest. The boy is ill, but the local peasants have shown pity and send in presents of eggs and milk for him.'

In order not to upset Galena – for he knew she was a Tsarist – Dmitri told me privately that, if the White Army moved much closer to Yekaterinburg, then the Imperial Family would be taken to Moscow, where the Tsar would be tried for treason.

It was mid-July now. The weather was warm and the evenings bright with late sunsets. I thought of

Alexei, cooped up indoors, and imagined how bored he would be.

'I could let them have some of Papa's story booklets,' I said. 'It will be an outing for me if I ride in with them myself. I will not stay,' I reassured Galena. 'I will hand over my gift and leave.'

Dmitri and Galena were forced to accept that they could not stop me.

As I put the folk tales into a satchel I had a sudden thought. I would give the Rasputin dagger to the Tsar! In truth it belonged to him. If the old, old stories were true it might even save his life. When the Imperial Family were free again he could sell it. Depending on what happened they might have need of money. Crossing the hall to my bedroom, I took Rasputin's sash from my travel bag and unwrapped it on my bed. I recalled that on my first visit to the Alexander Palace I'd feared the soldier on duty might search my bag – but he hadn't. The guards in Yekaterinburg would be more wary. I would have to hide it well.

Drawing a deep breath, I made to pick up the dagger. 'I must be strong,' I said aloud. I seized the dagger, quickly tucked it inside the top of my skirt and folded the waistband over several times.

When I reached Yekaterinburg I left my horse in the care of the stationmaster. He'd hardly time to acknowledge me, as an army supply train was long overdue from Moscow and the tracks were jammed with carriages full of soldiers arriving to be deployed towards the zone of fighting. I wrapped my green and purple shawl around my head and shoulders and covered most of my face as I walked past their ranks. They looked like farmers and peasants recently taken from the land to make up hastily formed battalions. The Bolsheviks must indeed be worried that their regime could be overthrown if these men were all they could muster for defence against the more experienced forces of the White Army.

The merchant's house was easy to find, for it stood on the slope of a hill. It was obvious that this was where the prisoners were being kept as there was a high fence around it and the windows had been painted with whitewash. Possibly this was to give privacy to those inside; more likely to stop any signal for help being seen from outside. Poor children! What wrong had they done? By accident of birth their lives were pre-destined. I thought of Alexei − despite his infirmity he loved to play in the open air. I shuddered as I realized how confined and claustrophobic he must feel.

I decided I would try to go inside and speak to him.

The guard at the house gate made me empty my pockets and searched my satchel most thoroughly. He was a surly old fellow, but I remembered Dmitri's words of long ago and let slip my shawl so that my hair came down over my shoulders as I made my request to exchange a few words with the children.

'By your favour, not many minutes.' I smiled my widest smile. 'Just to talk about the storybooks.'

'Uh,' the guard grunted. 'Have you identification?'

'She is Nina Ivanovna, the daughter of the man who was the story collector,' a voice called from the scullery door.

'Denis!' I recognized a young lad from our village. 'What are you doing here?'

'I am the kitchen boy,' he spoke proudly. 'Apart from preparing the meals I do everything that is needed.' To the soldier he said, 'Nina Ivanovna is a friend of the people. She and her papa fed us when we were starving. I can take her inside the house.'

'Don't be too long.' The guard stepped aside to let me pass.

Chapter 51

STEFAN

By ill luck I'd been posted to a unit serving in a remote area of the Front and it took weeks for our mail to reach us.

Nina's first letter, telling me that she was not marrying Tomas, made me decide to declare my own feelings. With the terms of the Armistice between Russia and Germany finally agreed in March, the ambulance trains began to be decommissioned and the medical staff disbanded — and so my intention was to tell her in person that I loved her.

I replied to say that I was coming home.

As soon as I received Nina's second letter I knew I had to get to her as fast as possible. The moment I read the words *I am a Romanov* I realized that she was in the most extreme danger.

She and Galena and Dmitri must be unaware of what

was happening in the wider world or the letter would never have been sent through the public postal service. The superintendent of the Hospital Train Service distributed the mail to the staff. Officers and medical personnel had privileges, which included uncensored letters. Even so, I was relieved to see that the seal on mine was unbroken, for there was no guarantee that outgoing or incoming correspondence wouldn't be read. This superintendent was a Bolshevik from the top of his head to the toes of his boots. His enthusiasm for the cause made Fyodor appear lukewarm. During the day he'd compile lists of superior officers who'd slighted him in some way, or whom he suspected were sympathetic to the Imperialist cause. He'd send these to the Cheka Secret Police and report with glee if he got word that their execution squads had used his information. At night he would drink himself stupid and chant the names off with sadistic satisfaction.

That's how I learned that the Romanovs were to be exterminated.

All of them. Not one member of any branch of the family was to be left alive. Every person bearing the name of Romanov was to be sought out, captured and killed. There was to be no chance of restoring the monarchy in any shape or form.

With deepest regret I burned Nina's letter. But first I tore out and kept the part where she'd written:

I love you . . .

Then I hitched a ride to Yekaterinburg on a troop train, stole a horse from the army stable, and rode the beast into the ground to reach Nina's house.

Her home was easy to find. A long, low building set back from the road, with a paddock, an orchard, and a meadow full of flowers – the places I'd heard her speak of many times.

How brave she must have been to undertake such a long journey to find Dr K, immediately after her papa died, after living here in isolation all her life! My cheeks burned with shame at the way I'd treated her, and the things I'd said when she'd first arrived on our doorstep. I dismounted from the horse, combed my fingers through my hair and wiped my face with my hands. I expected she wouldn't care about my appearance, but I didn't want to look like a ragamuffin when I asked her to marry me.

There was no response when I knocked upon the front entrance, and I recalled her saying that the door to their kitchen stood open in the summertime. I hurried to the rear of the house.

Galena, and an older man I didn't recognize, stood close beside each other at the sink. She was naming ingredients while she placed them in a mixing bowl and he made a reply which caused her to laugh. My heart rejoiced when I heard that sound. It was so long since I'd heard Galena laugh, or indeed anyone enjoy a light-hearted moment.

'Good evening,' I said.

Galena screamed, dropped the bowl, and then flew at me. 'Naughty child!' She hit me on the head with a dishcloth. 'Sneaking up on a person like that! You have given me a heart attack!'

'Galena, if this is the doctor boy that you speak of endlessly,' the man said, 'then possibly he knows the best way to help you recover.'

'I think I do know how to help her recover,' I said. Overcome with joy, I hugged Galena, burying my face in her shoulder to hide my tears.

'I am Dmitri,' the man said, 'and you are Stefan. In the absence of my lady, Nina Ivanovna, may I welcome you to her home.'

'Absence?' I said. 'Nina is not here?'

'Nina rode into Yekaterinburg earlier,' said Galena, 'to . . . deliver a package. I would have thought she'd be on her way back by now.'

Dmitri frowned. 'Stefan, did you notice anyone on the road?'

I shook my head. 'Who was she visiting?'

Dmitri and Galena exchanged glances.

'There is something amiss.' I turned to Galena. 'Why are you concerned? You must tell me.'

'She . . . may have dallied to talk to the stationmaster,' said Dmitri.

'I doubt that,' I said. 'The railway terminus is chaotic. Soldiers are piling in, but they cannot be moved out because the supply train is overdue.'

'I will go into Yekaterinburg,' said Dmitri.

'Who was she visiting?' My voice now shrill with anxiety. 'What package was she carrying?' I turned to

351

Galena. 'Please tell me. I do love Nina, you know. And I believe she loves me.'

'Konstantin and I knew long since that you loved each other,' Galena replied. 'The only people ignorant of that fact were the two of you.'

'Then tell me where she is!'

'Nina Ivanovna took some of her father's story booklets to give to the Imperial Family, who are being kept as prisoners in a house in Yekaterinburg,' said Dmitri. 'As you know, she became fond of the son, Alexei. I am beginning to worry that she may have persuaded a guard to let her inside to speak with him.'

His words stunned me to silence.

'Stefan?' Galena looked at me anxiously. 'You have turned pale.'

'There is an order out that every Romanov must be killed!' I choked on the words.

The three of us looked at each other in horror.

'I see that you both know the secret of her birth,' I said. 'That Nina Ivanovna's mother was a Romanov.'

'*I* did not know it.' A stranger wearing a light overcoat walked unannounced into the kitchen. 'But it is a piece of information that will serve me very well.' His cunning eyes raked over me. 'Allow me to introduce myself. I am the family lawyer, Viktor Ilyich Volkov.'

Chapter 52

NINA

'Nurse Nina! My storyteller!'

Alexei cried out a greeting when he caught sight of me at the door of their living room. His face showed delight, even though his leg was bandaged and his forehead damp with fever.

The Tsar was in a corner chair reading some papers while the children were seated around a table, engaged in doing a jigsaw puzzle with their mother. One of the girls turned her head. Her shoulders were rounded, her complexion grey.

'Nina?' she said. 'Is it really you?'

By her voice alone I recognized Olga, the eldest daughter of the Tsar. Her time in captivity had changed her, as indeed it had all of them, physically and mentally.

The Tsar's haggard face resembled the melting portrait he'd once drawn of himself upon the window of the

Alexander Palace. Although she maintained her courage, the Tsarina was thin as a flower stem. Olga and her sisters had dark shadows under their eyes and an air of listlessness. But they became animated when they insisted I sit with them to answer questions and bring me up to date with their circumstances.

'We live as we must,' said the Tsarina. 'And we thank the Lord for anything we receive.'

'And Father Grigory too,' said Olga. 'We think he is watching over us from above.'

'He was a martyr,' the Tsarina declared. 'Father Grigory Rasputin died for the cause of righteousness.'

'His spirit is near,' said Maria. 'I can sense his presence.'

'That must give you comfort,' I replied politely. My hand strayed to the waistband of my skirt.

'They took Nagorny away,' said Tatiana. 'Alexei misses him, but Dr Botkin and two of our personal servants are living with us in this house.'

'And our cook too,' added Anastasia, 'which means that Alexei's food can be prepared as he likes it.'

'There is much to be grateful for,' said the Tsarina.

It touched my heart that they were so glad to see me and displaying forbearance while in such reduced circumstances. As I rose to leave the Tsar took me to one side and asked me privately if I knew what was happening with regard to the fighting.

'Your Imperial Majesty—' I began.

'Nurse Nina,' he replied, 'there is no need to address me thus. The guards refer to me as "Citizen Romanov" and I'm told we are spoken of in the town as "Mr and Mrs Romanov and the children Romanov".'

'Sire,' I replied, 'it would make be uncomfortable to address you in that way.'

'In truth,' the Tsar sighed, 'I might have had a more comfortable existence if I'd always been plain "Mr Romanov". Now, please tell me of outside events, and' – he moved further out of earshot of his family – 'spare me no details. We won't share it with my family if the news is bad, but I want to know both fact and opinion.'

'The news is not so bad.' I lowered my voice to a whisper. 'The White Army is making steady progress towards Yekaterinburg.'

'We can hear the thunder of shelling. I am familiar with warfare for I spent time at the Front when I led my own army to defend my country against the invaders.'

'Are you aware that Russia has agreed an Armistice with Germany?' I asked the Tsar.

'I am,' he said. 'Lenin and his team have made a shameful peace. Shameful! Shameful!' He crumpled the paper he was holding in his hand. 'The Baltic States, most of the Ukraine, Poland and Finland: millions of acres of land and people – the Bolsheviks gave these away. It has made a mockery of the blood sacrifice of my soldiers. Ironic, isn't it? My wife was accused of being pro-German. They claimed *she* was a traitor, when now we see that the Bolsheviks' revolution has been financed by the Germans. My cousin, the Kaiser, should have care, for Lenin's words have fallen upon German ears as well as Russian ones.

His people may rise up against him and the pestilence of Communism be spread worldwide.'

I thought of Fyodor, who very much desired Communism to be spread worldwide, but as a means to a fairer society.

'Soldiers of the Red Guard are amassing to defend the town,' I told the Tsar. 'But to me they look untrained, and I heard that their supply train has not yet arrived.'

'Ah!' His tone lightened. 'A glimmer of hope?'

'Yes, sire,' I said. 'Indeed, yes.' I decided not to mention Dmitri's belief that the Tsar would be sent to Moscow with his family to stand trial for treason.

'My people here may rise to support the White Army.' The Tsar spoke more confidently. 'When we first arrived in Yekaterinburg our train had to halt on a line some distance away to prevent a hostile mob reaching us. However, the peasants found out that my son is unwell so they send in some of their own produce. Possibly they are denying their own children some treats in order to do this.'

With blinding clarity I saw how an observation like that would anger Stefan to the point where he would shake with rage and frustration. He would consider the Tsar's ignorance of the conditions in which his people lived to be culpable. For myself, I experienced an overwhelming sadness that this man who was responsible for the welfare of millions of people could think that his peasants in their grinding destitution could afford 'treats' for their children. Had it not been for the social conscience of my father, Denis the kitchen boy's family would have literally starved to death.

'There is sympathy,' I said cautiously. 'And I too have something that may help you.' Turning my back to the table where his family sat, I took the dagger from the waistband of my skirt and presented it to the Tsar. 'This could be sold for money.'

'Rasputin's dagger!' he exclaimed.

'His daughter brought it to me after Rasputin died. She said her father had wanted me to own it.'

'Then you must keep it for yourself,' said the Tsar.

'I believe it belongs to your family and you have greater need than I do.' I held it out to him.

The Tsar recoiled from me. 'No,' he said. 'Our hatbands and clothes are secretly studded with jewels, well-hidden. The Rasputin dagger is too obvious for us to carry and would be discovered. And in case' – he hesitated – 'I do not want to take ownership of it. Originally there were two daggers. They were kept in a case in the Golden Hall of the Alexander Palace below the portrait of Tsar Ivan. The servants' nonsense gossip was that one dagger would take a life and one dagger would save a life.' The Tsar made a dismissive gesture with his hand. 'Idle tittle-tattle. But the pair was stolen by a certain cousin of mine – a greedy and violent man. He tried to murder his own daughter with one, but she was saved by a young man who, in the struggle to protect her, accidentally killed her father.'

'How do you know this?' I whispered.

'On the night of the murder they ran away and were never heard of again. But she wrote to the local priest to explain what had happened. He told his bishop who, seeing that the letter was signed by a Romanov, brought it to my attention. I knew my cousin's nature and took his daughter's testament to be true. The charge of murder was lifted from the man's head, but he was wise to remain hidden, for the girl's brothers would have killed them both if they'd found them. There was a superstition that bad fortune followed the daggers, so when the second one was found among my cousin's goods and returned to me I gave it to the same bishop as a gift for the Church. He sent the dagger far away, to be kept at the monastery of Verkhoturye.'

'The Verkhoturye Monastery?' I repeated, my mind in a daze as I heard the final pieces of my parents' life story.

'I see you recognize the name.' The Tsar gave a wry smile. 'It is the same monastery where Father Grigory Rasputin went on retreat. I think the monks gave it to him because it was a source of conflict among them, with some wishing it kept for display and others wanting it sold to provide alms for the poor.'

I folded the Rasputin dagger into my waistband. There was no doubt that the Tsar's assessment of the daggers was correct. Stories of their power were built on half-truths and flights of fancy. The monks had got rid of their dagger for a very ordinary reason: it was causing dissent. And as Rasputin liked costume and striking clothes, he was pleased to wear the dagger stuck in the sash across his chest in order to appear dashing and dramatic. All the rest – the visions and trances – were the result of my emotional stress at losing my papa and having to make monumental changes in my life.

'Nina, you may keep the Rasputin dagger,' said the Tsar, 'as a token for what you have done for us.'

'I must go now,' I said.

'If you might stay a little longer' – the Tsar glanced towards his son – 'it would please us if you could tell Alexei a story.'

Given the Tsar's generosity, I could not refuse.

Chapter 53

STEFAN

'So Miss Nina is a Romanov on her mother's side of the family!' the lawyer gloated. 'I *knew* Ivan Izmailov was covering up something in his wife's background. He would never discuss her family, but it was obvious from her photograph that Valentina was cultured and affluent.'

'Viktor Ilyich Volkov.' Dmitri moved purposefully towards the man. 'You are no longer lawyer for this family. Please leave.'

'Mind your place, you upstart serf.' The lawyer glared at him. 'When I collect what I came for, then I will leave.' He pulled a pistol from his coat pocket. 'After the first time you bullied me out of this house I swore it would never happen again. I will use it,' he went on with determination. 'And I do not care who I fire at. Yourself, the young man, the woman . . .' He waved the pistol in the direction of Galena.

Dmitri stopped in mid-step.

'A Romanov, eh?' the lawyer chortled. 'Miss Nina will pay a high price for my silence on that subject. Where is she?'

I glanced at Galena and Dmitri. This man must only have heard the last sentence of our conversation. He wasn't aware where Nina might be.

'She went to visit friends,' said Galena.

'And might not return until tomorrow,' added Dmitri.

'Walk ahead of me to her bedroom,' said Viktor Ilyich. 'She won't have carried the object I am looking for with her. Go on now!' he ordered as we hesitated.

'What is it that you want?' Dmitri asked as we filed through the hall and into Nina's bedroom.

'A dagger,' the lawyer replied. 'A scimitar-shaped dagger of ancient origin, its handle studded with a single ruby encrusted in a circlet of pearls.'

Galena started at his words while Dmitri said, 'I never saw such a thing among my master's possessions.'

Viktor Ilyich had heard Galena's intake of breath. He regarded them both with narrowed eyes. 'You I believe,' he said to Dmitri, 'for Nina's father kept it concealed and I only ever saw it the once. 'But you' – he pointed the pistol at Galena – 'you have seen this dagger in Nina's possession, haven't you?'

Galena didn't answer him. As if in a dream, she walked forward and picked up an embroidered sash which lay discarded on the bed.

'You have no claim on anything or anyone in this house,' said Dmitri angrily.

'By refusing to give me that dagger you put yourself and everyone in the house at risk,' said the lawyer. 'I will report you to the Soviet Council in Yekaterinburg.'

'You'd be advised to stay well clear of the Soviet Council,' I said. 'Dr K told us that you embezzled the money for the grain which was harvested to feed the army. The old Imperial Government would have imprisoned you for that offence. Our new Soviet Government has proclaimed that anyone who steals from the State can be executed without trial.'

The lawyer was not the least downcast by my statement. 'It depends on how "facts" are presented. When your doctor friend alerted me to that hazard, I reported myself to the Yekaterinburg Soviet Council to tell them exactly what I had done.'

'That you were a liar and a thief?'

'That I was a patriot, for I had taken the wealth of the landlord to redistribute it to the people.'

Dmitri laughed out loud.

'You may laugh,' said Viktor Ilyich, 'but not for long. I told them that I'd been waiting and hoping for the Revolution and, as a sign of good faith, I gave them a large sum of money. Each man has his price. Over time I won their trust. See!' He opened his coat to reveal the uniform of the hated Cheka. 'I am favoured personnel with a special pass to the merchant's house if I choose to go there.'

'The merchant's house?'

'The place where the Imperial Family are imprisoned.'

'I didn't realize they were held as prisoners,' I said sarcastically. 'The official story is that they are being kept somewhere for their own protection against mob rule until a case is prepared against them.'

'You're not another dupe that thinks our ex-Tsar will be brought to formal trial?'

'If not that, then what is the Bolsheviks' intention?' I knew the plans that were being put into place regarding the Romanov family, but I was trying to keep this man talking while I edged closer, that I might spring suddenly upon him. I glanced at Dmitri, hoping he would understand my intention. He tilted his head a fraction and I guessed he too was readied to pounce.

'It will become clear soon enough,' the lawyer said smugly. 'I am preparing papers to verify that what will be done is perfectly legal under emergency measures that have been passed by the Soviet Government in Moscow. I am the official lawyer for the Yekaterinburg Soviet branch, so you'd better do as I say.'

'But you have not informed the Yekaterinburg Soviet of the existence of this dagger, have you?' I said.

He shifted his feet and I knew that what I said was true.

'And you will not inform them, for you do not want to share its value.'

Again I saw that I'd correctly judged the situation.

'So your threats are empty. You cannot speak out, for you will lose the thing you most desire.'

Viktor Ilyich raised his pistol and aimed it at Galena. 'I

will shoot her if you do not find the dagger and give it to me now.'

'It is impossible for us to do that,' said Galena. She indicated the sash which lay on the bed. 'I only caught a glimpse of the object which was wrapped in this. On the day before we got on the train to come to Yekaterinburg I saw Nina sitting on her bed, holding what I thought was a large brooch with a ruby stone. She hid it so quickly from my view that I didn't recognize it as a dagger. But I do believe that Nina has taken it with her, for she was going to visit the Imperial Family and had mentioned bringing them something of value.'

'The dagger is not here?' Disbelief was in the lawyer's tone.

But there was no doubting Galena's conviction that what she said was true. She sat down on Nina's bed and began to weep. 'It is not here,' she said, 'and now Nina is in terrible danger. The girl with a thousand kindnesses in her heart, who risked her life more than once to help others.'

'I will not be thwarted in this!' Viktor Ilyich shouted. 'If Nina has indeed smuggled the dagger into the merchant's house, then I will use my pass to enter and confiscate it. And while I am there I will denounce her as a Romanov. She will suffer the same fate that is being meted out to the Imperial Family tonight!'

A look of wild alarm crossed the faces of Galena and Dmitri, and my own heart began to pound.

'Tonight?' I repeated.

'Yes, tonight,' the lawyer repeated with venom. 'The Tsar's brother has already been executed, as will the Tsarina's sister, who also married a Romanov.'

'But she is a nun!' Galena protested.

'No matter. Nagorny, the sailor who carried the Romanov boy about, has also been executed.' Holding the pistol aimed at Galena, Viktor Ilyich backed towards the door. 'A Cheka execution squad is scheduled to arrive in Yekaterinburg shortly. They are all to be killed – every member of the Imperial Family, and whoever else is in the house with them tonight.'

Chapter 54

STEFAN

The lawyer had reached the door. In seconds he would be gone, no doubt locking us in as he went. Dmitri and I were poised, but the pistol was aimed directly at Galena.

Behind his back, with the fingers of his free hand, the Viktor Ilyich groped for the handle. He smirked.

In a swift movement Galena picked up the sash from the bed and flung it directly in his face.

The explosion deafened me.

'Galena!' Dmitri roared.

She had fallen to her knees. Dmitri bent to help her and the lawyer kicked him in the head. Dmitri crashed down, knocked unconscious by the blow. I grappled the gun from the lawyer's hand and it skittered across the floor. But he was heavy and my thin and fatigued frame couldn't hold him. He smashed my legs from under me and I curled up in agony as he trod heavily on my ribs.

Galena picked up the pistol. 'It is more than you deserve but I give you warning,' she cried out at him. 'You must not leave this house.'

'Silence, you peasant,' he answered her, and opened the door.

And so Galena shot him between the eyes.

Dmitri was the first to recover.

'You amaze me!' he said to Galena. 'Is there no end to your talents?'

Galena dropped the gun and stared at the dead man.

'Are you hurt?' Dmitri went over and touched her on the shoulder.

She shook her head. 'My grandfather was a farmer. He taught me how to bring down a running rabbit. It required small skill to shoot that snake.' Dragging a sheet from the bed she spread it over the lawyer's body. 'Now we must think what to do.'

I levered myself onto my feet. 'I will ride into Yekaterinburg and get Nina out of that house.'

'How long have you known that Nina bears the name of Romanov?' Galena glanced at me anxiously.

'Nina wrote and told me. She wanted to be completely honest with me.'

'You should be proud of how you helped to bring her up,' Galena said to Dmitri.

'I am.' He smiled at her.

'Is that why you came here, Stefan?' Galena asked me. 'To speak to Nina about her being a Romanov?'

'I came here because I love her,' I said simply.

'Love alone will not get you past the guard at the merchant's house,' said Dmitri.

'They are expecting the lawyer and he carries a Cheka pass . . .' I was thinking aloud.

'Dressed as the lawyer, you might at least gain access and plead for her life,' said Galena.

Dmitri searched in Viktor Ilyich's pockets and found his identity papers. 'You are not similar.'

'Not so dissimilar,' I argued. 'The main difference being my age. But the writing with the date of his birth is blurred.'

'Probably deliberately,' said Galena. 'Nina said he was a vain man.'

'Perhaps . . .' said Dmitri. 'He has a small beard and, with your present scruffy unshaven look . . .'

'It will have to do.' I began to unbutton the coat on the lawyer's dead body.

Galena took his cap and put it on my head. She kissed me as she did so. 'God go with you, my son.'

'Stefan,' said Dmitri, 'you ride ahead as fast as you are able. I will follow on the lawyer's horse and bring one of our own. The merchant's house is easy to find for it is set into the slope of a hill. Opposite the front gate there is a field of grass with a large tree and a path leading to the forest. I will wait there with the second horse. Nina knows the countryside very well. She can take you through the villages where she and her papa travelled. They were known and loved among the people and they will help you on your way.'

Galena embraced us both, calling after us to be careful and saying she would light a dozen candles for each of us.

Night was coming on, but the sky was lit by that late low glow which comes with summer sunsets in northern latitudes.

The guns had quietened. Whatever bombardment was taking place had ceased until morning. Perhaps Dmitri was right. With the intimate knowledge of the country-side that Nina possessed we might be able to slip between the opposing armies and win our way through the war zone.

I was halfway on the road to Yekaterinburg when I realized that in my haste to leave I'd forgotten to bring the gun.

Chapter 55

NINA

Alexei had gone to the window, where a section of the shutter was open to show a slit of daylight.

'They allow us that much so we can breathe some fresh air,' the Tsar told me. 'It is fixed to go no wider lest we try to climb out and escape.' He beckoned to his son. 'Alexei,' he said, 'I have persuaded Nina to tell you a story before she leaves us tonight.' ·

Alexei shrugged his shoulders. 'What good are stories when they have whitewashed the window panes so that I cannot see the sky?'

'You think that is whitewash on the windows?' I asked him with great surprise in my voice.

'Of course it is, Nina,' he replied. 'What else could it be?'

'You once told me that you owned all the snow in Russia. And because you love snow, I assumed that you'd commanded it to fall so thickly that it had drifted as high as the rooftops. Just like in the second story of *Masha and the Bear . . .*'

The child turned from the window with a look of mild interest on his face. 'Was that the tale you were about to tell us on the evening when Father Grigory frightened Mama with the story of the dagger he carried in his sash?'

'It is,' I said. 'But my story is even scarier . . . so perhaps I'd better not tell you what happens when Masha meets the Bear in the steep snow-covered mountains.'

'But now you must.' Alexei limped over and seated himself on the couch with his bandaged leg resting on a stool.

I opened my satchel and took out the story booklets. These handwritten stitched sheets were so important to me – a vital aspect of my childhood. The rustle of the sheaves with their neatly curved script triggered my childhood memories; I could smell our log fire and see my father, spectacles perched on the end of his nose.

One midwinter night my father had looked up and said: 'Nina, daughter of mine, this is my most precious legacy to you, and to Russia – the country that I love.' He spoke quietly but with great passion. 'These tales are passed from generation to generation. They are an essential part of the fabric of life, an expression of our identity.' He set down his pen, took off his spectacles and rubbed the bridge of his nose. 'My hope is to preserve our history and our culture through the written word. Oppressive regimes consider words to be dangerous,' he said, 'and they are right. A person with a book in their hand wields more power than the one who holds a gun.'

Through a mist of tears I found the story I was searching for. I held it up for Alexei to look at, and saw that the Tsarina and her daughters had turned from the table to listen. The Tsar himself had set aside his paperwork and was gazing fondly at his son.

'Here it is,' I said. '*Masha and the Bear of the Snowy Mountains.*'

Chapter 56

STEFAN

My desperation made me bold. When I found the house I tethered the horse and marched to the gate.

The barrier that had been erected around the garden made it look more like a stockade than a gated building. I realized that they weren't so concerned about people breaking out as they were about rescuers breaking in. My stomach cramped with fear. I blotted Nina's face from my mind for I didn't want to think what might be happening to her.

The soldier on duty at the gate took the papers and the pass which had belonged to Viktor Ilyich. He began to examine them. Too closely. I turned my head away from the lamp and his direct gaze, and saw that next to the guardhouse his fellows were cooking a meal over a burning brazier.

I said, 'Are we boiling socks for supper tonight?'

It was an old joke, exchanged between battle-weary soldiers used to existing on short rations in the trenches for days. Not particularly funny, but it was the key to my entry.

'Where did you serve?' the guard asked me.

'The Balkans,' I said. 'You?'

'Galicia.' He spat on the ground and then pushed open the gate to let me pass. 'Get this dirty deed over with and rid us of the Romanovs, that we can bring this bloody business to an end tonight.'

I walked slowly to the main entrance to give him time to close the gate. Then I swerved to the side of the house. Dmitri said they were being held in five rooms on the first floor. In the gathering gloom the whitewashed windows stared out like the empty eye-sockets of a skull. A window stood open. I would need a ladder to reach it and there was the chance that I might be seen from the street. In any case, the gap was too small for anyone to climb out. I forced my brain to think only of the next step, avoiding the problem of two people attempting to exit through the guarded gate. I would circle the house and see if there was another way in. I pressed myself flat against the wall and crept on, to be brought up short by a gun poking into my back:

'Put up your hands and turn round, Stefan Petrovich, or I will kill you where you stand.'

Chapter 57

NINA

The window shutter banged.

'There's a storm coming,' I said.

Alexei rose to go to the window. He peered through the narrow opening. 'There are soldiers coming through the gate.'

'There are always soldiers,' the Tsar responded wearily.

'These are different,'

The Tsarina glanced up from the table. 'What is different about them, my love?'

'I don't know,' said Alexei. 'They're just . . . different.'

I went to the window and looked down.

The soldiers who were arriving weren't in the uniform of the house guards. Their clothes, their manner, everything about them was unusual. One of them spotted the kitchen boy. He cuffed him on the ear and sent him scampering out of the gate. Then he stood fiddling with the loading mechanism of his gun. Another was wiping the blade of his bayonet while a third checked and rechecked the ammunition. They sprang to attention as their officer appeared. He spoke to them and then looked directly at our window.

I recognized him. He was the commissar who had shot Dr K. Approaching the house was a Cheka execution squad! I took Alexei's hand and stepped back. Alerted by my sudden movement, the Tsar raised his head from his papers. I was aware that my breathing was becoming more rapid – a terrible dread had entered my body.

'You're holding my hand too tightly, Nina.'

'I'm so sorry, sweetheart.' I released my grip and knelt down in front of Alexei. I brushed his hair from his face. 'I am so, so sorry.'

The door of the room opened. The Cheka commissar stood there. He spoke abruptly to the Tsar. 'You, your family and your servants are being transferred to a new location. You must all come with me now.'

The Tsar and the Tsarina exchanged glances.

'Get up and come at once!'

The Tsar rose to his feet. He reached out for his wife and she ran to him. He held her in his arms and kissed her hair.

'Father Grigory told us what would happen,' the Tsarina whispered. 'The holy monk gave clear warning: "Disaster for the Romanovs follows the death of Rasputin."'

'My children,' the Tsar said in a brave, calm voice. 'We must do what this man says. But' – he smiled at his wife and children – 'we will do it together, as a family.'

His daughters linked hands and gathered round their parents. I helped Alexei to his feet.

'That girl' – the Tsar pointed to me – 'was only visiting for an hour.'

'When I said all of you, I meant all of you.'

'Nina is not a member of our staff,' said the Tsarina.

'Everyone within the household is to travel on to Moscow tonight.'

'But I live in Yekaterinburg,' I protested. 'This is my home.'

'Do as I say.' The commissar put his hand on his gun. 'I will not ask you again.'

Tsar Nicholas hoisted Alexei into his arms. The child's face was pinched with fear.

'Alexei,' I spoke softly. 'Once again you are higher than everyone else.'

The young Tsarevich looked at me seriously and said, 'In the stories of Masha and the Bear, does the Bear represent Russia?'

'I do believe it might,' I answered him.

'It is appropriate,' he said. 'I am happy with that.'

The Tsarina allowed her husband and son to leave the room first. She too went out and indicated for me to follow her. Behind me came, one after the other, Olga, Tatiana, Maria and, lastly, Anastasia.

Chapter 58

STEFAN

I turned round.

His face had changed: older, harder, but I recognized the man who held the gun.

'Fyodor?' I said.

He pointed the muzzle at my stomach. 'If you move I will fire.'

'Hey!' I tried to joke. 'We both worked in the wards in the Winter Palace. We've seen the damage done by a bullet to the stomach. You'd end up having to sew up my intestines.'

'And no doubt you think you'd do that better than I could,' said Fyodor. 'You were always a snob.'

'My mother was a factory worker. I've never denied my origins.'

'We were all aware that you're working class. But you escaped to comfort and security before reaching adulthood.

It was a false image you projected, for you were too aloof to really care about ordinary people.'

'Me?' I said in astonishment. 'Ever since I qualified as a doctor I've worked in the City Hospital of Petrograd caring for ordinary people.'

'Arrogance!' He thrust his gun at me. 'You spoke as though you were doing these people a favour by touching them. The Almighty and Marvellous Stefan Petrovich descending from on high to cure the sick.'

I saw that he despised me and would shoot me dead without further thought. Dispassionately I wondered how long it would take me to bleed out and which organs would fail first. But I had to win him round. 'I do care about people, Fyodor, but we differ in how we interpret the politics of how to do that.'

'You once said that you detested the Romanovs and wished them dead.'

'I admit it – but it was before I witnessed the killings of the battlefields.' I looked at Fyodor and it dawned on me why he was in Yekaterinburg. 'You hold a post as Medical Adviser to the Bolsheviks,' I said. 'Your loyalty is legendary. Have you been sent here to examine the bodies of the Imperial Family after they have been murdered and check that they are definitely dead?'

'Not murdered,' said Fyodor. 'Executed for treason.'

'And Nina?' I asked him. 'Don't *you* care about *her*?'

'Of course I care about her. It was I who arranged her escape from the Alexander Palace.'

'You wrote the letter?' I asked. And then another

thought entered my head. 'That means you also sent the note to warn Dr K. You are a compassionate man, Fyodor.'

Fyodor didn't reply. His face had misery etched in every line.

'I know we argued,' I went on. 'I was angry and said things I shouldn't have. But, Fyodor, may I remind you that it was me who saved you from the Okhrana that famous day, a year ago in February.'

'Go away then.' He holstered his gun. 'There. My debt is paid, but if I see you again I'll report you or shoot you myself. The White Army are closing in on Yekaterinburg and we've orders to kill anyone who tries to rescue the Imperial Family.'

'Fyodor,' I said, 'I'm not here to rescue the Imperial Family. I am here to save the life of Nina.'

'Nina!' He stared at me. 'Nina is in this house?'

'Weren't you aware of that?'

'No!' He became terribly agitated. 'No! That cannot be! The Cheka execution squad are already inside with orders that nobody must come out alive.'

'Help me, Fyodor,' I begged hm. 'If not for my sake, then for Nina's.'

He spoke quickly. 'The doors are guarded, but the hatch where the winter coal is delivered into the cellar is round the next corner. Go, now!'

Weakness in my limbs meant I had to hold onto the wall as I went past him.

'I'll let the soldier on the gate go for his break,' said

Fyodor, 'and take over myself. I reckon you have about ten minutes. No more.'

I dropped into the hatch and found the door to the house. It opened on to a half-landing. On one side was a staircase going up to the ground floor. On the other side a staircase going down. To the basement.

On tiptoes I inched down the stairs. The door to the basement room was open. Trunks and suitcases were stacked in one corner. They would be led there. The sight of their luggage would reassure them while the execution squad prepared to burst in. There was no escape from that basement room.

I must reach Nina and persuade her to come with me to the half-landing and outside before they assembled the Romanov family.

I got to the top of the staircase and was about to step into the ground-floor hall when, in the corridor, a door opened.

'I will bring them to the basement. When I have settled them there I will return and we will carry out the orders. Until then be silent so that they suspect nothing.'

This man stumped along the corridor and upstairs to the family rooms, and began to knock on their doors.

I was too late.

Chapter 59

NINA

'Go all the way downstairs to the lowest level of the house.'

The Cheka commissar's order was not to be disobeyed. Keeping my place in the line, I descended from the ground floor to a turn on the staircase. Below me I saw the Tsarina glance into a basement room.

'Our suitcases and outdoor capes are here,' she said in relief. She held the door open as the Tsar, carrying Alexei, passed through. 'We will be together as we travel onwards.' Imperiously she waved her hand at me before following her husband and son inside. 'Nina, make sure the girls are coming.'

I stopped and looked up. Above me something had delayed the procession. On the way downstairs the Cheka commissar had ordered the doctor, the cook and the two servants from their rooms to join us. I could hear the voice of the doctor. The cook and the maids were doing as they were bidden, but Dr Botkin was protesting, and the line was stalled in the hall.

Yet the girls came on. Olga led the way and joined me on the half-landing. One of the younger girls stumbled and let out a mewling cry. Olga turned round and climbed back up a few stairs. She raised her hand and stretched it above her head. Her sisters, Tatiana and Maria and Anastasia, reached out to her with their hands. And the fingers of the sisters interlaced with each other. They exchanged whispers in their secret language – closing the circle of their special bond, physically and emotionally.

I hesitated.

In that moment arms grabbed at me. A hand clamped firmly over my mouth and I was dragged through a hidden door.

Chapter 60

STEFAN

'Stop struggling, Nina, please.'

For answer she kicked my leg as hard as she could. I swore but held her more tightly. 'It's Stefan,' I hissed in her ear. 'Stefan. You understand?'

Nina relaxed and I loosened my grip on her.

'What are you doing here?' she asked.

'Trying to protect you.'

'Why?'

'Because I love you.'

'You do?' She twisted round and there were tears in her eyes.

From the other side of the door we heard the sound of footsteps as the remainder of the servants descended.

'Did you read my letter?' Nina asked me. 'I am a Romanov.'

'Hush!' I placed my hand over her mouth. 'I have been

at the Front, Nina. I will never wish death upon anyone ever again.'

'Not even a Romanov?'

'Not even a Romanov. And especially not you, Nina. If anything happened to you, then I would die too.'

'I have to help them,' she said. 'They think they are being moved to Moscow but the man who came to tell us this is the Cheka commissar who murdered Dr K. I think they are being taken to the basement to be murdered.'

'You are right.' I held her close. 'That is why I came to rescue you.'

'I must warn them.' She tried to get past me.

'You cannot,' I replied. 'Nina, you *must* not. You will get us both killed if you try.'

'Let me be with them.'

Above us a chair scraped across the floor.

'Leave them together with their last few minutes of hope.'

'What about Alexei?'

'You cannot save him.'

'But I cannot go without him either; he's only a little boy.' She leaned her face against the door. 'Alexei!' she whispered. 'Alexei!'

I half carried Nina out of the cellar and round to the front gate where, true to his word, Fyodor was the lone solider on duty. I could hear the rest of them inside the guard house, talking as they ate their supper. He turned his face away as we went past him.

In front of the house was a grassy field. An oak tree stood by the fence and beside it, as Dmitri had described, was the path leading to the forest. We were almost abreast of the tree when, from its leafy shade, a soldier stepped out. He raised his rifle. 'Halt or I shoot!'

Chapter 61

NINA

Stefan pushed me behind him.

'Don't move!' The soldier's voice wavered. He was just a lad, and a young lad at that.

'I will walk towards him,' Stefan spoke under his breath. 'When he shoots at me, you must run along the path to where Dmitri is waiting with horses.'

'I will not leave you.' I clung to the belt of his coat.

'Go! Please, Nina.' He put his hands behind his back to try to disentangle my fingers. 'We have nothing to defend ourselves with.'

From the basement window of the prison house came a searing flash.

Fiery red.

The ruby's light exploded in my mind.

And instantly there was sound there too. Bursts of fire-cracker noises.

Gunfire!

Voices – insistent . . . pleading . . . A rattling, clattering . . .
The howling of a wolf which changed eerily into a thin, distant
high-pitched scream.

'Ah!' I bent over with the shock. It was the same vision
I'd had on the day Rasputin's daughter had brought me
his gift from beyond the grave.

My fingers felt for the Rasputin dagger and I drew it
out from the waistband of my skirt.

Rasputin's words rang in my ears: *One dagger to take a*
life. One dagger to save a life.

I wasn't able to stab anyone with it. The shortness of
the blade meant it was only useful for fighting at close
quarters. This soldier could shoot us from a distance. He
raised his rifle, tucked it against his shoulder and took
aim. Stefan and I were going to die.

And yet . . . in my hand I held the Rasputin dagger . . .
One dagger to save a life.

I grasped the dagger's hilt and, slipping past Stefan, I
brandished the blade at the soldier.

'What have you there?' He hesitated.

'A dagger,' I said, with no clear idea of what I might do
next. I could not throw the weapon far enough, and even
if I could, it wouldn't pierce his rough clothing.

Stefan caught at my sleeve. But I shook him off. I had
this boy's attention. Perhaps Stefan could go free and live
his life for both of us.

I raised the dagger. The moon shone on the blade and
the ruby flashed brimstone-red.

'What kind of dagger is that?' Although the barrel still pointed ahead, the boy had lowered his rifle and was walking towards us.

One dagger to save a life.

Suddenly I understood. The meaning of the words was clear in my mind. And I knew what to do.

'It is the Rasputin dagger.' I spoke distinctly. 'A dagger with a single red ruby surrounded by pearls. It is worth more than the Imperial Crown of the Tsar himself.'

'It's a fake.' The boy laughed and once more raised his rifle.

'Nina,' I heard Stefan say in my ear. 'He will shoot us and take the dagger from you.'

'If this soldier fires his rifle,' I murmured, 'it will alert the other men. He knows he'll not be allowed to keep the dagger for himself. Move away and get ready to run.'

In response Stefan came near and took hold of my free hand. 'Not without you,' he said.

'This is no fake. Look at it,' I urged the boy. 'But' – I lowered my voice and glanced around me – 'don't let anyone else hear us. Else they will steal it from you.'

'How can I believe you?'

'I was a nurse who cared for the young Tsarevich, Alexei.' The truth was evident in my voice. 'And so did the monk, Father Grigory Rasputin. This dagger belonged to him.'

'Rasputin!' The name enticed the boy even closer. His rifle was dangling by his side. He was getting ready to snatch the dagger from my hand.

'Yes,' I said. 'It has magical powers.'

'Give it to me. Give me the Rasputin dagger!'

'Here it is!'

I drew back my arm and, with all my might, I threw the Rasputin dagger high in the air – beyond and behind the soldier, deep into the long grass at the side of the path.

As the boy swivelled his head to see where it would fall, Stefan pulled on my hand and we turned and raced away. We didn't need to look back to know that the boy would not pursue us or shout for help. He'd be frantically searching for the dagger to claim it before his fellow soldiers noticed what was happening.

And so we ran, Stefan and I, towards the forest and freedom.

AFTERMATH

In order to conceal the murder of Tsar Nicholas, and his family and servants, their bodies were hidden – two of the children in separate locations. This gave rise to the rumour that at least one of the four sisters had managed to escape, and for many years after the Russian Revolution several imposters pretended to be members of the Imperial Romanov Family. It is only relatively recently that DNA tests were conducted to identify what are believed to be the remains of the last members of the Imperial Family. They will lie together, reunited in death, within the special memorial built for the victims of the assassination in the Cathedral of Saints Peter and Paul in the city of St Petersburg.

Father Grigory Rasputin remains an enigmatic and controversial figure. Lately, material has been discovered which suggests that the British Secret Service may have been involved in his murder, as Rasputin was actively in favour of Russia making peace with Germany. During the turmoil of the revolution, Rasputin's grave was desecrated. His body was dug up and its whereabouts are unknown.

St Petersburg, the city founded by the Russian Emperor Peter the Great, had its name changed to Petrograd during the First World War in order to make it sound less German. For a time it became Leningrad. Eventually the city's name was changed back to the original, and is known today as St Petersburg.

After bitter fighting between different factions, the state of the Soviet Socialist Republic was established. In modern times Russia has adopted a more federal style of government.

One war to end all wars.
Five lives that are
changed for ever.

Remembrance
Carnegie Medal-winning author
THERESA BRESLIN

NOMINATED FOR THE CARNEGIE MEDAL

Summer 1915, and a group of teenagers meet for a picnic. But already the sound of gunfire on the Western Front can be heard across the Channel, and soon the horror of the Great War engulfs them. From the grimness of the trenches to the devastating reality seen daily by those nursing the wounded, they struggle to survive – and nothing will ever be the same again.

A powerful, engrossing and truly epic novel of love and war.

With book notes.

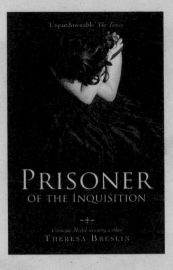

SHORTLISTED FOR THE CARNEGIE MEDAL

VOTED FAVOURITE BOOK BY CARNEGIE
MEDAL SHADOWING GROUP

Spain, 1490.

Zarita, teenage daughter of the town magistrate, is an
only child, indulged and spoiled by her parents.

Saulo, son of a pauper, sees his father wrongfully judged
and brutally dealt with. Hauled off to be a slave at sea, he
swears vengeance on the magistrate and his whole family.

With the cruel agents of the Inquisition bringing
suspicion, terror and death, Zarita and Saulo will meet
again, amid the intrigues of the royal court, to face final
acts of betrayal and revenge . . .